BETWEEN THE LIES

A J WILLS

Between the Lies
Copyright © A J Wills 2018

All rights reserved. No part of this publication may be reproduced, stored in a retrieval system, or transmitted, in any form or by any other means, without the prior written permission of the author, nor be otherwise circulated in any form of binding or cover other than that in which it is published and without a similar condition being imposed on the purchaser.

This book is a work of fiction. Any resemblance to actual persons, living or dead is purely coincidental.

1

Jez Hook woke with his heart trying to punch its way out of his chest. He sat up, and gasped. It was early, 2:57am, according to his phone on the bedside table. He collapsed back onto his pillow, and stared through the gloom at three ugly watermarks on the ceiling, wondering at the cause of the fear spiking through his veins.

The house creaked and popped; claws scratched in the attic. But there was another noise he couldn't quite place.

'Alice, are you awake?' He tapped her on the shoulder. 'Did you hear that?'

She withdrew her arm into the warmth under the duvet, and rolled away with a soporific murmur. Her breathing deepened and slowed into a steady rhythm. In the next room, Lily's bed groaned.

There.

He heard it again.

Like the brush of cloth against a wall.

Then a thud. Dull and hollow.

Jez imagined a scrawny, heroin-addled junkie rummaging through their drawers, looking to fund his next hit, all tracksuit bottoms, gelled hair, and earrings, eyeing up the television set, their stereo, the iPad, and his Xbox. In an instant, fear resolved itself into outrage.

He slipped a leg out of bed, the stripped floorboards icy on his bare feet.

'I think there's someone in the house,' he hissed. 'I'm going to take a look. I'll be back in a minute.'

Jez pulled a t-shirt on. As he reached the door, Alice gave a little snort, scrunching up her face, and rubbing her freckled nose with the back of her hand.

He sidestepped a loose floorboard on the landing. He should probably call the police. But how long would they take to arrive? And what if the noises were a product of his overactive imagination?

Lily's door was ajar. He pushed it open with a trembling hand. The four-year-old, on her front in a tangle of sheets, had her legs drawn up under her chest, and her bottom stuck up in the air in that peculiar way she had of sleeping. A thumb wedged in her mouth and her favourite stuffed toy tucked under one arm.

Jez backed out of the room and winced as the latch clicked shut. Over the banister, he could see light haloing around the lounge door. The flicker of a shadow. Someone moving around.

He picked up one of Alice's dumbbells next to her trainers on the landing. It weighed barely a couple of pounds, but felt reassuringly heavy. Then he took the stairs one at a time, his muscles wound up like springs, his senses supercharged.

He noticed the bolt on the front door was drawn, so the intruder had either come through a window, or more likely, vaulted the garden wall at the back of the house, and forced the tired old lock on the kitchen door he'd been meaning to replace.

The floor tiles in the hall were gritty with dirt. He put an ear to the lounge door, and listened.

Silence.

No, wait. Maybe a slight rustle. The sound of footsteps softened by the carpet?

He pushed the door open. A figure stood hunched over Alice's oak sideboard. Not the gaunt, skeletal physique of a desperate drug addict Jez had expected to find, but an older man, his greying hair neatly cut, and smartly dressed in a blue jacket, beige trousers, and brown brogues.

'Hey!' said Jez, with an assumed bravado.

The man stiffened, then turned slowly, a framed photo in his hand, removed from the collection of family pictures on the sideboard. Jez recognised it as one of his favourite images of Alice and Lily. He'd taken it on his phone in the first flush of their romance. Mother and daughter with the same button nose, and dimples that pinched their cheeks when they smiled. Only their eyes were different. Alice's were the colour of coral oceans. Lily's a chocolate brown.

'Put that back,' said Jez.

The man stared at him with dark, glassy eyes.

'I said, put it back.' Jez raised his voice.

'She's pretty.' The man traced a finger across Lily's face. Jez caught the rank odour of alcohol and stale sweat. 'What's she called?'

'You're drunk. Get out!' Jez reached for the man's arm, but he swatted it away, his face contorting into an ugly snarl.

'Let me see her.'

'I've called the police. They're on their way.'

The man dropped the photo. The glass in the frame cracked. Then he lunged at Jez, who was momentarily caught off guard, but instinctively pushed the intruder back with a firm hand on his chest.

'I have to see her!'

'Last warning. Get out.'

When the man rushed at him a second time, Jez didn't hesitate to use the dumbbell. He swung it like a boxer aiming a fight-winning uppercut, letting its weight create its own momentum.

But he was too slow.

The man saw it coming, parried it away, and rammed a hand into Jez's face. His palm caught him under the chin, and snapped his head back.

Jez yelped as fingers dug into his eyes. He fell back over the side of the sofa, and the stranger dashed past, into the hall, the stairs in his sights.

In a few quick bounds, he would be in Lily's room.

Jez screamed, rage boiling in his veins. He had to protect his family. He blinked away the tears, and launched after the vanishing figure. He caught him on the bottom step, and with a cry of rage, brought the dumbbell crashing down on the back of the man's skull.

It connected with a crack, and the man's legs buckled. He collapsed to his knees, and Jez hit him again.

A splatter of blood patterned the wall. Jez lashed out once more. Unable to stop. Venting his fury. Until exhausted, breathless, and burning with sweat, he dropped the dumbbell. It thudded on the floor, and rolled away.

2

A light sparked on, and Alice appeared on the landing, rubbing her eyes. 'What's all the noise?'

Jez, standing in the hall, opened his mouth, but couldn't speak.

She started down the stairs, her pyjama bottoms flapping around her legs, but a plaintive cry halted her mid-step.

'Mummy! Mummy!'

'Great. Now Lily's awake.'

She turned and ran back up, her feet dancing on the steps. The bedroom door latch clicked open, and the soothing murmur of her voice calming her daughter back to sleep carried through the house.

When she returned, Jez hadn't moved.

'What is it?' she asked, her head tilted, her hair hanging loose.

When she saw the crumpled body on the stairs, she clamped a hand over her mouth to stifle a scream. 'Oh my God!'

A single bead of sweat rolled down Jez's back. 'I didn't mean to,' he said. He needed her to understand it had been an accident.

'What have you done?' A tremor in Alice's voice.

Jez tried wiping the blood on his hands on his t-shirt, but couldn't get them clean.

'For God's sake, call an ambulance,' said Alice, frozen to the spot.

Jez stared at the body. Everything was a bit fuzzy. None of it seemed real. He fixated on the smallest details. Tiny black hairs that sprouted from the top of the man's ears. A cluster of moles on his neck. A gold band on his ring finger. He noticed the elbows of his jacket had been worn shiny smooth, and that he had holes in the scuffed leather soles of his shoes. Specks of blood peppered the Farrow and Ball cream walls, and had seeped into the seagrass carpet on the stairs.

'Jez!' said Alice. 'Where's your phone?'

'He was drunk. He was going for Lily. I had to stop him.' Jez swallowed hard, forcing back the urge to vomit. 'He found that picture of the two of you together on the beach. He said this horrible thing about Lily being really pretty.'

'What?'

'He was trying to get upstairs. I had to stop him.'

Alice said nothing.

'It was an accident.'

Jez blinked, forcing away the memory of how his rage had taken hold, possessing him. How he'd been unable to stop himself even as the man lay unconscious.

Eventually Alice said, 'We should call the police.'

Jez clenched his hands into tight fists, his nails digging into his palms until the pain drew him back to the moment. Alice was right. They had to do something.

Without thinking, he grabbed the man's ankles, and pulled him off the stairs, grimacing when his face thudded on the floor. He straightened his legs, and unfurled his arms. It seemed like the right thing to do. He'd looked so awkward, bent and twisted on the stairs, lying in his own blood.

'How did he get in?' asked Alice, descending slowly.

'He probably forced the back door,' Jez snapped.

'You were going to fix the lock.'

'Yes, I know.' His skin prickled with irritation.

He knelt on the hard floor by the man's side, and reached into his jacket pocket. He found a well-worn brown leather wallet bulging with cards. Inside, tucked behind a clear plastic panel, was his driving licence.

'His name's Marcus Fenson. He's from Broadstairs.'

When he glanced up at Alice, she'd frozen with eyes wide. Her skin was deathly pale. 'You okay?'

After a second or two, she seemed to come to her senses, and forced a smile. 'Sure,' she said.

The pixelated thumbnail picture on the licence made Marcus Fenson look a lot younger. In the photo he had fewer lines around his eyes, and his hair was a dark, lustrous black that fell over his ears.

Alice floated down the last few steps, and tiptoed over the blood that had seeped into the carpet. She tucked a loose strand of hair behind her ear, and crouched next to the body. With a trembling hand, she reached for his neck.

'He's dead,' she said after a moment. She wiped her nose with the back of her hand, her eyes red.

'Shit,' said Jez. He rocked back on his haunches. 'Are you sure?'

'Yes, of course I'm sure,' Alice snapped. 'What were you thinking?'

'I ... I ... I don't know.'

'How could you have been such an idiot?'

'Alice, I'm sorry. It was an accident.'

Her shoulders shuddered as tears flowed hot and fast down her cheeks.

'I was trying to protect you,' said Jez. He reached for Alice's hand, but she recoiled from his touch.

They sat in silence for a few moments, lost in their own thoughts, Alice's gentle sobbing the only sound breaking the silence.

'What do we do now?' Jez said eventually.

Alice stood suddenly, and with a deep breath her tears ceased. She pulled her shoulders back, and with her jaw set defiantly, said, 'You'll have to get rid of the body.'

3

It hadn't exactly been love at first sight, at least not for Alice. She'd been more concerned about the damage to her car than the strange man who'd distracted her attention as she reversed out of a parking space. Fortunately, the damage had been mostly cosmetic, and the Renault she'd hit had escaped without so much as a scratch.

'I'm so sorry, but you forgot these,' said Jez, holding up a bunch of flowers in a cellophane wrapper.

Alice frowned. 'Sunflowers?'

'I was behind you at the checkout. They were on the floor. I thought you'd dropped them.'

'No,' she said.

'Oh,' said Jez. 'Well, I've paid for them now. You should have them anyway.'

'Right.' She took them, and threw them on the passenger seat. 'Thanks, I think.'

'I really am sorry about your car.'

'Don't worry about it,' she said, inspecting the scuffed paint and dent in her bumper. 'It's only a lump of steel and plastic.' The words tripped lightly off her lips, but it was obvious she didn't mean them. It was an eight-year-old Mini Cooper with sports trim, a chunky leather steering wheel, and polished red paint that gleamed in the sun. It suited her personality, although she'd since sold it, after deciding they didn't need the cost of running two cars.

'No, I insist, I'll pay to get it straightened out.'

'There's no need. The insurance will cover it.'

'I want to.'

'Look, thank you for the flowers.'

'I'll leave you my number in case you change your mind.' Jez conjured up a business card from his wallet.

'I should have guessed. We're in the same line of work.'

Jez raised an eyebrow. He thought he knew all the estate agents in town, and would have certainly remembered her face.

'Lambert and Steele. I'm a legal secretary.'

'Right,' said Jez. 'I thought you meant…'

'No,' she said, pulling a face. 'Not an estate agent.'

'My name's Jez. I mean, it's Jeremy, but everyone calls me Jez.'

Her face finally broke into a smile. 'Alice,' she said, offering him a delicate hand with immaculate red painted nails. 'I'd better get going.'

'At least let me buy you a drink.' The words tumbled out of his mouth before he realised what he was saying. It wasn't like him to be so bold. She was well out of his league. Glamorous and sophisticated, with lustrous brunette hair, and delicate make-up. He didn't think he'd have much chance with a woman like that, especially one who took so much care over her appearance just for a Saturday afternoon supermarket dash.

'Please?' he said, and regretted the desperation in his voice.

Alice glanced at a slim silver watch on her thin wrist. 'I don't know. It'll have to be a quick one. I have to be somewhere at six.'

They found a bar on the quay overlooking the creek, and drank champagne sitting in high-backed chairs. He discovered she liked dancing barefoot in the sand, and lying on a beach watching the clouds race across the sky. She hated January - 'the longest, coldest month' - spiders, fennel and insincerity. He told her his idea of a perfect weekend was a lazy Sunday morning in bed. He explained his loathing of football, aubergines and birthdays - he despised being the centre of attention - and that his favourite band was The Killers. He liked his coffee strong and black, and regretted having never learned to sail. She laughed at all his jokes, and two hours passed in the blink of an eye.

'It was fun,' she said, as she stood to leave. 'But I really have to go.'

They exchanged an awkward handshake, and when Alice leaned in to kiss his cheek, they bumped noses, and collapsed in a fit of giggles.

'I don't suppose you'd like to go out for dinner with me sometime?' said Jez, emboldened by the champagne.

'I'd like that,' she said, without hesitation.

Four days later, they met at an Italian restaurant on the water's edge, ate pasta, barely taking their eyes off each other all night. They held hands under the table, and at the end of the evening shared their first kiss. Two weeks later, Alice introduced him to Lily.

Within four months, Jez had signed the rental agreement on their house in Abbey Street, an idyllic location in the historic quarter of the town neither of them imagined they'd ever be able to afford. And suddenly, Jez had everything he thought he wanted from life. The woman of his dreams, a ready-made family, and a house they both adored. But everything had moved so quickly, he'd hardly had time to draw breath.

He studied Alice's expression, as she stood with the dead body at her feet, not sure he'd heard her correctly.

'What do you mean, get rid of it?'

'Well, you're going to have to do something with it,' said Alice.

'I'll call the police,' said Jez, trying to think where he'd left his phone.

'No.' The force in Alice's tone took him aback.

'What?'

'Look at him,' she said. 'You beat him to death.'

'I didn't mean to. I told you, it was an accident.'

'I'm not sure the police will see it like that. You went too far. They'll most likely charge you with manslaughter.'

Jez's mouth fell open. She had to be kidding. He was only trying to protect his family. They couldn't prosecute him for that, could they?

'He was deranged,' said Jez, panic rising. 'He was going to hurt Lily. They'll understand I had no choice.'

'Are you really willing to take that chance?'

'Yes.'

'You used a weapon,' she said, pointing at the blood-stained dumbbell at the foot of the stairs. 'You attacked him from behind, and bashed his skull in. It's hardly reasonable force.'

Jez's head was spinning. Surely he had a right to defend his home if someone broke in threatening his family. There must be some kind of precedent, even if he did go over the top a little. He certainly hadn't meant to kill the guy.

'This is madness.'

'Just think about it for a minute. How's a good lawyer going to paint this in court?' said Alice. 'He was unarmed, drunk maybe, and a bit confused. But you were the one who lost his temper, picked up a weapon, and attacked him from behind. I'm sorry, Jez, it doesn't look good.'

'So, what I do?'

'Listen,' she said, lowering her voice conspiratorially, 'no one knows he was here. If you do this right, everything will be fine.'

'What do you mean?'

'Dump the body.'

'You mean bury him in the woods or something?' It felt as if Jez's world was falling apart. His legs were weak, and his breathing was coming shallow and fast.

'You'll think of something. Just make sure you lose the body somewhere it will never be found,' said Alice.

'What about when someone reports him missing?' said Jez, shaking his head.

'He broke into our house —'

'His name's Marcus. He's wearing a wedding ring. For all we know he has kids too.'

'I know.' Alice's eyes narrowed into fierce slits. 'The point is, he's hardly going to have told anyone he was coming here to break in. So, there's nothing to connect him with us, or this house.'

'But his blood's all over the walls, and in the carpet. It's everywhere.'

'We'll clean it up.'

How could she be so detached? So emotionally vacant?

'What about DNA? They can still find traces of it,' said Jez. 'I've seen it on programmes on the TV.'

'Only if they suspect we had something to do with it, and search the house. But what are the chances of that? No one knows he was here.'

Jez staggered backwards, the enormity of what Alice was asking sinking in. He'd killed a man in a fit of fear and anger. Even if the carpet and walls came up clean, he'd never be able to forget the sight of the blood.

'I don't think I can do it,' he said.

'Do it for Lily. Do it for us as a family.' Alice moved close. She buried her head into his neck. Her fingers stroked the back of his head. 'But you have to do it now. It'll be light soon. I'm going to get dressed, and make a start on cleaning the carpet. Where's the car?'

Jez couldn't remember. His thoughts were jumbled, like the pages of a book thrown into the eye of a tornado. 'I think I parked it at the end of the road,' he mumbled.

'Bring it to the front of the house,' said Alice. 'We can put him in the boot together.'

This wasn't happening. It couldn't be happening. Were they seriously contemplating trying to dispose of a dead body? Maybe if he went back to bed, everything would have sorted itself out when he woke up.

'Jez! Are you even listening to me? Lily will be awake soon. Get a move on.'

4

Street lamps picked out a swirling mist that had rolled in from the estuary like Victorian smog. Against the chill, Jez hurried along the deserted street with his hands shoved in his pockets, and his chin nuzzled onto his chest. He couldn't have parked the car much farther away from the house if he'd tried, two wheels on the pavement, wedged between a black Range Rover, and a rust-coloured hatchback.

The exhaust rattled with a bronchial wheeze as the engine kicked into life. He flicked the wipers to clear a watery film from the windscreen, and half expected to see the twitch of a curtain or the flicker of a bedroom light. But no one stirred.

He manoeuvred out of the space, and hunched over the steering wheel to negotiate a tight path through a string of cars parked nose to tail.

Alice was waiting on the doorstep with her hair tied back. She'd thrown on a pair of skinny jeans with one of Jez's hooded tops, arms folded, her face drawn.

'Did anyone see you?'

'No,' said Jez, pushing past with an opaque plastic box filled with his Wellington boots, waterproof trousers and a torch, cleared out from the boot of the car. He rammed it into the cupboard under the stairs where they kept the ironing board, and an ever-growing supply of reusable supermarket bags.

While he was gone, Alice had wrapped the body in a white sheet, and left it in the hall looking like an ancient Egyptian mummy, with the material collapsed around his face, creating hollows around his eyes and mouth that gave Jez the creeps.

'Let's get this over with,' he said.

'You grab his top half, I'll take his legs,' said Alice.

The body was heavier than Jez had anticipated. A dead weight with arms that dragged along the floor. It was worse for Alice, who had to stop twice to catch her breath.

'Come on, Alice. Hurry,' hissed Jez. It would only take one curious neighbour to sneak a peek at the commotion outside, and they were done.

Eventually, they folded Marcus Fenson's body into the boot, bending his legs at the knees, and pressing his head onto his chest.

'Hang on,' said Alice, rushing back into the house.

She returned wiping the pink dumbbell with a tea towel. 'Make sure you get rid of that as well,' she said, tossing it in with the body. 'No loose ends.'

Jez took one last look, and slammed the boot shut with a shudder. Alice kissed him chastely, and gave him an encouraging nod.

'Do you think I should take a spade?' Jez asked. 'I mean, if I have to bury him.'

In truth, Jez didn't even know if they owned one. There was a shed in the garden, under the old apple tree, but he'd never been in it. It was possible Alice had brought one when they moved in. She'd brought so many things. A whole life's worth of belongings that made Jez's contribution to their new start together appear pitiful.

'Christ, Jez, I don't know. Just get him out of here, will you. And watch your speed.'

'All right, all right, I'm going.' Jez raised his hands in submission, jumped into the car, and wound down the window. 'Are you sure this is a good idea?'

'Jez, go! I'll see you later.'

Alice turned for the house, leaving Jez on his own, with no idea what he was going to do.

He reached the end of the road before he remembered the headlights. He fumbled for the switch on the dashboard with clammy hands, and sat for a moment staring at the street ahead. Where the hell was he supposed to go now?

Alice had made it sound so simple, like dumping a body was easy; no more testing than disposing of an old freezer at the recycling depot. If only it was that straightforward.

He could imagine it as a fun conundrum played out as a game of consequences in the pub after a few pints.

So, if you'd bludgeoned someone to death, and had to get rid of the body, what would you do?

Easy after a few drinks. A bit of a laugh. But Jez was

tired, his nerves shot, and his mind blank. He'd never even picked up a speeding ticket, and now he was contemplating burying a body.

He should have called the police as soon as he heard someone in the house, and let them deal with it. It's what they were trained for. But he couldn't turn back the clock. What was done, was done. Time to man up, and deal with it.

His foot hovered over the accelerator, and his hand gripped the handbrake. Maybe it wasn't too late to involve the police. The station was only a few minutes' drive away. He could explain how he'd been attacked in his own home. He could even inflict a few scratches on his arms and face to give his story some authenticity. Maybe he could go back to the house, trash it a bit, and make it look like there had been a struggle.

The alternative was to find an isolated spot in the woods and dig a hole. But how long would that take? It would be light in a few hours. And what about the spoils? A big pile of dirt was going to be certain give-away, that is if dogs or foxes didn't find the body first.

Jez banged his head against the steering wheel, and cursed his stupidity. If only he'd not lost control of his temper in the first place, Marcus Fenson would still be alive.

Jez slammed the car into first gear, and pumped the accelerator. The car pulled away in a screech of tyres, hurtling past the brewery, and bumping over a pedestrian crossing so fast he felt the body shift in the boot.

The lights at the crossroads by the Post Office turned red as he approached, and he lurched to a halt. He might have just killed a man, but his stupid sensibilities wouldn't allow him to jump a traffic signal.

As he waited impatiently, doubt crowded his mind. One way or another he was going to have to pay for what he'd done, either in the courts, or tormented by his conscience for the rest of his life.

He checked the fuel gauge. Half a tank of petrol, which would give him at least two hundred miles. Far enough to disappear, and start a new life. But then what? Life without Alice and Lily would be pointless.

His attention was distracted by a flash of pink in the passenger footwell. Jez reached down, and picked up one of Lily's sandals. Open-toed and stitched with red roses. One of her favourite pairs.

Before Alice, he'd had little interest in kids. He'd never imagined having a family of his own, nor considered raising someone else's child. Other people's children generally irritated him. But not Lily. She was different, and he'd grown surprisingly fond of her in such a short time. She was sassy like her mother, and unintentionally hilarious. The thought of her tucked up in bed with her bottom in the air, oblivious to the adult drama going on around her, made him smile.

When the lights turned green, he'd made up his mind. He had to do the right thing.

He turned left, past the Indian restaurant, and pulled up outside an imposing red brick Victorian villa set back from the road. Typical of a town steeped in so much history to house its police station in such an ancient building. Jez shivered as he stepped out of the car, and pondered what he would tell the duty sergeant.

It was important his story added up, so he ran through it in his mind again, how he'd woken to the sound of someone breaking into the house. The crack of the back door being forced open, the crash of cupboard doors, and how Alice had been terrified, and sent him to investigate. When the intruder, his eyes wild and crazy, had attacked him, Jez had grabbed the first weapon that came to hand. He'd not meant to hurt him. It had been an accident. That much was true.

But no matter how he framed it, there was no escaping the fact he'd beaten the man to death, hitting him repeatedly with a dumbbell, and then with Alice's help, bundled him into the car with the intention of burying his body.

It was ridiculous to think there could be any outcome other than his arrest on a manslaughter charge. They'd lock him up for a long time. He'd be an old man by the time he tasted freedom. He might never see Alice and Lily again.

Jez jumped back into the car, and yanked his seatbelt on. He couldn't do it. If he confessed, his life was over.

Maybe Alice had a point. There was nothing to connect Marcus Fenson with either of them. If he held his nerve, and found somewhere to safely hide the body, he could get away with it. The hole he'd have to dig would need to be deep. A shallow grave wouldn't cut it.

And then it struck him. He knew the ideal place where, if he did it right, the body would never be found.

5

For half a mile, Jez sat in the slipstream of a slow-moving articulated lorry, willing it to go faster, but not daring to overtake. It turned north onto the bypass, no doubt heading for the logistics depot on the outskirts of the town, close to the boatyard where Jez was heading.

Coming off the roundabout, it crunched through its gears, gradually building speed, until the road straightened, and Jez took his opportunity. He pulled out around the truck, and accelerated hard, ignoring the screams of protest from his aged Astra. He hit a downhill section, and watched the lorry's headlights fade in his mirrors.

Trees flashed past in a blur, picked out by his own lights, and on his right, the ghostly shadows of vast white warehouses appeared. Around a sweeping bend, the wash of flashing blue lights came into view. A police car blocked the road, and an officer in a hi-vis yellow jacket stood with legs planted apart, and a hand raised.

Jez glanced in the mirror, and eased off the accelerator. Too late to turn around without raising suspicion. His mind raced, but all he could think about was the body in the boot.

He slowed to a halt, and wound down his window. The female officer, whose over-sized jacket was buttoned to the neck, approached the car with a powerful torch in one hand.

'Good evening, Sir.'

'What's going on?' asked Jez, forcing a friendly smile. He had the sudden and terrifying thought that his clothes might be splattered with blood. He'd never thought to check, and it took all his willpower not to check now. Maybe she wouldn't notice in the dark.

'The road's closed, I'm afraid.'

Jez peered past the police car angled across the road. More blue lights ahead. Two police cars and an ambulance alongside a lorry dwarfing the mangled wreckage of a small saloon.

'We're dealing with an ongoing incident,' the police officer said, offering little in the way of explanation.

'Anyone hurt?'

She leaned on his car, and peered in through the open window. An attractive blonde with cold, blue eyes, her hair pulled back in a ponytail under a peaked cap. 'Can't say at this stage,' she said.

'Any idea how long it's going to be closed for?'

'Shouldn't be too long.'

'Right,' said Jez.

The entrance to the boatyard was on the opposite side of the junction. No way to reach it until they cleared the accident.

The officer gave him a long, hard stare, sizing him up, and eventually said, 'It's late to be out.'

Jez rolled his wrist to check his watch before remembering he'd forgotten to put it on. 'Is it?'

'Where are you going?'

Jez's mind went blank. He didn't have a cover story. It never occurred to him he'd need one. 'What?' he said, cocking his head as if he'd not heard.

'It's past four in the morning. Where are you going at this time of the morning? Work?'

'No, I don't have to be in until nine,' said Jez, without thinking. He should have told her he was a shift worker at the logistics depot. She'd have been none the wiser. Instead she raised an eyebrow, her interest in him piqued.

Two paramedics lifted a stretcher into the back of the ambulance. A figure wrapped in a red blanket had an oxygen mask strapped to their face.

'I'm an estate agent,' said Jez. 'I couldn't sleep. I have a lot on my mind at the moment. I thought a drive might help.'

She looked at him as if she didn't believe a word of it. But then most police officers had perfected that sneering look of disbelief, sceptical about anything they were told. It was probably a symptom of being lied to so often.

'Have you been drinking, Sir?'

'No, absolutely not,' said Jez, affronted. Then he remembered the two cans of beer he'd drunk the previous evening. But that was such a long time ago, surely that didn't count?

'So where are you going?'

'Nowhere.'

The ambulance pulled away, heading south on the bypass. A recovery truck took its place, appearing from the direction of the town, flashing orange lights strobing in the dark. A man in dirty blue overalls jumped out of the cab, nodded at two police officers, and lumbered around the crashed vehicles, inspecting the damage.

'Listen, it's fine. I can go back the way I came,' said Jez. He reached for the gear lever.

'Are you okay?'

'Yeah, I'm fine,' he said. 'A little wired, that's all.'

'Wired?' Her eyebrow shot up again.

'Stressed. I told you, I couldn't sleep. You know what it's like. Four in the morning, and the worries of the world racing around your brain.'

'Please switch off your engine, Sir.'

'What?' Jez's heart was pounding so hard, he was sure she'd be able to see it under his jumper.

The police officer reached into the car and snatched the keys from the ignition. 'Have you been taking drugs?'

The powerful torch beam seared Jez's eyes. 'No, of course I haven't. I'm just tired.'

Her hand travelled towards a radio clipped to her jacket. She sensed something was wrong. Jez had never been a good liar. The guilt must have been written all over his face.

'Is there a problem?' Jez's voice came out an octave higher than normal.

The officer took her hand from the radio. She'd had

second thoughts, as behind, the hiss and grunt of air brakes heralded the arrival of the lorry Jez had overtaken. Its headlights illuminated the inside of the car, and threw heavy shadows across the seats.

'Could you step out of the vehicle.'

This was it. She was definitely onto him. He should have followed through at the police station. No way of explaining away the body in the boot now.

Jez stepped out of the car. The officer was shorter than he'd first thought. Standing face-to-face, her head barely reached his shoulder. He guessed he could easily outsprint her, and be away into the cover of the old gunpowder works in a few strides. Her colleagues attending to the accident were paying no attention, and he doubted the lorry driver would have any interest in getting involved.

'Do you own the vehicle?' the officer asked, taking a notepad and pen from her jacket pocket. She noted down the number plate.

'Yes,' said Jez, tasting the salt of the sea on his lips. If she made him open the boot, he had no explanation. What could he possibly say?

'Can I see your licence?'

Jez fumbled for his wallet, and handed over his licence. Less than an hour before, he'd been staring at Marcus Fenson's licence. His fingerprints were all over it. Why hadn't he thought to wipe it clean? But it was the least of his worries, right now.

'And your insurance documents, Mr Hook?'

Jez dived into the car, and opened the glove box. He rummaged through a mess of old CD cases, empty sweet wrappers, and crumpled receipts. He found the brown envelope containing the insurance certificate wedged under the service logbook.

The officer gave it only a cursory glance, and handed it back.

'Everything okay?' asked Jez.

'Happily for you, all your paperwork is in order,' she said without the glimmer of a smile.

'So, I can go?'

'I'd like to take a quick look inside the vehicle.'

'Why?' He shouldn't have snapped. It sounded defensive.

'Because I have reason to believe you may be in possession of drugs,' she said.

'I told you, I don't do drugs.'

'In which case, you've nothing to hide.'

'Is this really necessary?'

'Step away from the vehicle.'

Jez hesitated. 'Fine,' he said. 'But it's a bit of a mess.'

He glanced at the lorry, its engine idling with a noisy rattle. Its bright headlights were dazzling. Even shielding his eyes, he couldn't see into the cab, but he was sure the driver was enjoying the show. He'd be in for a shock if Jez had to open the boot though. From where he was sitting, he'd have a grandstand view of the body.

The officer took her time rooting around all the places Jez might have hidden a stash of drugs. In the pockets in the door, the glove box, and behind the sun visors. She checked under the seats, and in the cubbyhole by the cigarette lighter, shining her torch into the darkest corners until she was satisfied there was nothing to be found.

Jez smiled as she pulled herself out of the car, and adjusted her cap. He was aiming for friendly, but was worried he might have come across as arrogant. He couldn't afford to fail the attitude test.

'Find anything?' he asked.

Over her shoulder, the guy in the recovery truck was hooking up the mangled car to a steel cable, ready to winch it onto the back of his low loader.

The officer ignored his question. She drifted to the back of the car, and checked the number plate against the record she'd made in her notebook.

Jez swallowed hard, hoping for a miracle; anything to distract her attention. She ran a finger along the paintwork of the boot, and inspected the dirt on her finger.

'Could you pop it open for me?' she said.

Jez froze.

'Mr Hook? Could you open the boot?'

His legs went weak, and for a second, he thought he was going to collapse. This was it. It was all over. Nothing to look forward to apart from a miserable prison cell, and a weekly visit from Alice, if he was lucky.

'Look,' he said, clenching his hands into tight fists. 'There's something I need to tell you.'

6

The house was silent, and in darkness, apart from a single light in the hall which revealed all too starkly a dark stain on the stairs, and a damp patch on the wall where Alice had scrubbed clean the splatters of blood. Jez kicked off his shoes, and was jolted by a flashback, like a surge of electricity through his veins. His hand gripping the dumbbell, striking bone and soft tissue, at once both brittle and spongy. A spray of blood. A pattern of scarlet on the walls, like a Jackson Pollock painting.

He screwed his eyes shut, and pinched the bridge of his nose, trying to shut out the memory.

With a deep breath, he brought his panic under control. He prised open his eyes and noticed that actually, apart from the wet patches, the hall was spotless. Alice had done a good job.

And yet everything had changed.

He was a killer, and the guilt gnawed his insides. No matter how many times the rational part of his brain reminded him that Marcus Fenson had brought it on himself the moment he broke into their house, he couldn't shake the dark cloud depressing his spirits. The euphoria he'd felt when the police officer had taken an urgent call on her radio as Jez was about to confess, had long since passed. It had sounded like some kind of urgent domestic issue. She'd raced off with blue lights blazing, and without a second thought about him.

Alice had tidied the lounge too. She'd plumped up the sofa cushions, and stacked his Xbox games in a neat pile by the television. Lily's dolls had been swept off the floor, and pushed into the corner. In the kitchen, dishes left to drain had been cleared away.

Jez assessed the damage to the back door. The wooden frame was splintered, the paint cracked and dented revealing the bruised timber beneath. Remarkably, the lock still worked, but it would need replacing. For now, Jez wedged the back of a chair under the handle, and headed for bed.

Alice woke when he walked into the bedroom. She was lying on her back with her hands resting on her stomach. Her bedside light was still on.

'Did you do it?' she asked, sitting up.

'Yeah.' Jez perched on the edge of the bed, and combed his fingers through her hair, sensing her melt at his touch.

'What did you do with him?' she asked.

'Let's not talk about it.'

'Tell me.'

'It's late, and I'm tired. I need to sleep. We can talk about it in the morning.'

Jez pulled away, and threw his clothes in the corner. He climbed into bed in his boxer shorts, and lay on his back, staring at the ceiling. Alice rolled over, and tucked her head into his shoulder.

'Are you okay?' she said.

'I'm fine.'

'Are you sure?'

His mind was in turmoil, and he felt sick to the pit of his stomach. But the last thing he wanted was to talk. He needed to work this out in his own head. Compartmentalise his feelings, and move on.

'Let's get some sleep before Lily wakes up,' he said.

Alice squeezed his arm, and within a few moments, he could tell from the pattern of her breathing, she was asleep.

But Jez was too wired with adrenaline, every neuron in his brain firing. He was beyond sleep, although he ached for its numbing, restorative comfort. But somehow it just didn't want to come.

He must have finally dozed off shortly before Alice's alarm jerked him awake from a dreamless, restless sleep. He woke with a vague sense of foreboding, and then the memory of what had happened hit him like a slap across the face. The darkness of despair returned like an eclipse blocking the light from the sun.

'Did you manage much sleep?' asked Alice, rolling over, her eyes narrow slits.

'Not much.'

She kissed him, and he pulled her against his body, her skin soft to his touch.

'I keep seeing his body lying at the bottom of the stairs,' he said.

'What did you do with him?' Alice took his hand, and examined his fingers one-by-one.

'You don't want to know.'

'No dirt under your fingernails. No blisters on your hands. I'm guessing you didn't dig a hole?'

'Not exactly.'

'Why won't you tell me?'

'Because it's better you don't know.'

'I didn't think we kept secrets?'

'You'll be implicated. What do they call it?'

'Being an accessory?'

'Yeah.'

'It's a bit late for that,' said Alice, dropping his hand. 'You think I'll tell someone, don't you?' She pulled away from him, and gathered her hair in her hand.

'Of course not. But if the police start asking questions, you won't have to lie.'

'I scrubbed his blood from the carpet, Jez. I'm already implicated.'

'I took care of things, that's all you need to know.'

'Fine.' Alice swung her legs out of bed, and sat up. 'I need to get to work.'

'Don't be like that. I'm protecting you.' But she'd already gone.

He listened to the patter of water from the shower, and sank back into his pillow, pain building behind his eyes.

When Alice returned, he was still lying in bed.

'Not getting up?' she asked. Her shoulders glistened with water droplets. 'You'll be late. Again.'

'I'm not going in. I can't. Not today.'

Alice scrunched up her face as she towelled her hair. 'Seriously?'

'I've barely slept a wink, and my mind's all over the place. I'd be useless in the office.'

Alice sat on the bed, a dark scowl forming over her face. A bead of water ran down the back of her neck. 'I'm not sure that's such a good idea.'

'I've only got a couple of appointments today. The others can take care of them. I'll tell them that I'm not feeling well. It's the end of the week. They won't mind.'

'You should go in,' said Alice. 'Even if you have to leave early. We shouldn't do anything out of the ordinary.'

'I can't. It's all right for you. You didn't kill him.'

'Don't say that.'

'That I killed him? Well, I did. You can't pretend it didn't happen.'

'Stop it.'

'How can I?'

'You have to get a grip or it's going to drive you mad.' Tears formed in Alice's eyes.

'I see his face all the time. And the blood. It's all I can think about.'

'Don't torture yourself.'

'I can't help it.'

'You have to be strong, for me and Lily. We need you,' said Alice.

'I know, but one day. That's all I need. Seriously, I can't face seeing anyone today.'

'One day. You promise?' She pouted, and made those sad, puppy eyes he couldn't resist.

'One day, that's all. Just to get my head together.'

'All right, but I need to get Lily to nursery.'

Jez grabbed his phone, and pretended to scroll through his Facebook feed, as Alice dropped her towel, and stood naked at the end of the bed, picking through her underwear drawer.

'The thing I still can't understand is what he was doing in our house in the first place,' said Jez. 'It's odd, I didn't get the impression he was trying to burgle the place.'

Alice floated to the wardrobe, and chose a grey pencil skirt and a pink cashmere sweater.

'Alice?'

'No,' she said.

'He was fascinated by that picture of you and Lily.'

'Hmm?'

'I mean, he stank of booze, and was probably off his head on drugs too.'

'Right.'

'Are you even listening to me?'

'Of course I am, but I have to get ready. Let's talk later.'

Alice gathered her hair in a ponytail, and fixed it in place. Then, after a few minutes with her make-up, managed to conceal how tired and pale she'd looked first thing.

'You look great,' said Jez. 'Come back to bed. Spend the day with me.'

That would help to take his mind off things. He shot her a lascivious grin as the bedroom door crashed open, and Lily ran into the room. She launched herself onto the bed with a toothy grin that instantly crushed Jez's ardour.

'Hey, Lily-Bear!' Jez smothered her head with kisses.

'Why are you still in bed?'

'He's not feeling very well, darling,' said Alice.

'What's wrong?' Lily pushed her glasses up her nose with a stub finger.

'Sore throat,' said Jez, as Alice tried to say he'd been sick in the night.

'He was sick last night, and now he's got a sore throat.' Alice shot Jez a look. 'Now why aren't you dressed? We're going to be late for nursery.'

'Don't want to go to nurs-wee,' said Lily.

Jez loved that she couldn't pronounce nursery.

'Want to stay here.' Lily clamped her arms around her chest in gesture of defiance.

'Jez doesn't feel very well. He's going to stay in bed to get better, but he'll still be here when you get home tonight.'

Jez loved hanging out with Lily, but he needed time on his own to straighten out his head today, not hanging on every whim and tantrum of a four-year-old.

'I'm staying.'

'Lily! I don't have time for this.'

'Come on, do as your mum says,' said Jez. 'We don't want her getting cross.'

'I want to stay and look after you.' She thought about it for a second and announced, 'I can make chicken soup and toast soldiers.'

'What a lovely idea, but I'm not very hungry, and I think your friends would miss you, wouldn't they?'

'Don't care.'

'Lily, for the last time, go and get dressed and leave Jez in peace.'

Lily pretended to burst into tears, and flounced out of the room.

7

Jez spent the morning in his boxer shorts and dressing gown, slumped on the sofa, flicking between daytime TV and battling an alien invasion on his Xbox. Tiredness had left his head woolly, but he couldn't sleep.

It was mid-afternoon before he summoned the energy to dress, and only then because he was worried what Alice would say if she came home and found him vegging out in his pants.

When he heard the key rattle in the lock, and the front door swing open, he was struck by a pang of guilt. He'd forgotten to call the locksmith. It was the last thing Alice had reminded him to do before she left, but it was too late now. They probably charged a small fortune for an emergency call-out.

Lily sprinted the length of the hall, and jumped into Jez's open arms. He swept her up, and swung her onto his hip. She smelled of the nursery, disinfectant and floor polish.

'How are you feeling?' she asked with genuine concern. Her pudgy hand felt clammy on his forehead.

'Much better now.'

She wriggled free of his grasp, and ran off into the lounge. 'Can we play on the Xbox?'

'You go ahead. I'll be there in a minute,' said Jez.

Alice looked exhausted, her hair unusually dishevelled, and her skin pasty.

'How was your day?'

'Busy,' she said, but Jez didn't register the curtness in her voice.

'I know, I've been knackered all day. But I couldn't sleep. Every time I closed my eyes —'

'You should have tried doing a day's work.' She cut across him before he could finish.

'I'm sorry. You're right. But you're home now.'

'Did you call the locksmith?'

'They couldn't come until next week,' Jez lied.

'You're kidding. Did you tell them it was an emergency?'

'Of course.'

'Did you try another number?'

'Come on, why don't you come and sit down. Put your feet up. I'll pour you a glass of wine.' Jez sloped off into the kitchen, and heard Alice's footsteps on the stairs.

He found an open bottle of Sauvignon Blanc in the fridge, and poured a large glass before hooking out a bottle of beer for himself, and joining Lily on the sofa. Her face was set in concentration as she held a grey controller in her lap.

When Alice returned, she'd changed into a pair of jeans and a thick woollen sweater. She fell into her favourite armchair in the corner, tucked her feet under her legs, and took a large gulp of the wine.

It was as close to normality as Jez could imagine; the three of them sitting together after a long day. And yet it felt far from normal. Jez's pulse threaded thick and fast through his veins. His palms were hot and sweaty. And when the timer on the oven pinged, he almost shot out of his seat.

'Calm down, will you,' said Alice.

Jez bit his lip, and wiped his hands on his jeans. 'I'll be all right in a bit,' he said.

They ate dinner watching TV, an inane game show which featured, in Jez's opinion, some of the country's most stupid contestants. But he knew how much Alice hated it when he shouted in frustration at the television, and kept his thoughts to himself for a change.

By seven-thirty Lily was yawning, and rubbing her eyes.

'Come on, time to get you to bed,' said Alice, folding up a tea towel as she finished drying the dishes.

'I'll take her,' said Jez. 'You've had a long day.'

It was rare, if not completely unheard of, for Jez to offer to oversee Lily's bedtime routine. It was the least he could do after forgetting to call the locksmith.

'It's fine,' said Alice.

'No, it's not. Leave it to me. We can manage, can't we Lily-Bear?'

For a change, Lily didn't argue. She raced up the stairs with Jez chasing her, roaring like a lion. Lily screamed, and almost toppled over her own feet as she reached the top step.

'Don't wind her up before bedtime,' Alice yelled.

Jez ran a bath, helped dress Lily in a pair of pink princess pyjamas, and read four pages of *The Gruffalo* before he felt his eyes growing heavy. He pulled the duvet under Lily's chin, and tucked her in with her favourite soft toy, a black and brown dog with matted hair.

Alice had stretched out on the sofa with a glass of wine resting on her stomach. The television was on low. Jez picked up her feet, and dropped them in his lap.

'Want to talk about last night?' she asked.

'What have we done?'

'It was an accident. You didn't mean to kill him. You said so yourself.'

'He had this crazy look in his eye, and when he went for the stairs, I guess I snapped.'

'You were only looking out for us.'

'But I killed him.'

'He broke into the house.'

'We should have called the police,' said Jez. 'If I'd explained what happened, they would have understood.'

Alice didn't say anything, but he knew what she was thinking. And she was probably right. Reasonable force was one thing. But Jez hadn't been able to stop himself, even when the man was unconscious. Blow after blow after blow. His loss of control terrified him.

'Listen, we couldn't call the police,' said Alice. 'You'd have been arrested for sure.'

'What we did was wrong. I wish you hadn't told me to get rid of the body,' said Jez.

'What else were we going to do?'

'I don't know. It seemed so … callous,' said Jez.

'So, it's my fault?'

'It was your idea.'

'You've got a mind of your own.'

'We don't even know who he is,' said Jez.

'Don't think about it.'

'Don't you think someone's bound to miss him, sooner or later?'

'He brought it on himself,' said Alice.

'But if anyone finds out what I've done …'

Alice pulled her knees up to her chest. 'How could they?'

'What if we missed something? What if someone saw us last night?'

'No one saw anything.'

'His blood was all over the floor, and the walls. It wouldn't take long for police to prove he'd died here,' said Jez.

'No one is going to find out, not unless they discover the body. But you took care of that, right?' Alice raised her eyebrows.

Jez couldn't meet Alice's intense gaze.

'I know you didn't bury him, so what did you do with him?' she asked.

'I can't tell you.'

'I thought we're in this together, aren't we?'

Jez shook his head. 'Don't, Alice.'

'I need to know you've done it properly.'

'Don't you trust me?'

'Of course I trust you.'

'Well, then, it's under control. I'm dealing with it.'

'What do you mean dealing with it? Is it done or not?'

'No,' Jez snapped. 'But it's in hand.'

'Now I'm worried.'

'You don't need to be.'

'Tell me what you've done with the body,' Alice pressed.

Jez squirmed in his seat.

'I want to help you through this,' said Alice, 'but I can't if you won't tell me.'

'Fine,' said Jez, jumping to his feet. If it was that important to her, he'd tell her. 'I left him at the yard.'

'What yard? You don't mean the boatyard?'

Jez said nothing.

'Where your uncle's boat's moored?'

'I'm going to take the boat out at the weekend, and chuck him overboard.'

Jez saw the panic in Alice's eyes. It was a good plan. He didn't see the problem.

'So, where's the body now?' Alice asked. Her mouth hung open in disbelief.

'The tide was out. I left it on the boat.'

Alice looked horrified. 'You're kidding me?'

'What's the problem? I'll take it out when it gets dark, and weigh his body down with some chains or something. There's no way they'll find it ten miles out in the estuary.'

'And in the meantime? For Christ's sake, Jez. You

can't leave a dead body festering on a boat on a busy mooring.'

'It's fine.'

'It's not fine. You can't take the risk. Apart from anything else, that boat connects his death to you.'

'I'll do it tomorrow night then, when it's dark.'

Jez had never taken the boat out, let alone at night. He began to doubt now whether he was capable of doing it on his own. Uncle Tony had made it look so easy on long summer days cruising around the Isle of Sheppey, running up the rigging when the winds picked up off Warden Bay. But Jez didn't have the first clue where to begin. He wasn't even sure he could start the outboard motor.

'No, that's not good enough. Do it tonight. You have to move him from the yard. Every minute he's there, is another minute he could be found.'

'Don't be ridiculous.'

'I'm not messing around, Jez. Do it tonight, or I'll call the police myself.'

8

Uncle Tony's heart gave up long before his zest for life had waned. He died alone in his bed, shortly before his seventieth birthday, and was found four days later after the postman noticed a build-up of mail.

A former merchant sailor, he'd travelled the world, and had shown little interest in settling down, or finding a partner. His true love was the sea, and in later years, his yacht, the *Fare Winds*.

He'd bequeathed the boat to Jez in the hope his only nephew would inherit his nautical passion. But he would have been disappointed. Jez cherished his childhood memories when the two of them had spent long, hot summers sailing the southern English coast, sporting sun-burned noses, and living on a diet of fish and chips.

Jez knew how to run up the main sail, to duck to avoid a swinging jib, and the importance of a decent mooring hitch. But that was the limit of his knowledge.

Even now, in his thirties, Jez found the idea of

learning how to sail overwhelmingly daunting. He'd once Googled it, but had never taken it any further.

Instead, he used the vessel as a place of refuge, where he could retire on a warm, sunny Sunday to read, sleep or lounge on deck with a beer. He'd never attempted to launch her. He wasn't even sure she was seaworthy.

Now he was committed to try, at night, under the most difficult of circumstances. He planned to leave the sails well alone, relying solely on the outboard motor. It couldn't be that difficult to navigate into the estuary.

With the moon bright in a cloudless sky, Jez unlocked the padlock on the flimsy wire gate at the entrance to the boatyard. He parked alongside a row of yachts propped up on wooden blocks for the winter, and threw a rucksack, packed with a flask of tea and a supply of digestive biscuits, over his shoulder to navigate the slippery wooden pontoon jacked up on the muddy banks of the creek.

As he approached the *Fare Winds'* yellowing hull, he felt the stir of potent emotions. He didn't care that her insides were slowly rotting, and the salt air had cracked and dried out her hull. She was the embodiment of happier, carefree times.

Jez sniffed the air. A familiar earthy tang of mud, salt and seaweed hanging thickly in the dark. But no foul stench of putrefying flesh. He had no idea how long it would take a body to start decomposing. Hours? Days? Weeks? Maybe the cool autumnal temperatures had slowed the process. But it was one less thing to worry about after Alice had stoked his fears.

He glanced up at the row of masts, at the little flags and spinning turbines.

A light breeze.

Nothing to worry about.

A bigger issue was finding the yacht was lying in thick mud, keeling slightly to starboard. In his haste, Jez had forgotten to check the tide times. He'd be going nowhere for a while. Nothing he could do, but wait for the incoming tide to refloat the vessel.

Jez tiptoed across the deck, careful not to trip on the rigging in the dark, and dropped into the companionway.

Strange. The cabin hatch was pushed back a few inches, and the doors ajar. He was sure he'd secured them before he left. In fact, he was certain.

His stomach lurched. Had someone been on board, poking around? He stood tall, and scanned the yard with the uncomfortable feeling he was being watched. In the distance an owl screeched, a haunting scream that carried across the marshes, floating on the mist. If someone had been on board, they would have certainly found the body.

Slowly, Jez reached for the torch in his rucksack, and shone it below deck. He imagined how the body might look now, cold and rigid, with waxy grey skin. He shuddered at the thought.

A cone of light danced over the galley sink and cooker, illuminating the old ship's bell hanging from a rope on the ceiling. A row of crinkled paperbacks on a shelf. Mildew-blackened flowery curtains hanging over the narrow windows.

The floor was bare.

No body.

No bloodstained sheet.

Nothing.

Jez stumbled down the steps, and fell onto his hands and knees. The heat of panic flushed his cheeks.

Impossible. How could it have disappeared? Had someone moved it? The police? An animal? But what kind of beast could drag the body of a fifteen-stone man out of the cabin, and off the boat?

He shuffled on his hands and knees in the semi-dark, with the torch casting eerie shadows, looking desperately for a sign he wasn't going mad.

Then he found a smear of blood. A rusty, terracotta smudge, roughly where he remembered the man's head had been. And the dumbbell too. Under a wooden bench where he'd thrown it.

So, where the hell was Marcus Fenson's body?

Jez rubbed his eyes. The pain was back, throbbing through his skull.

He popped his head up through the hatch, and scanned the yard, along a chain-link fence beside a pot-holed road, and as far as the car park, where the hulls of three yachts perched like beached whales.

Nothing.

Jez shone the torch into a tangle of brambles, and across the creek to the pitted mud flats where, during the lighter evenings, armies of sandpipers and curlews hunted for their dinner. Beyond, a bed of reeds rustled in the breeze.

He couldn't think straight. He scratched at an imaginary itch on the back of his head, his nails digging into his soft scalp until he broke the skin and drew blood. He had an overwhelming urge to run away. To get as far away as possible. He couldn't explain what had happened, and didn't want to hang around to find out. It was all too weird.

Trembling, Jez clambered back up on deck, and with shaking hands pulled the doors and hatch shut. He sprinted back to the car, not daring to look back.

'Keys, keys, keys,' he muttered to himself, patting down his jeans and coat, and wondering how he was going to explain to Alice.

He laid the torch on the roof of the car, and found the keys in his trouser pocket. A pigeon burst out of the vegetation climbing over an old wooden shed by the entrance gate. The panicked beat of its wings, and its plaintive warning cry made Jez jump.

'Stupid bird,' he muttered to himself, tossing the rucksack onto the back seat.

His hand reached for the torch, but he froze when he saw its beam had picked out a scrap of white material snagged on a sheet of corrugated steel hanging over a gaping hole in the shed.

Jez's eyes narrowed as the material wafted in the breeze, lifting and falling, like a ghostly apparition, luminescent under the chalky glow of the moon.

He tried to ignore it at first, but as he climbed into the car, and slid the key into the ignition, he couldn't help a glance over his shoulder. The flapping scrap of material snatched at his curiosity, begging him to investigate.

His hand faltered on the key.

'Shit!' he hissed, stepping out of the car, and shoving the keys back into his pocket.

The building was badly decayed. A corrugated steel roof had collapsed in places, and the whole thing looked as if it might blow down in the first serious gale of the winter. As he drew closer, his fears were confirmed. The scrap of material was a bed sheet, mottled with dark stains.

Mud? Blood?

With a shudder, Jez tore it down. It ripped with a wrenching tear.

'Hello?' he shouted, pointing the torch through a gap where the corrugated panel had been bent back far enough for a man to squeeze through. 'Is there anyone in there?'

No response, only a distant avian cry, and the orchestra of whistles, taps and rattles high up in the rigging of the boats on the creek.

Jez forced himself inside, ducking into the darkness with his breath coming in ragged gasps. He was struck by the smell of diesel oil and damp wood.

'Hello?' His voice came out a little strangulated. 'Who's there?'

Torchlight tumbled over piles of abandoned nautical junk. Barrels, rope, paint and bitumen cans, old machinery parts, faded lifebuoys, and sections of fibreglass hull.

What the hell was he doing?

At first, he didn't register the crumpled heap in the corner. He thought it was a pile of old rags and sacks.

But on a second sweep of his torch, the light reflected off something shiny, a button maybe, or a belt.

His vision adjusted to the darkness, and he pieced together the parts of a body. An arm. A leg bent at the knee. A head.

'Oh God,' Jez gasped, dropping the torch.

The light went out. In the dark, bats swooped low through the air. Jez dived onto his knees, feeling around over the slick mud that formed the base of the shed.

A low groan followed a slow, rasping breath.

Jez's fingers tripped over the torch, half buried in the mud. When he flicked it back on, he saw the body hadn't moved.

It was unmistakably a man, face down in the dirt, one arm raised up, the other tucked under his body. Blue jacket, crumpled and grubby. Beige trousers, coated in dirt. Brown brogues with holes in the soles.

Jez staggered backwards, his head spinning. How the hell had Marcus Fenson, supposedly dead, made it from the yacht, and into the shed?

9

Jez pressed two fingers to Marcus's neck. His skin was cool, but not cold. After a moment he detected a slow, weak pulse, and snatched his hand back, as if he'd been burned. Then, with all of his strength, he rolled him onto his back, his feet slipping on the muddy floor.

'Hey, wake up,' Jez shouted, shaking Marcus's shoulders. His head rolled back, and air wheezed through his chest.

He was in a bad way, but definitely not dead. Dried blood matted his hair, and was caked on the side of his face, his skin ashen, his lips blue. Aside from the head injury, it looked like he was probably suffering from mild hypothermia.

Trembling, Jez pulled out his phone. He didn't need a doctor to tell him Marcus needed help, or he was going to die.

His fingers hovered over the keypad, ready to call for an ambulance. But how the hell was he going to explain finding Marcus in the boat shed in the middle of the night without implicating himself? Finding him alive had been a huge let off, and if he walked away, chose to do nothing, he'd be signing the man's death warrant as surely as if he were to put a bullet between his eyes.

Jez rubbed a hand over his stubble, and chewed his lip. Marcus's breathing was ragged and wet. Choking sounds came from his throat. His eyes sprang open. Wild dark opals, confused and fearful.

'Help me!' he gasped, snatching Jez's arm.

Jez fell back, tearing out of Marcus's grip. He crashed into a stack of gas cylinders piled against the wall. They toppled over with a hollow thud that reverberated through the building. Jez scrambled to his feet, fishing in his pocket for his keys. He watched Marcus drift out of consciousness again, and came to a decision.

He tore out of the shed, and tumbled into the car park. Twice he dropped his keys on the gravel in his haste. Marcus was alive. He repeated it over and over in his head, hardly daring to believe his good fortune. He wasn't a killer. At least, not yet.

Jez jumped into his car, chasing his breath, hands clutching the steering wheel. He stared at a house nestled on the hill on the opposite side of the creek, shrouded in darkness, surrounded by bushes and trees, the light of the moon picking out its outline. He could drive away, leave Marcus behind, and he would surely die. It was almost guaranteed he wouldn't make it through the night. Eventually someone at the yard would find his body. They'd call the police, and there'd be an investigation. But would they be able to connect his death with him, or Alice? It was feasible Marcus had wandered into the yard while he was drunk, hit his head, and knocked himself unconscious. They'd certainly find alcohol in his blood, and with no explanation, would they come to the conclusion it was a tragic accident?

But what if the police found traces of his DNA on Marcus's clothes? Fragments of skin, or hair. How could he explain that away? He'd not taken any precautions inside the shed, and if they were at all suspicious about how he'd died, they'd start looking for forensic evidence, for sure. The risk was too great. And besides, Jez had been given a second chance to save Marcus's life. He couldn't let him down again, even if he had broken into their house and frightened the life out of him, threatening Alice and Lily. The decision would haunt him forever.

He reversed the car close to the entrance to the shed, and cranked on the handbrake.

Inside, Marcus was deteriorating fast. His breathing had become irregular and shallow. Time was running out. No time to lose.

He hooked his hands under Marcus's arms, and dragged him out with his feet trailing. He laid him on the ground behind the car, and had an unwelcome flashback to when he and Alice had bundled him into the boot first time around, legs bent at awkward angles, his head pressed down onto his chest. Only now Jez realised he'd not been dead at all. Better to give him some dignity this time.

He threw open the passenger door, bundled Marcus in, and pulled a seatbelt around his chest. He folded his hands into his lap, reclined the seat so his head fell backwards with his airway open, and carefully closed the door. He ran back to the shed to collect the bloodstained sheet, shoved it in the boot, then collapsed on the bonnet, letting his heart rate slow.

Shit. Now he faced the problem of delivering Marcus to the hospital without being seen.

He'd have to work it out on the way.

He rolled out of the car park, padlocked the gate, and used one hand to hold Marcus's head steady as they trundled along the potholed lane towards the main road.

He calculated they could make it to the hospital in thirty minutes with no traffic. He only hoped Marcus would survive that long.

10

Bright sunshine streamed through the kitchen window, flooding the house with an invigorating light, and with near perfect timing, the toaster popped up as the kettle boiled. Jez threw two pieces of hot toast on a plate, and whistled as he made tea in a mug.

'Someone's cheerful this morning.'

He'd not heard Alice silently pad into the room.

'What time did you get in last night?' she asked, standing in her cotton pyjamas, arms crossed over her chest.

'Late.' He poured a second mug of tea, and slid it across the counter for her.

'Was it awful?' she asked, cradling the mug in both hands.

'Do we have to talk about it?'

'I need to know you did it right.'

Jez pushed the plate of toast to one side, lowered his gaze, and drew circles on the floor with his big toe. 'You should sit down,' he said. 'There's something I need to tell you.'

'What?' she said, the smile she'd carried into the room fading.

Jez hesitated, unsure how to explain. 'Marcus is alive,' he said.

Alice shook her head. 'Is that supposed to be a joke?'

'I didn't kill him, Alice. He wasn't dead.'

'Stop it. It's not funny.'

'I'm serious. I went to the yacht, like we planned, but he'd gone. I found him in an old shed, barely conscious, but alive. I thought you'd be pleased.'

Alice stepped back, her expression clouded with an emotion he couldn't read.

'It's good news, Alice,' he said, moving to her. She shrugged away his attempt to take her hand.

'You're in shock,' she said.

'No, I'm not.'

'You're imagining it.'

'He was in a pretty bad way, but he was breathing, and I found a pulse. All I can think is that he came around on the boat, but the yard's locked up most of the time, so he wouldn't have been able to escape.'

'You're serious, aren't you?'

'Of course I am. Why would I lie?'

'But we put him in the boot of your car,' said Alice.

'I know. He must have been alive all that time.'

'Oh my God.'

'We should have called an ambulance.'

Alice paced a small circle, her head thrown back, staring at the ceiling. 'What did you do with him?'

'It was a chance to make things right.'

'What did you do with him, Jez?'

'I drove him to the William Harvey.'

'You drove him to hospital? Are you insane?'

'Well, I could hardly leave him there, could I?' said Jez, raising his voice, then checking himself, worried Lily might hear. 'What was I supposed to do? It's been a living hell, thinking I'd murdered him. I've hardly slept a wink. But now —'

'You've redeemed yourself,' said Alice, with a sneer he didn't much like. 'Your conscience is clear, and we can all go back to playing happy families.'

Jez frowned. 'If you want to put it like that.'

'You're an idiot. How long do you think it will be before the police come looking for you now? You attacked him, and left him for dead. I'd say that's grounds for an attempted murder charge, and that makes me an accessory.'

'Don't be ridiculous. The state he was in, I doubt whether he'll remember anything.'

'What about the cameras around the hospital? There's CCTV everywhere. All they'll have to do is look back and see who brought him in.'

'I didn't take him in. I left him in the park, near the hospital, and called an ambulance.'

'On your mobile?'

Jez had made the call brief, and hadn't left his name. It was unlikely they could trace his number, wasn't it? He said nothing.

'And what's he going to tell them at the hospital when they ask what happened?'

'You think I should have left him there to die?'

'No,' said Alice, 'you should have finished what you started.'

'What the hell does that mean?'

Alice turned away, dabbing at her eyes with the corner of a tissue. 'It doesn't matter,' she said.

'It does if you meant what I think.'

'We need to get away from here,' said Alice. 'We can start over. Just the three of us. You, me and Lily.'

'Leave? What about Mum and Dad?'

'I forgot, you can't do anything without the approval of your mum, can you?'

'Don't be like that. I just don't understand why we need to leave.'

'Fine, we'll go on our own. We don't need you anyway. It was you who got us into this mess in the first place.'

'I wanted to call the police, but you wouldn't have it,' said Jez.

'You hit him.'

'I was scared. God knows what he'd have done if I hadn't stopped him.'

'You overreacted.'

'I was protecting you.'

'Really? Not just your temper getting the better of you then?'

'Don't leave,' said Jez. 'I won't let you.'

'I have to, for Lily's sake.'

'Lily's fine where she is.'

'You don't understand.'

'If you leave, I'll tell the police everything,' said Jez. 'I'll tell them it was your idea to hide the body.'

'You wouldn't.'

Jez shrugged.

'I'm scared he'll be back. And I can't risk that,' said Alice.

'I'll get the door fixed. I'll put up some cameras, and fit some proper locks,' said Jez. 'You'll be safe, both of you. But I doubt very much he's ever coming back.'

'He knows where we live, and he'll find a way of getting to me, and Lily, no matter what you do.'

Jez shook his head. 'He doesn't care about us. He's not coming back.'

'He will. I know what he's like.' The words snapped out of her mouth with a ferocity that took Jez by surprise.

'How do you know what he's like?'

'Oh, forget it.'

Alice turned for the stairs, but Jez was across the room in a flash. He snatched her wrists, and wrestled her arms to her sides.

'You're hurting me!'

'Alice, how can you know what he's like? Do you know him?'

'Let me go!'

'I want the truth. Who is he?'

'Please, Jez,' said Alice.

'You were screwing him, weren't you?' He'd had his suspicions about her, but nothing like this.

'You bastard!' screamed Alice, snatching her wrists free.

He was a fool to think she could ever be satisfied with a man like him. He'd noticed the way she eyed up other men when they went out. A flirtatious smile. A flutter of her eyelids. He'd done his best to ignore it, but this was something else.

'What was he, a bit of fun on the side who took it a bit too seriously? Come to profess his undying love, had he?'

'Mummy! Mummy!' Lily's footsteps sounded on the stairs, and she thundered down them like a herd of wild cattle.

Alice slapped him hard across the cheek. 'How dare you,' she said, indignation burning in her eyes.

Lily burst into the room, and froze when she saw the two adults squaring up to each other.

'Tell me the truth,' said Jez.

'You wouldn't believe the truth,' she hissed, scooping Lily up in her arms. 'I think you should move out.'

'What?'

'Until I can find some place for me and Lily. If that's honestly what you think of me, I don't want to be with you anymore.'

'Alice, can't we talk about this?'

'There's nothing left to say. Pack your things, and get out.'

11

The couple, Tim and Maria, were waiting on the pavement, hand-in-hand, when Jez arrived fifteen minutes late. He sorted through a large bunch of keys without apologising, and let them into a tired-looking end-of-terrace Victorian cottage.

'Welcome to the house of your dreams,' said Jez, ushering them into a small lounge with a shocking pink carpet. The room had been emptied of furniture, the ceiling was a swirl of yellowing plaster, and the decor looked like it hadn't been updated in forty years.

'It's not the biggest property I've shown you, but on your budget your options are limited,' said Jez. 'But you're the first to see it, and at this price it's going to sell quickly. So, if you like what you see, I suggest putting in an early offer.'

'I can definitely see potential,' said Maria, who Jez had determined worked in finance somewhere in London.

Her boyfriend, Tim, who did something with

computers, eyed the room as if someone was holding a bag of festering meat under his nose.

They'd already viewed and dismissed at least thirty properties on Jez's books, which made them the type of buyers he loathed, first-timers so paralysed by the fear of making a mistake that they refused to commit to a purchase, whilst the market spiralled further out of their reach.

'The kitchen could do with modernising, but it's all just cosmetic really. Nothing new cupboard doors and a lick of paint wouldn't sort out.'

Jez led them to the back of the house, where Tim jammed his nose up against a window overlooking a scrubby patch of lawn, laughingly described in the details as a garden. It was hardly large enough to accommodate a shed.

'Not much of a garden, is there?' Tim said.

'It's what you get for your two hundred grand,' said Jez. 'I can show you a house with a garden twice the size, but we'd be looking outside of your preferred area, and sticking another fifty thousand on the price. Is there any more money in the pot?' Jez raised a hopeful eyebrow, knowing full well the house was at the top of their budget.

'No,' said Tim.

'Then this is what you get for your money, particularly in a popular location like this. It's very close to the town, and within easy walking distance of the station.'

'Can we take a look upstairs?' asked Maria.

'Be my guest.' Jez directed them towards a narrow staircase in the lounge.

When they'd disappeared, he checked his watch, and made a small wager with himself. It wouldn't take long for them to check out the twin box rooms and the tiny bathroom with its 1980s-style avocado suite and mould-mottled ceiling. Without question they would dismiss it out of hand, just like all the previous properties.

While he waited in the kitchen, listening to the patter of their footsteps, Jez pinched the bridge of his nose, and rolled his neck. He hated fighting with Alice, but he was no mug. He was glad to have finally seen through her deceit. It was Lily who would suffer, but he convinced himself that moving out was best for all of them.

Everything had moved so fast when he'd first met Alice. He'd been swept up in her momentum, and never really had a chance to adjust to his newfound role as a family man. He should have listened to his mother. He was still young. It was too soon to settle down.

His thoughts were interrupted by his phone ringing in his jacket pocket.

'Mick, can I call you back? I'm in the middle of a viewing.'

'Working on a Saturday again?' said the voice on the other end of the line.

'Some of us don't have a choice.'

'It's just that me and a couple of the lads were popping out for a few lunchtime jars. Want to join us?'

'I can't. I don't finish till five,' said Jez, although the offer was tempting. 'Maybe later.'

'Yeah, whatever.'

'I could do with a drink.'

'You all right, mate? You sound a bit down.'

'I broke up with Alice.'

'Seriously?'

'We had a row this morning.'

'Want to talk about it?'

'Not right now. I've got to go. I'll call you later.' Jez hung up as Tim and Maria trouped boot-faced down the stairs.

Jez slipped his phone back into his jacket, and forced a smile. 'What do you think?'

'Well, it's definitely a good area for us,' said Maria, always the diplomatic one. 'We've looked at houses in St John's Road before, and we like a period property with a bit of character, and as you say it's close to the station and the town.'

'But?'

'There's a lot of work to do,' said Tim. 'For a start the carpets are hideous. They'll all need ripping out and replacing.'

'Not a major job though,' said Jez, through gritted teeth.

'And that's before we even begin looking at the kitchen and bathroom. And with the house being at the top of our budget, there's not going to be much left for doing the place up. Besides the garden is very small.'

'We want a bigger kitchen too. And I'm not sure about being on the end of a terrace,' said Maria.

'Anything else?' said Jez, feeling a headache coming on.

'Is there anything on the other side of the street?' Maria raised her eyebrows with optimistic hope.

'No,' said Jez. 'I've shown you every house that's come on the market in your price range for the last nine months, but the house you want doesn't exist. So, unless you're expecting to win the lottery anytime soon, you're going to have to compromise on something.'

Maria's face fell, and for a split-second Jez felt bad about knocking the wind out of her sails. But he pushed on, regardless.

'If it's not the toilet that's in the wrong place, then it's the bedroom painted in the wrong shade, or you don't like the shape of the roof,' he said. 'You're making excuses, and wasting my time. At some point you're going to have to bite the bullet. Maybe you'll make a mistake, maybe you won't. But for God's sake, make a decision before you drive me insane.'

Maria looked close to tears.

'I'm sorry you feel like that,' said Tim. His face had turned sour. 'I'd hate to think we're wasting *your* time.' He grabbed Maria's hand and dragged her to the front door. 'Come on, I've heard enough. Let's get out of here.'

The front of the building shook as the door slammed behind them.

'Shit! Shit! Shit!' Jez banged his head against his clipboard. Still, someone needed to point out the facts. He was doing them a favour.

When he caught up with them, halfway down the street, they were climbing into their car.

'Tim! Maria! I'm sorry, I probably shouldn't have said that. It's been a stressful morning,' he said. 'I'll go back through the books when I get back to the office and give you a call if I find anything else.'

The car pulled away with a screech of tyres, leaving Jez standing forlornly on the pavement, his clipboard hanging at his side.

'Idiots,' he muttered under his breath, as he turned away and trudged back to the office.

12

Five o'clock came around slowly. None of Jez's other viewings had looked remotely like resulting in a sale, so ignoring the flashing red voicemail light on the phone on his desk, he closed up the office and headed for the comfort of the Rising Sun. He picked a table by the log fire, and nursing a pint, checked his mobile for any messages or missed calls from Alice.

Not a word. Not even a text.

That made up his mind. He thought after a day to dwell on things, she might have come to her senses, but if she wasn't prepared to apologise for throwing him out, he wasn't going to go back with his tail between his legs.

He finished his beer, and pushed his way outside through a swelling early evening crowd. He retrieved his car, and drove straight to his parents' house on the other side of town.

His mother answered the door drying her hands on a tea towel.

'Jeremy! Why didn't you phone? What a lovely surprise.'

'Sorry, Mum. It was a spur of the moment thing.'

She noticed the overnight bag slung over his shoulder. 'Are you staying the night? Where are Alice and Lily?' She craned her neck to look past him.

'They're at home. It's just me. I need to stay for a couple of nights.'

'Did you fall out?'

'Jez?' His father stuck his head around the lounge door. 'Good timing, son. I'm struggling with this one.' He held up a tiny jigsaw piece between his thumb and forefinger.

'Richard! Let the poor boy get in the door. You should have told me you were coming. I only went shopping this morning. Never mind, you know you're always welcome.'

'Don't fuss, Mum.'

'Take your things upstairs. Tea won't be long. I've made plenty.'

Jez's room was largely as he'd left it when he'd moved out. The world atlas tacked to the wall by the wardrobe, the shelves thick with dust, and his bed still made up. Only his TV, Xbox console and CDs were missing, his limited contribution to the new life he'd begun with Alice and Lily. She'd brought everything else into their new home together; beds, wardrobes, chests of drawers, sofas and chairs. All from a previous life Jez was all too conscious he had played no part in.

He threw his bag in the corner, and collapsed onto the soft mattress, his beer buzz rapidly evaporating.

'Mum! Has the wifi code changed?' he shouted from his bed, struggling to load his Facebook feed on his phone.

He heard the clattering of plates from the kitchen.

'Mum!' he shouted again, convinced she was going deaf.

When she still didn't reply, he conceded defeat. He found her in the kitchen, the windows thick with condensation, pans boiling on the hob. The smell of roasting chicken and simmering vegetables evoked a nostalgia of childhood, a memory of uncomplicated comfort food when his mother always served meat, veg and gravy at every meal because his father wouldn't have it any other way.

'There you are,' she said, looking up from mashing potatoes. 'Can you set the table? And ask your father to open a bottle of wine, as if he'll need any encouragement.'

They ate around the family dining table, in their usual places, just like old times. Before Alice and Lily.

'How long are you staying?' his mother asked, skirting around the real question he knew she was dying to ask.

'I don't know. A couple of days maybe,' said Jez.

'More wine, Jezza?' His father topped up his glass without waiting for an answer.

His mother scowled. She hated it when his father called him that.

'Jeremy, just tell me what's going on. I am your mother, you know.'

'It's nothing. We had a row. That's it,' said Jez.

'About what?'

'It's not important.'

'Of course it's important if you've walked out.'

'I haven't walked out. We're just giving each other some space for a few days,' said Jez.

'Sounds like you've walked out,' said his father, unhelpfully.

'Really, it's nothing to worry about.'

'What about Lily?' said his mother. 'Poor child, caught up in the middle of it all. I warned you this would happen, rushing into living together without giving yourselves a chance to get to know each other properly.'

'Yeah, thanks Doctor Freud,' said Jez.

'How's Alice?' His mother stood to gather their empty plates.

'Okay, I guess. I've not spoken to her since this morning.' Jez pushed his chair back, and took a large gulp of wine. 'Well maybe on this occasion, you're right. Perhaps we did rush into things.'

Their romance had blossomed far too quickly, and Jez had been swept along on the euphoria of a new relationship with a woman he was surprised had given him a second glance. She was beautiful, and funny, passionate and caring.

Alice who had taken the reins, driving the relationship at a frantic pace, introducing him to Lily within their first few dates, and proposing they moved in together. Jez had tumbled along in the wake of her enthusiasm and energy, with questions rolling around his head about her past and the sadness he saw in her eyes.

She never mentioned Lily's father, and Jez didn't like to ask. On the rare occasion he'd raised the subject, Alice dismissed it with the wave of a finely-manicured hand. He thought he could be happy not knowing, but realised now he'd been storing up problems for the future. Secrets and ignorance were no basis for a lasting relationship.

'But are you sure walking out on Alice is the solution?' his mother asked.

'Whose side are you on? I didn't think you approved of her anyway?'

'That's not fair. I thought things between you happened too quickly, but you were happy. You should fight for that.'

'Some things aren't worth fighting for.'

His mother put the plates down, and sat on the edge of her chair. 'You don't mean that.'

'She made it quite clear she wanted to break up.'

'Why? What happened?'

Jez shrugged.

'There must have been a reason,' his mother said. 'People don't just break up. If you've done something stupid, perhaps you should apologise.'

'Why do you think this is my fault?'

His mother raised an eyebrow. 'Isn't it?'

'No!'

'So, what happened?'

Jez folded his arms across his chest, and stared at the reproduction Monet hanging on the wall, its colours faded by sunlight and age. 'She's been seeing other people behind my back.'

At first his mother didn't react. She blinked a couple of times, then laughed. 'Don't be ridiculous,' she said.

'Why's that ridiculous?' Of all people, he expected his mother to be on his side.

'Alice isn't like that.'

'How'd you know?'

'Women's intuition. I know Alice, and she wouldn't do that to you. She loves you.'

'She's got a funny way of showing it.'

'Why do you think she's been unfaithful?'

'I don't want to talk about it,' said Jez.

'You must have good reason if you've accused her of something so serious.'

'I've seen the way she looks at other men,' said Jez, struggling to put into words the jealously that had secretly wormed inside his head. 'I mean, how can I expect she was ever going to be satisfied with someone like me?'

'What on earth are you talking about?'

'You know what she's like. She puts this spell on people when she walks in the room. What do you think she saw in me? I'll tell you - a mug to bring up her daughter. Someone to play daddy. That's it.'

'That's ludicrous. Can you even hear yourself?' said his mother. 'She loves you. You're good for her. You're good together. You swallow your pride, and tell her you're sorry.'

'Tell her I'm sorry? You're kidding me?'

'Don't be so petulant, Jeremy. You're acting like a child.'

'I'm not.'

'Suit yourself.' His mother gathered the plates, and stomped into the kitchen, leaving Jez and his father sitting in an awkward silence, punctuated by the noisy clatter of crockery being thrown into the dishwasher.

'Any more where this came from?' said Jez, finishing his glass of wine.

'Sorry, Jezza. It was the last bottle.'

'Terrific.'

'And don't think you're going to mope around here feeling sorry for yourself,' his mother said, storming back into the room, a tea towel twisted tightly around one hand. 'You need to have a long, hard think about things.'

'Great, thanks for the pep talk, Mum.'

'I'm serious, Jeremy. I won't stand back and let you ruin the one decent thing that's happened to you in years. Go back to her, and talk it through, for God's sake.'

'I've heard enough of this.' As Jez stood, his chair toppled backwards, scraping the wall.

'Mind the paintwork, son,' said his father.

'Sorry, Dad.' He righted the chair, and pushed it under the table. 'I'm going to bed.'

Jez stomped up the stairs, and slammed his bedroom door shut. He'd come home for some sympathy and a compassionate ear. But his mother was worse than Alice, treating him like a teenager.

The fact was, Alice had lied to him. He'd caught her

out, and she didn't like it. And if she'd lied about knowing Marcus Fenson, how many more lies had she fed him that he'd swallowed like a gullible fool?

His mother was wrong. It wasn't up to him to apologise. If Alice wanted him back, then she had to make the first move. And she'd need a pretty good explanation.

13

An oppressive blanket of cloud hung low on the horizon as a keen north-easterly wind carved through the town. Jez sat on a park bench overlooking the recreation ground with his shoulders hunched and his collar pulled up over his neck to keep out the chill. The heat from a takeaway coffee in a cardboard cup warmed his hands, but the rest of him was freezing. Still, it was infinitely better than spending Sunday morning with his parents. He'd only been home a few hours, and they were driving him mad already.

He suspected his mother had woken him deliberately, running the vacuum cleaner around the house at some unearthly hour, banging into skirting boards and doors. He'd tried to cling onto the last threads of sleep, burying his head under the pillow, but his mother had put paid to that when she barged in and pulled open the curtains.

'Still in bed? You'll miss the best of the day. I'll open

a window. It smells like something's died in here,' she said.

Jez groaned, and reached an arm from under the duvet to grab his phone. The picture on his lock screen taunted him. Three grinning faces taken on a sunny afternoon in April on the beach at Whitstable. Lily up front, smiling with crooked milk teeth. Jez trying to look cool behind a pair of aviator sunglasses. And Alice. Immaculate. Perfect. Like a model on the front of a magazine. Jez swallowed the lump in his throat, and threw the phone down.

No messages.

No missed calls.

He gave up on any ambitions of a Sunday morning lie-in, showered, dressed, and found his father spread out on the sofa in the lounge, drowning under a sea of Sunday supplements. The radio was on, droning in the background. Dad's favourite soap.

The final straw was discovering they were out of coffee, and the only cereal his mother had in was a box of supermarket-brand cornflakes. Jez did not do supermarket brands of anything. So he snatched his coat from the hook by the door, and took off, not really knowing where he was going.

A grey whippet, shivering in the cold, sniffed around his legs before shooting him a worried look, and trotting off. From the opposite direction, a toddler approached unsteadily on stiff legs, arms outstretched, targeting a pigeon pecking through fallen leaves. The toddler's parents, all rosy cheeks and relaxed smiles, followed pushing a pram. The picture of perfect family life.

They meandered with no particular hurry towards an enclosed playground where fathers were bent over roundabouts and swings, with protective arms ready to catch their uncoordinated offspring, while gaggles of conspiratorial mothers gathered in huddles, gossiping and laughing.

The children came in all shapes and sizes. Any one of them could have been Lily, her brow knitted in concentration as she navigated each piece of equipment with her glasses perched on the end of her snub nose, her hair a tangled mess. As the screams of laughter and joy drifted across the park, Jez realised how much he missed her. More than he imagined he would. She wasn't his child. He was simply a surrogate. Her next dad in what would probably be a long list in her life.

The toddler, who'd been chasing pigeons, froze when he approached the playground, mesmerised by the sight and sound of so many older children. His mother took him by the hand, and encouraged him on. Jez smiled to himself. He wished he'd known Lily at that age. So cute.

His legs were so numb with cold, he stood and stamped his feet. He dumped his coffee cup in a bin, and with no conscious thought followed the path that wound its way through the park. Without realising it, he was heading towards the playground, unknowingly drawn by the excited joy of children's laughter.

A football whizzed past his legs, startling Jez from his thoughts.

'Hey, mister, over here,' said a young lad in an

Arsenal shirt, standing with a group of half a dozen other youngsters.

Jez stared at them for a moment, alarmed that a teenager was yelling at him, until he understood they wanted him to kick their ball back.

He jogged across the dewy grass, and awkwardly side kicked it out of a divot, suddenly conscious that he'd never been much of a footballer. His sporting skills were virtually non-existent, and so he'd always shied away from any form of physical activity for fear of being ridiculed.

'Over here, mate!' one of the other teenagers shouted.

Jez eyed up the ball, and took a step back. The boys were standing less than twenty metres away, but it might as well have been the length of the park. It had been a long time since Jez had kicked a ball, and he was terrified of making a fool of himself.

'Come on, mate. Hurry up,' another one shouted.

Jez focused, and tilted his head. Nothing to be worried about. It was only a football.

He planted his left foot firmly on the ground, and swung his right leg, concentrating on making a decent contact. But he judged it all wrong. Instead of the solid punt he was aiming for, he wrapped his foot around the ball, and sliced it left, sending it away to the boys' right, towards an elderly couple walking arm in arm by the tennis courts. The boys stood with hands on hips watching the ball soar away. One of them clapped sarcastically.

'Cheers for that,' said another voice, dripping with irony.

Jez held up an apologetic hand. 'Sorry,' he said.

He sauntered back to the path, his cheeks burning with shame. When he glanced up at the playground, he noticed a flash of red. A scarlet coat. Something about the cut and shade of it triggered a reaction in his head. The woman had her back to him, tending to a child on a swing. Lily, wrapped warmly in a scarf and mittens.

He doubled his pace, and pushed through a swinging gate into the playground where the little girl was whooping with delight.

'Guess who?' said Jez, approaching the woman from behind, and clamping his hands over her eyes.

The woman screamed, and as she spun around, Jez realised too late that the little girl on the swing wasn't Lily. There was definitely a passing resemblance, but she was much younger, and her build more slender.

'I'm so sorry,' said Jez, backing away. 'I thought you were my girlfriend. She has the same coat.'

The woman stared at him with terror in her eyes. She snatched the little girl off the swing, and clasped her protectively against her legs. 'What the hell do you think you're playing at?'

Jez became aware that the playground had fallen silent, and several of the mothers who'd been in a huddle in the corner were staring.

'I'm sorry,' Jez said again.

'Get away from me,' said the woman.

He noticed she was trembling. A total over-reaction.

'Everything okay here?' said a deep voice from behind.

One of the fathers with broad shoulders and thick, callused knuckles appeared at Jez's side.

'Yeah, it's all fine. Just a misunderstanding,' said Jez.

'I wasn't talking to you. Are you all right, love? Is he bothering you?'

The woman seemed too shocked to answer.

Another man sidled up, his nose bright red from the cold. 'Where's your kid?' he asked.

'I don't think she's here right now,' said Jez, without thinking. Then realising how it might look that a childless man was hanging around a children's playground, pouncing on single women, added, 'I thought she was my girlfriend. She has the same coat.'

It sounded pathetic, even as he said it.

The woman, who Jez had accosted, had regained a little composure, and seemingly emboldened by the growing crowd said, 'He attacked me.'

'No, I didn't,' said Jez. Describing it as an attack was a little harsh.

'I saw him,' said another woman, who'd broken away from the huddle of mothers in the corner. 'I had my eye on him. He was lurking around the park watching the children.'

'I wasn't lurking,' said Jez, affronted.

'Is that right?' said the man with callused knuckles.

'Look, it was an honest mistake. I'm sorry if I frightened her. It was a stupid thing to do.'

'Call the police,' said the man with the red nose.

The idea was greeted with a murmur of assent. A

strong hand gripped Jez's bicep. 'Get off me,' he said, shrugging off the hand.

A third man, with a bald head and woollen scarf wrapped around his neck, was already on his phone. Things were spiralling out of control. Jez couldn't afford the police to get involved. He had to think quickly.

'Why don't I call my girlfriend, and she can confirm we were due to meet here, and that this is all a silly misunderstanding?' he said.

'Go on, then,' said one of the mothers with an unnaturally deep tan and heavily-drawn eyebrows.

Jez dug in his jeans' pocket for his phone, but fumbled with it in his urgency. It fell face down in the grass. Jez dropped to his knees, and wiped away a smudge of mud from the handset with trembling fingers. He checked the screen for any missed calls, and was more disappointed than ever to find that Alice hadn't been trying to contact him.

'I'm calling her now,' he said, finding Alice's number at the top of his list of contacts.

He pressed the phone to his ear, and had to check twice that it was connecting. Eventually he heard a click, and he smiled at the crowd.

'The person you are trying to call is unavailable. Please try again later,' said the automated voice in his ear.

Jez's stomach flipped. He hung up, and redialled, praying it was a momentary glitch, that Alice hadn't switched off her phone.

He waited through a long pause for a connection, and heard the same distant click. Jez held up a finger to indicate to the crowd that he was through, and was about to speak.

'Hey, Alice, it's me,' he said.

'The person you are trying to reach is unavailable,' said the voice in his ear.

'I'm here at the park waiting for you and Lily. Are you going to be long?' Jez smiled at one of the mothers, standing with her arms folded, and an unpleasant sneer on her face.

'Please try again later.'

'Okay, see you in a minute then. I'll wait for you in the playground. Love you,' he added, for effect.

He sensed the crowd relax a little. But nobody moved. A dozen pairs of eyes were watching him. Judging him. It was a most uncomfortable sensation. Jez calculated the distance to the low iron fence was no more than five long strides away. He slipped the phone back in his pocket, and snatched his opportunity, pushing past the woman in the red coat.

He vaulted the fence with one hand, landed on his toes, and sprinted as hard as his legs would pump, heading across the playing fields towards the main road.

'Oi! Get back here!' shouted one of the dads.

Admittedly, it didn't look like the behaviour of an innocent man, but he couldn't face the police, not after everything that had happened in the last few days. What if they started poking around his home life, asking awkward questions? He couldn't risk it, after all, he'd done nothing wrong. It was best to make a run for it. The crowd in the park would soon forget.

But they weren't in the mood to let him go easily. He

heard the rapid thud of someone running behind him, but he didn't look back. If he could make it to the road, and into the estate beyond, maybe he could lose them.

He made it halfway there before a sharp pain stabbed him in the ribs, and took his breath away. He winced and gripped his side, but pushed on, ignoring the stitch, and the burning sensation in his thighs.

His feet slid and turned on the rough field, churned up through the autumn by football and rugby teams. Finally, he made it to the street, expecting to be tackled to the ground at any second. He tumbled down a low grass bank, and ran straight out into the road, in front of a white van which slammed on its brakes to avoid him. Jez swerved around its bonnet, caught his balance, and pushed on. Behind him, a car horn blared, accompanied by the screech of brakes and howl of rubber.

Jez put his head down, and ran hard, ignoring the pain radiating through his shins as he pounded the hard pavement. His wheezing lungs felt fit to burst. He'd let himself grow fat and unfit, and he was paying the price. But he couldn't stop now. If they caught him, he was sure they would hand him over to the police, and they were bound to draw the wrong conclusions when they found out he had made a run for it. His only option was to push through the pain, and keep going.

At least two sets of pursuing footsteps echoed off the walls of the terraced houses. Jez could hear they were close behind. Ahead, the road ended at a T-junction. A decision to be made. Left or right? He didn't know this part of town, a sprawling nineteen-fifties council estate of dreary semi-detached houses crammed into a network of back roads.

What he did know was that he couldn't go much farther. His hip had started aching, adding to the catalogue of discomfort from his protesting body. He either needed to find somewhere to hide, or face his accusers.

As he reached the junction, he feinted left, then turned right, based on a sense it would lead him deeper into the estate, and provide more options to escape his pursuers.

For a moment or two, he was out of sight of the chasers. He had to make a split-second decision, but his options were limited. The houses all looked identical. Cheap two-storey boxes with tiny front gardens. No obvious places to take cover.

He slowed up with his stitch shooting daggers through his gut, and dived over a low privet hedge into someone's garden, rolling on the grass and curling up into a ball.

He clamped a hand over his mouth to silence the sound of his wheezing, and heard the pounding of feet slow, and come to a stop.

Jez held his breath, and waited.

14

The men were close. No more than a few feet from where Jez was hiding. The sound of their breathing, heavy and laboured, gave them away.

'He's gone,' said one, between gasps.

'He can't have got far.'

If they'd peered into the scrubby garden with its patchy lawn and clumps of leafless shrubs, maybe they would have seen Jez cowering, tucked up in a ball under the hedge with his knees drawn up to his chest.

'Start looking around. He's here somewhere.'

The men drifted away, their footsteps fading as they moved down the street.

Jez brought his breathing back under control, as his cramping stitch eased. Relaxing a little, he unfurled from his protective ball. His coat and jeans were covered in mud from the unsightly dive he'd taken over the hedge, and a chill dampness seeped through his clothes from the wet grass. But it was the least of his worries.

Lifting his head, he found he was lying in the garden

of an exposed brick, semi-detached house with white plastic window frames, greying net curtains, and a red door faded pink with age. Jez eased himself onto his hands and knees, and risked a glance down the road. The two men were prowling the street, scanning left and right into each of the houses and gardens. Jez willed them to keep walking. If they made it to the next junction, it might buy him some time to give them the slip. If he was lucky, he could sneak back towards the recreation ground without being noticed.

The closest of the pair, the man with callused knuckles, stopped without warning between two cars parked on the pavement. He made a call on his mobile, close enough that Jez heard every word.

'Robbie, it's me. Listen, we chased a kiddie fiddler out of the playground on the rec, but we've lost him in the estate opposite. Round up some of the guys and get over here, will you.'

Jez swallowed hard. Kiddie fiddler? Could there be anything worse? Even when he thought he'd killed Marcus Fenson, it hadn't seemed as serious. But touching up small kids? That's what real monsters were made of. Those kinds of allegations could ruin people. He could lose his job. He'd never be able to show his face in town again.

The man on the phone turned a slow circle. Jez dropped out of sight, and rolled onto his back, watching the clouds racing over the roof tops. A net curtain twitched in an upper window of the house, and a woman appeared, her grey face lined and wrinkled with the folds of aged skin.

Jez watched with bated breath as she noticed the two men stalking the street. She studied them with the curiosity of someone used to knowing everything that happened in the neighbourhood. Jez prayed she wouldn't notice him curled up in her garden.

For a few long moments, she remained motionless, half hidden in the shadows.

Eventually, she turned her head. He noticed her eyes were wet and rheumy as her gaze fell on him. But she showed no sign of shock or surprise. Her expression remained impassive, as if it was nothing out of the ordinary to find a stranger cowering on her lawn.

Jez pulled an apologetic grin, willing her not to raise the alarm. She'd only have to bang on the window to alert the two men down the street, and it would be game over. He wasn't sure he had the legs to run any farther.

But after a brief moment, the old woman's gaze shifted to a spot beyond where Jez was lying on the grass. She tapped on the window pane with a bony finger, pointing. He rolled over, and saw a small wooden shed partially obscured behind an ornamental Japanese maple tree that had been stripped of most of its leaves. Perfect.

He turned to mouth, 'thank you', but the net curtain had fallen back into place, and the old woman had vanished.

Jez stuck his nose over the hedge. The men had moved even farther down the road, so he took his chance, rose into a crouch, and duck-waddled across the lawn. He fumbled with the shed door, cringing at the metallic creak of the latch, and found it was crammed full. A lawn mower took up most of the room among stacks of old plant pots, garden furniture, tools, and assorted junk. Just enough space for Jez to squeeze in. He collapsed on a builder's bag half-filled with damp sand, and pulled the door shut.

There was a strong smell of cut pine, and the silence of an enclosed space echoed around his head. Out of the wind, it felt several degrees warmer. If he needed to, he could probably last it out in there for several hours. But a plan had formed in his head. He wiped his nose with the back of his hand, sniffed, and dug out his phone.

In the dark, the screen seemed unusually bright, throwing shadows against the rough, wooden walls. With his thumb, Jez navigated to his contacts, looking for someone he could trust.

The name at the top of the list was Alice's. In any other circumstance, she would have been the first person he'd have phoned. For the past nine months she had been his rock. He'd been devoted to her, and thought she was equally devoted to him. How wrong he'd been.

He scrolled past, putting the sour thoughts to the back of his head. Besides, what would he say? They'd not spoken for more than twenty-four hours, having parted under a dark cloud. Now was not the time to try to clear the air. He needed to find someone who would act first, and ask questions later. Someone he could rely on.

For a fleeting moment, he considered calling his boss. Terry Neil was reliable, but he couldn't imagine explaining his predicament to him. In the office, behind his back, they called him 'Serious Terry'. Even now, on a Sunday morning, he was probably dressed in his three-piece suit.

'You can't change a first impression, Jeremy,' he'd told Jez on his first day. The mantra had stuck with him. So typical of Terry.

Jez carried on looking, soon realising he possibly had the smallest group of friends on earth. He'd lost touch with most of his mates from school. They'd either moved away, or settled down with wives and kids, and Jez had lacked the energy and motivation to keep in contact.

He knew, in reality, there was only one person he could call to spring him out of this mess. He started a new message, and typed:

- I'm in big trouble. Need ur help asap.

He hit send, watched the message spiral into the ether, then stared at the screen, willing a quick response.

Mick didn't let him down.

The phone buzzed twice.

- Whats up?

- You won't believe it but Im hiding in a shed from two guys who want to kill me. Explain later over a beer. Right now I need a lift. Arden Rd. Near the Rec. Hurry.

- Seriously?

- Yes. Really need ur help. Please.

- On my way. Be there in 10 mins.

He knew he could rely on his old friend, Mick. He'd put so much business his way, he owed Jez quite a debt of gratitude. The steady flow of recommendations from

Jez's office had seen Mick Denham's removals firm transformed from a small-time, one man and his van operation to a thriving business with six full-time staff, and four vehicles.

Jez nudged the door open with his foot, but through the narrow crack couldn't see either of his pursuers. He doubted they'd gone far, but not being able to see them made him nervous.

A car roared into the street, travelling too fast, its engine over-revving. Brakes screeched, and an adrenaline spike sent Jez's pulse soaring. He heard two or three car doors open and slam shut. More voices. Deep and serious.

Jez's stomach lurched. He regretted now not having made a run for it while he had the chance. If they found him in the shed, he had nowhere to run.

He eased the door open a couple of inches wider, and an ugly brute strayed into his line of view. A gorilla of a man, with meaty bunched fists dangling by his sides, a squat neck, and a pumped-up chest developed either from too much time in the gym, or a little steroid assistance. With a determined purpose, he strode into the garden where Jez was hiding, and knocked on the front door of the house.

Jez heard the door open, but struggled to hear the muted voices as they presumably discussed the search to find him. Right now, the gorilla was probably telling the old woman he was a pervert who'd been approaching kids in the park. He only hoped she wouldn't believe him, nor give away his hiding place.

The gorilla stepped back into Jez's line of view, his

hands in his pockets, and his brow knotted in a serious frown. He gesticulated with his arms, pointing up and down the road, and Jez guessed the old lady was playing ignorant. He made a note that if he made it out of this alive, he'd send flowers.

Jez was concentrating so hard on trying to catch snippets of their conversation that at first he didn't register the low rumble of a worn-out diesel engine, and the racket of a blown exhaust. Mick's van pulled up right outside the house, blocking Jez's view of the opposite side of the street. He immediately recognised the paintwork, caramel cream with dirty black scrapes down the side.

Mick, a man with a barrel chest and an even larger barrel stomach, jumped out of the cab. He lifted his cap with a chubby hand, and scratched his head.

Jez scrambled for his phone, and fired off another text.

- I'm in the shed in the front garden of the house by ur van. At least 4 men r looking for me.

Mick read the message, and casually glanced to his right. He located the shed, dipped his head in acknowledgement, and tapped out a reply with a stubby finger.

A few seconds later, Jez's phone buzzed.

- will cause a diversion. Wait till they're distracted then get in back of the van.

Mick hauled himself back into his vehicle, and fired up the engine. It belched thick, black diesel smoke from the exhaust, as he reversed a few metres down the road.

The handbrake ratcheted on, and the rear door clattered open. Mick waddled back into view with his enormous stomach hanging over his grubby jeans.

'I'm looking for Gordon Avenue,' he called to the gorilla, who'd moved along to the next house in the row. 'You know it, mate?'

'What?'

'I promised a mate I'd pick up a fridge for him.' Mick hooked a thumb over his shoulder towards his van.

'No idea.'

'Must be close,' said Mick, undeterred. 'But I've been driving around in circles for the last twenty minutes.'

'Honestly, mate, I can't help you.'

'Don't you live around here?'

'Nah, we're looking for someone.'

'Yeah?' said Mick.

'My mate said some pervert was touching up the kids at the rec. He ran off down here, but now they've lost him.'

'Youngish bloke? Mid-thirties? Dark hair?'

The gorilla shrugged. 'Yeah, I guess.'

'Think I saw him in Abbots Road. He looked a bit shifty. Must have been him.'

'Yeah?' said the gorilla, a hesitancy in his voice.

'He certainly looked like a pervert. I reckon you could still catch him if you ran.'

'Right.'

The gorilla rocked from one foot to the other, as if he was trying to make up his mind. Eventually, he ran into the street, shouting, 'Lads, come on, he's down here.'

He vanished from Jez's view as a roar of excitement went up, and heavy footsteps pounded the hard ground, echoing off the houses. Mick stood with his hands on his hips watching the men disappear.

After a few seconds, he nodded in Jez's direction.

Jez didn't need any more encouragement. He bolted from the shed, vaulted the low hedge, and clambered into the back of the van. He dived under a pile of dust sheets at the back and curled up, lying still on the cold, metal floor.

The rear door clanged shut, and Jez felt the van lurch forward. It swung around in a wide arc, bumping off the pavement, and then pulled away, picking up speed as Mick dropped through the gears.

15

Mick planted two pints of beer on the table, and almost knocked them flying as he negotiated his way into a chair. Jez, sitting in the corner with his back to the wall, nervously watched the door.

'You going to tell me what's going on?' asked Mick. 'I guess this has something to do with you breaking up with Alice?'

'Kind of.'

'Well? I'm all ears.'

'It's complicated,' said Jez, savouring the taste of his beer.

'You guys had a fight or something?'

'She kicked me out, so I'm back with my parents.' Jez thought he caught the beginnings of a smirk on his friend's face. 'It's not funny, Mick.'

'I'm sorry, but you only managed to escape a few months ago. Even I didn't think you'd be back quite so soon.'

'Neither did I.'

'I thought things were going well between you two?'

'Me too, for a while.'

'You guys were totally loved up. Christ, you even stopped coming to the pub with your mates,' said Mick. 'You had it bad.'

'If I'm honest, I think I made a mistake. I mean, we barely knew each other, really, and there we were playing happy families.'

'Life's short. If it feels right, you've got to go for it, or you'll regret it forever.'

Jez chewed his lip as the door swung open, and a shadow fell over the threshold. He was relieved when two ramblers with ruddy cheeks, boots thick with mud, and bulging rucksacks stepped inside.

'The problem is, I went into it with my eyes shut. I mean, why would a woman like Alice look twice at a bloke like me?'

'Yeah, maybe you've got a point there,' said Mick, with a cheeky grin.

'Thanks.'

'Oh, come on, the self-pity is killing me. She loved you.'

'No, I don't think she did. Not really.'

'What makes you say that?'

Jez sighed, and rubbed his eyes. The headache that had been nagging him since his row with Alice had become a dull throb. 'You've met her. She could light up a room walking through the door.'

'She's a good-looking girl, for sure.'

'It's more than that. She has this aura, like a magnet

that draws people in. And I see men looking, like they're imagining being with her.'

'So what? She chose you. You should be flattered. She worshipped you,' said Mick.

'I wanted to believe it, I really did, but you can't ignore that sort of attention. Could you, if women were throwing themselves at you?'

Mick almost choked on his beer. 'Yeah, right,' he said. 'Chance would be a fine thing. But I think you've got it all wrong. Men weren't throwing themselves at her.'

'I suppose I shouldn't blame her. It's human nature.'

'Blame her for what?'

'Seeing other people behind my back.'

'Are you insane? Alice wouldn't do that.'

'I don't think she could help it. It's like a curse.'

'Come on, do you seriously believe Alice was cheating on you?'

'I can see now what she was up to. She wanted someone to be a dad to Lily. That's all I was to her. A convenience.'

Mick pushed back his chair, and folded his arms over his bulbous stomach. 'Are you sure this isn't all just in your head?'

A memory of Marcus Fenson, laying bleeding in the hallway, flashed across Jez's mind. 'I'm sure.'

'How?'

'I don't know. Call it instinct.'

'Instinct?'

'I know of at least one guy,' said Jez, defensively. He

expected Mick to have lent him a more sympathetic ear. 'He's called Marcus.'

'Who's he?'

'It doesn't matter. What's important is that I found her out. She told me she didn't know this guy, and later she let it slip that she did.'

Mick stared at Jez blankly, and then laughed, his whole body shaking, rolls of fat wobbling under his clothes.

'What's so funny?'

'That's it? That's your evidence she was shagging behind your back?'

Jez's jaw tightened. 'It's difficult to explain,' he snapped. 'But I know what's been going on. I'm not stupid.'

'All right, calm down. I'm just saying, maybe you got things wrong.'

Jez finished his pint, and slammed the glass on the table. 'You're right, I did get things wrong, like getting together with Alice in the first place. It was a big mistake.'

'Mate, you're angry and confused. I can see that. But honestly, you're overreacting. Whatever this argument was about, you should talk to her. Clear the air.'

'I can't.'

'Why not? Don't be so stubborn.'

'You wouldn't understand.'

'Try me.'

Jez tugged at a snag of skin around the nail of his finger. 'You want to know the truth?'

'Sure,' said Mick.

Jez leaned across the table, and jabbed a finger at his friend's chest. 'I nearly killed him. I should have finished him off, but I couldn't even get that right.'

Mick's arm froze in mid-air, his pint halfway between his mouth and the table. 'Who?'

'Marcus,' said Jez, exasperated. 'The guy who she claimed she'd never seen before. He broke into the house, and I hit him with one of Alice's dumbbells.' Jez rattled out the words like bullets from a machine gun, a fury welling from deep inside him as he recalled the confrontation.

Mick put his glass down slowly, and lined up his beer mat against the edge of the table. 'Seriously?' he said, his face darkening.

'I thought he was dead at first, and she tried to get me to cover it up. Can you believe it?' Jez heard the words spilling from his mouth, and felt powerless to stop. He was on a roll. The floodgates were open, and it felt good to be sharing what he'd done with someone else. 'But it turned out he wasn't dead at all.'

'Slow down,' said Mick. 'I'm not sure I'm following this.'

'And when we talked about it, she let it slip that she knew him. So, we had this massive fight. I tell you, the woman's a bloody psychopath.'

'Are you saying she'd been seeing this bloke behind your back?'

'Yeah. Well, probably. I don't know. I didn't want to hear the details. I had to get out,' said Jez.

'You said she threw you out.'

'Same difference.'

'She could have known him from anywhere.'

'So why didn't she say something earlier, if she didn't have anything to hide? She had plenty of opportunity.'

'What did she say when you accused her?' asked Mick.

'She didn't exactly deny it.'

'But she didn't admit it?'

'She didn't have to. It was written all over her face.'

'And this bloke, Marcus? What happened to him? Is he all right?'

'I got him to the hospital. I'm sure he'll be fine.'

Mick stood, and picked up their empty glasses. 'For what it's worth, I think you two need to talk, straighten this mess out. You ought to find out what's really been going on before jumping to conclusions.'

'Whose side are you on?'

'I'm not on any side. But you two had a good thing. I'd hate to see you throw it away for nothing.'

'It's hardly nothing.'

Mick returned from the bar with two more pints. He eased himself back into his chair, which strained under his weight.

'You know, I've never met any of her family,' said Jez, 'and she's never even introduced me to her friends. It was like she was holding me at arm's length. I never really understood why, but I can see it now.'

'Did you ever ask her why?'

Jez shook his head. Alice was an intensely private person. If he ever raised the subject, she'd always dismiss it as unimportant, and change the subject. 'What about *your* missus? If she'd had a kid by another bloke, you'd want to know who the father was, wouldn't you?'

'Donna? Yeah, I suppose so.'

'Of course you would. It's the sort of thing couples tell each other, even if it is hard to hear. But not Alice. She's a complete closed book.'

'Women are strange creatures, mate. Maybe she'd got good reason not to want to talk about it. You don't know what Lily's real father was like. But don't be an arsehole, Jez. Maybe Alice is keeping secrets from you, but perhaps she has good reason. I think you may have gone off on the deep end. And what about Lily? How's this going to affect her?'

'You're beginning to sound like my mother.'

'All I'm saying is, why throw away something that's been so good for the sake of the green-eyed monster.'

'This isn't about me being jealous.'

'Really? Then find out what's going on. Talk to her, properly,' said Mick.

'I don't think I can trust her.'

'Running back to Mum and Dad's isn't going to solve anything. You know, me and Donna have been married for twenty years. There were plenty of times I wanted to run away, get the hell away from it all, especially when the kids came along. It wasn't glamorous, we didn't have much money, and we were getting hardly any sleep. More than once I thought about legging it. Maybe she did as well. But what would that have solved? Would I have been any happier? Unlikely. We stuck at it, and we're still sticking at it, through the good times and the bad.'

'Aren't you happy then?'

'Of course I'm happy. We argue like all couples, but what I'm saying is, ultimately, we're better together. Everyone has their wobbles. It's only human. It's how you come through it that matters. Call Alice. Swallow your pride, or kiss her goodbye forever. Tell her how you feel. You have to try, or you'll regret it.'

Jez finished his pint, and watched a frothy residue slide down the inside of the glass. 'I'm not sure she'll listen,' he said.

'Try.'

'She could have any bloke she wants.'

'But she wanted you,' said Mick.

'I don't know,' said Jez. 'I said some harsh things.'

'Apologise. Tell her you said it in the heat of the moment because you love her.'

'I do.'

'I know,' said Mick.

'I need a slash,' said Jez, sliding out from behind the table.

He wasn't going to be played for a mug, by Alice or anyone else, but perhaps he had overreacted. Although, if Alice had nothing to hide, why hadn't she called? Maybe he should try talking to her. He'd bite the bullet and speak to her.

'What was all this nonsense about this morning,' said Mick, when Jez returned.

'I thought I saw Alice with Lily on the swings in the park. There was a bit of confusion with some of the parents, and it all got out of control.'

'And they chased you off the rec?'

Jez sighed. 'They thought I was a paedophile.'

'Why?'

'Because I was in the playground on my own, and some woman reckoned she saw me watching the kids. I mean, so what? Doesn't make me a pervert. Anyway, they got themselves worked up, and tried to call the police.'

'And you ran away?'

'Yeah.'

'Great. Why didn't you wait for the police to come and sort it out?'

Jez glanced up from his empty glass. 'Why do you think? I nearly beat a man to death. The last thing I needed was for the police to start poking their noses around. I panicked, and ran.'

Mick sniggered.

'I'm glad you can see the funny side of it all.'

'It's just the thought of you hiding in some stranger's shed while a load of goons were poring over the estate looking to tear you limb from limb.'

'Hilarious.'

'I'm sorry. But it is pretty funny.'

'You're right, Mick. I need to speak to Alice.'

'Good man. And really listen to what she has to say.'

'I should go and see her, sort it out face-to-face.'

'Sober up first. Don't turn up on the doorstep stinking of booze and bullshit. Never a good combination. And maybe change out of those muddy clothes.'

Jez glanced at his jeans, streaked with grass stains and mud. 'Okay, I'll call her later. You're right.'

Mick stood, and hooked the keys to his van out of his pocket. 'Right, I've got a family to get home to.'

'Do me a favour and walk?'

'What? Yeah, right, of course,' said Mick, shoving the keys back in his jeans. 'Do me good anyway.'

Jez's phone buzzed on the table. He snatched it up, and pressed it to his ear. 'Alice?'

Mick raised an eyebrow.

Jez checked his watch. It was almost one-thirty. 'Yeah, Mum. I'm on my way.'

16

Terry Neil sat with a rigid back, and his hands clasped lightly on the desk. 'You look tired, Jeremy. Are you sleeping?' His moustache quivered when he spoke.

'I've got a few things on my mind,' said Jez. 'But I'm fine.'

'Good, now don't slouch, and straighten your tie. This isn't a holiday camp. First impressions count in our business, and you know what I say?'

'You can't change a first impression,' said Jez.

Terry had called him in first thing, and asked his secretary to hold all his calls, so it must be important. Jez just wished he'd get to the point.

'That's right. We trade on our professionalism here at Parker Cheshunt. It's all about standards.' Terry was silhouetted by the light streaming through a small, barred window overlooking a narrow alley. 'And I take a dim view when those standards drop. Look at the state of you this morning. Did you even look in the mirror before you left the house? It looks like you've been dragged through a hedge backwards. Your hair's a mess, your shirt needs an iron, and you've left half of your breakfast down your tie. You need to buck up your ideas, Jeremy.'

Jez ran his fingers through his hair, and squirmed in his seat. Thirty-one years old and he was still being spoken to like a child in front of the headteacher. 'If this is about being late this morning, I'll make it up at the end of the day,' he said. 'I'm sorry,' he added as an afterthought.

Terry glanced at a computer screen, angled in such a way Jez couldn't quite read it. 'It seems to me this is symptomatic of your lax attitude of late. What's wrong with you? Problems at home, is it?'

Jez forced himself not to roll his eyes. He'd been a sales negotiator with the company for six years, and the role suited him well enough. The pay wasn't great, but the job was hardly taxing. And besides, he could top up his meagre salary with commission on his sales, although there'd not been many of those lately. But then the market was struggling.

'You're cruising, Jeremy, and I don't much care for cruisers. Where's your ambition, lad? When I was your age, you couldn't stop me. I was hungry for it. I wanted to be top seller in the south east. I hated it if a sale slipped through my fingers. That's why they put me in charge here. With a bit of hard work, you could have your own branch. You're not a bad salesman, but you lack commitment.'

Jez picked at the sore bit of skin around his finger nail.

'You need to knuckle down and start treating your clients with respect,' Terry continued.

Jez zoned out as Terry droned on. He'd still not heard from Alice, even though he'd left three messages on her phone the previous evening, apologising through gritted teeth. The least she could do was return his calls. Maybe the relationship was doomed to failure after all.

'... and this is the first time I've ever had to deal with a complaint from a customer about one of our sales team. Are you listening to me?'

'What?' said Jez.

'A complaint, Jeremy, from the couple who had a viewing in St John's Road on Saturday. They said you were rude and disrespectful.'

'I wouldn't say I was rude,' said Jez.

'But you know who I'm talking about?'

'I'm guessing Tim and Maria?'

'Mr Corbett and Ms Timms, yes.'

'They're wasting our time. They're never going to commit. I merely pointed out that they need to make some compromises, or they're never going to find a house. You know I've shown them about forty properties already?'

'That's not the point, and there are ways of guiding clients without being rude.'

'They've not made an offer on the property then?'

Terry gave him a withering look. 'No, and I don't suppose they'll be making an offer on any of our properties after your behaviour. I'm afraid I can't let this go unpunished.'

'I'm sorry,' said Jez. 'Look, you're right, I am having

a few problems at home at the moment. I shouldn't have brought it into work, I know that, but it won't happen again.'

'No, it won't. You can write a letter of apology for a start, and I'll be noting this incident on your record. Consider this a formal and final warning. Any more nonsense like this and you're out. Understand?'

'But Terry ...'

'Do you understand?'

'Yes,' said Jez.

'Really, you're not a bad salesman,' Terry said, his tone softening. 'But you need to pull your socks up. I can't afford weak links in the team, nor am I going to let you undermine the reputation of this branch.'

Jez was lost for words. What he wanted to say was Terry could stuff his job where the sun didn't shine. But he sat in dumb silence. How dare Terry speak to him like that. He wasn't even interested in hearing Jez's side of the story. What the hell, he could find another job easily enough. Something completely different perhaps, where he could take a fresh perspective. Alice had wanted them to move away and start over. Maybe it wasn't such a bad idea. The town was beginning to feel claustrophobic anyway. A change would be good for them all.

'I'll email you the form, and you can add any comments you'd like recorded,' said Terry, tapping at his computer keyboard.

Jez had plenty of comments he'd like to add, and most of them concerned Terry's lack of ability as a manager. He was a corporate whore intent on securing his way up the greasy pole at the expense of the rest of the staff who did the real work in the branch. When was the last time Terry was out on the front line, actually selling houses?

'Now go on, get out of here. And let this be the end of it.'

Jez stood sulkily, and kicked the chair as he left. He slammed the door, and returned to his desk, where he slumped into his chair and sat with his head in his hands.

17

Jez woke early with a clarity of intention, determined to put things right. After four days, he'd still not heard from Alice, who was neither returning his calls, nor responding to his texts.

He made it to the office early, dressed in a neatly pressed shirt, and a clean tie. Throughout the day, he kept his head down, answered the phone with unusual enthusiasm, and resisted the distraction of the internet for once. He even worked through lunch, grabbing a sandwich from the delicatessen next door, rather than spending an hour in the pub, as had become his custom in recent months. And so, when the clock rolled around to four-thirty, Terry was happy to let him leave early.

He stopped at a stall in the market on the way to his car, picked up a bunch of red roses, then drove straight to Lily's nursery, guessing that he'd make it well ahead of Alice.

He parked in a side road where she wouldn't spot his car, the anticipation of seeing her again fizzing through his veins. He imagined her face when she saw him with Lily, and the peace offering of flowers. How could she resist?

On neutral territory, he hoped to diffuse her anger. He'd tell her he was sorry, that he was an idiot to ever doubt her, and that he loved her more than he realised. He would suggest they grab a takeaway pizza, and eat slobbed out in front of the TV. He had it all planned out. Everything was going to be perfect. What could go wrong?

As he approached the nursery, he expected to hear the excited chatter and joyful screams of children playing, but he was unsettled by a heavy silence from the building. It was getting late, and he dismissed the quiet as a result of most of the children having been collected early by their parents.

Jez checked his watch. Alice would be leaving work in less than five minutes. His stomach bubbled.

The nursery was housed in a converted Victorian villa at the end of a long terrace of cottages, with big bay windows overlooking the road. Jez let himself into the garden through a side gate, and was surprised to find the front door wide open. He hesitated, uncertain.

'Hello?' he called.

Something wasn't right. The staff were normally so careful with security. It seemed such an unusual lapse.

He peered inside, and was struck by an evocative smell from childhood, of floor polish and disinfectant, a trace of steamed cabbage, and musty carpets. A red-faced woman appeared in an oversized blue polo shirt and jeans that clung to a pair of wide hips. A shock of grey hair had been piled on her head, and tied in place with a thick band.

'Yes?' she said, forcing an uncertain smile, and drying her hands on her thighs.

Jez remembered he was holding the roses, and dropped them to his side. 'I've come to pick up Lily,' he said.

'Mr Hook,' said the woman, her frown vanishing as she seemed to recall his face. It had been a while since Jez had collected Lily, and it was no surprise she couldn't immediately place him.

'Has she had a good day?' he said, craning to see into a room from where the woman had emerged.

'Lily's not here,' she said, tilting her head as if she suspected Jez was having a joke at her expense.

'Where is she then?'

'I'm sorry, didn't anyone tell you? We've had to close for a few days. None of the children have been in.'

'Of course,' said Jez, trying to make it sound as if he knew all along. But he had no idea what she was talking about.

'We've cleared up most of the mess, but I don't think we'll be able to have the children back until at least Monday.'

Jez stood mutely in the hallway, not sure what to say.

'Why anyone would want to vandalise a nursery though is beyond me. Not that the police took any interest. They didn't even bother sending anyone. I thought they might be able to dust for fingerprints, or look for clues.'

Jez shrugged, and followed as the woman retreated

into a spacious room at the front of the building. It was used as the children's main play area, but now miniature tables and chairs had been piled up out of the way, and plastic boxes full of toys and games stacked up by the door. One woman was scrubbing at a scrawl of black graffiti on the wall, and another was sponging the carpet. In one corner, he noticed a pile of broken furniture, and piles of black rubbish sacks. Dirty smears of paint had crusted on the floor and all over a pair of curtains pulled from the window.

'Were you insured?' asked Jez.

'It's not the money,' said the woman with the ruddy face, 'it's the inconvenience. I just don't understand the mentality of anyone who'd want to do something like this.'

Jez shook his head as he assessed the damage. 'Any idea who might have done it?'

'I don't know. Kids probably, bored and looking for trouble. We're an easy target here.'

'Didn't any of the neighbours hear anything?'

'Apparently not.' The woman perched on a window ledge, and sipped a mug of tea. 'Didn't Miss Grey tell you we were closed?'

'Probably. I'm sure she said something, but I wasn't listening. And there was me thinking I could surprise them both tonight.'

'In the doghouse?'

'What?'

The woman nodded at the flowers.

'Not exactly. Do you know who's looking after Lily?'

'Afraid not. Some of the parents have made childcare arrangements between themselves, but we've had our hands full here. Sorry.'

'It's okay,' said Jez. 'I'll phone Alice, and find out what's going on.'

He backed out of the room, his head spinning, and his hand reaching for his phone. He was already dialling Alice's number as he stepped outside. Why hadn't she called to tell him the nursery was shut, and more importantly, what had she done with Lily? Maybe she'd taken a few days off, but she should have told him. He might have been able to help, rather than sending Lily off with some stranger.

Her phone went straight to voicemail.

'Alice, it's me. For God's sake, where are you? I'm at the nursery, but Lily's not here. I'm beginning to get worried now. Look, whatever's happened between us, we need to talk. I can't go on like this. Phone me. Please. As soon as you pick up this message. I need to know everything's all right.'

He hung up, and checked his watch again. It was gone five. If Alice had been at work, she'd be home soon. If he hurried, he could be waiting on the doorstep when she returned.

He jogged to the car, threw the flowers on the passenger seat, and battled with the early evening commuter traffic. He found a space almost immediately outside the house, but had a sense no one was home. He banged on the door, and when no one answered, hollered through the letterbox.

'Alice, it's me. Are you there?'

Feeling like an intruder in his own home, he reluctantly let himself in with his key. After being away for the best part of a week, the house felt oddly unfamiliar. Even its smell was alien to him. He swept up a large pile of mail from the doormat.

'Alice?' he called, ignoring the bleached stain on the carpet at the bottom of the stairs. 'Lily? Is anyone home?'

He listened for signs of movement. A creak of floorboards, or the sound of running water. But he heard only hollow silence. He crept into the lounge, guilty for not slipping off his shoes, and discovered the cushions on the sofa had been left crumpled and untidy. Two of Lily's dolls had been abandoned on the floor by the fireplace, and a ream of letters had been stacked next to the microwave on the breakfast bar. Jez flicked through them absentmindedly. Mostly bills and junk mail. Nothing of importance. He put them back with the letters he'd picked up from the doormat.

He paced up and down, hands on his hips, and a worry growing in his gut. It felt odd to be home, especially when he knew he wasn't supposed to be there. After five minutes, and with no sign of Alice or Lily, he sat in the comfy chair in the corner, where he had a good view of the hallway, and the window onto the street.

With the light fading, he tapped his foot impatiently on the floor. The boiler in the kitchen kicked in with a loud click, and the radiators clunked and gurgled.

Another half an hour passed. Jez had chewed most of his nails down to the skin. Where was she? It had been almost an hour since she should have left work. He expected her to have been home with Lily by now, putting on the dinner, settling in for the night.

And then an irrational thought hit him. When they'd rowed, Alice had talked of moving away, starting a new life in a new town. What if she'd been serious, dropped everything, and taken Lily with her?

Jez vaulted out of the chair, and crept upstairs. Their bedroom door swung open with a gentle push. The bed was made, and the quilt smoothed down. A hint of Alice's favourite perfume, citrus with an undertone of vanilla, hung in the air. Opposite the bed, the dressing table had been left in an unholy mess of lotions and creams with exotic names. Jez picked up a silver-handled brush, and ran his fingers across the bristles matted with her hair. If she'd left, she must have gone in a hurry. It wasn't like Alice to travel anywhere without her cosmetics.

He hurried to the wardrobe, and pulled open the double doors. It was bursting with cotton dresses, silk blouses and tailored skirts, all crammed on a single rail. Jez ran his hand through the fabrics, but Alice had so many clothes it was impossible to tell whether anything was missing.

Below the rail, a dozen boxes were stacked up in piles where she kept her most expensive high heels. Packed in around them were an assortment of boots, sandals and trainers. More shoes than Jez had any idea what she could do with.

Jez reached up for a high shelf, feeling for Alice's suitcase. He pulled it down in a shower of dust that made him sneeze. It seemed unlikely she would have gone without taking her suitcase, and at least some of her clothes. She loved her designer labels, and never set a foot outside without her make-up immaculately applied. But Jez's relief was tempered by a dreadful sense that something was wrong.

He slumped on the bed, and held Alice's pillow to his cheek. The scent of her hair swelled a familiar ache in his stomach. He'd do anything now to turn back the clock and retract the horrible allegations he'd made about her fidelity. If only she would answer his calls, or come back home.

A sharp knock on the front door brought him crashing back to the moment. He jolted upright, and was racked with a guilt that he wasn't supposed to be in the house.

A second knock followed, a little louder, and a little more urgent. At first, he thought it might be Alice, but why would she be knocking on her own front door?

Jez eased down the stairs, and with a shaking hand reached for the latch.

'Is Alice in?' said the little old lady standing on the pavement outside.

'Mrs Dobson,' said Jez, not even trying to disguise the disappointment in his voice. 'What can I do for you?'

'I wanted to speak to Alice.'

'She's not here, I'm afraid.'

'Oh, will she be long? Only I was hoping she might have finished the book I lent her.' She stepped closer, her eyes wide with anticipation.

'Well, I'll let her know you called.' Jez attempted to

close the door, but she pushed it open with surprising strength.

'You see, we're doing it in the reading group this week.' She peered past Jez as if she didn't really believe he was in the house alone.

'Can it wait? I'll get Alice to drop it around when she gets back.'

'Perhaps I could pop in, and have a look around for it?'

Jez sighed. He could have done without this. 'Look, what's the book called? I'll have a look, and see if I can find it.'

Marilyn Dobson, a prim, former teacher who lived next door, broke into a wide smile revealing a perfect set of dentures too big for her mouth. 'If it's not too much trouble. It's an Agatha Christie. *And Then There Were None*. Have you read it?'

'No,' said Jez. 'Hang on here, I'll take a look.'

He strode purposefully into the lounge, and scanned the room. After a brief search through the bookshelves and the junk on Alice's oak dresser, he finally located the novel under a stack of magazines on the coffee table.

He was surprised to find Mrs Dobson had let herself in, and was standing in the lounge doorway.

'Here it is,' said Jez, holding the yellowing paperback triumphantly, and trying not show his irritation.

'Thank you,' she said, snatching the book. She shoved it in the handbag hanging off her arm, and examined Jez with watery, blue eyes. 'Is everything all right, Jeremy? You look a little pale.'

'I'm fine, but a bit busy, if you'll excuse me.'

She made no attempt to leave. 'And Alice?' she asked, raising a pair of whiskery, white eyebrows.

'Fine,' said Jez, ushering her towards the front door.

'It's just we couldn't help but hear all the shouting the other night. You know, the walls are so thin, it's difficult not to hear.'

'Shouting?'

'Alice sounded upset.'

'Did she?' Jez concentrated on keeping the emotion from his face, but he'd never been much of a poker player. 'We had a bit of a row. I'm sorry if we disturbed you, but everything's fine.'

'It sounded serious.'

'Not really. It was one of those silly arguments. In fact, I can't even remember what it was about now,' Jez lied.

'We were concerned, that's all.'

Jez reached for the front door, and opened it wide. 'That's kind of you, but honestly there's nothing to worry about.'

Mrs Dobson studied Jez's face. 'Are you quite sure?'

She wasn't going to let it go. She was fishing for scandal, and Jez couldn't help himself. 'Actually, can I be honest with you?' he said, lowering his voice.

'Of course,' said the old woman, her eyes lighting up with anticipation.

'And you won't tell anyone?'

She looked affronted. 'You have my word. You can tell me.'

'I don't know,' said Jez, beginning to enjoy himself.

The old crone was positively foaming with expectation of a good dollop of gossip.

'The thing is,' said Jez. He beckoned her closer, and put his lips to her ear. 'I've killed Alice, and buried her under the patio.'

Mrs Dobson sprang back with a look of horror etched across her face. 'Jeremy!' she gasped.

For a moment he wondered if she'd taken him at his word. 'I'm kidding,' he said, allowing himself a self-satisfied smile. It would teach her for poking her nose in. 'Alice is fine.'

The old woman composed herself, smoothing the fabric of her coat over her hips. 'That's hardly something to joke about,' she said, through pursed lips.

'I know, I'm sorry. She'll be home soon. I'll tell her you called.'

'Yes, you do that.' She hurried out of the door, and scurried back to her house without a backwards glance.

Jez shut and bolted the door. 'Stupid old bat,' he muttered to himself.

18

Jez spent the next hour calling every hospital in the county, battling through automated switchboards and harassed receptionists, until he'd ruled out that Alice had been involved in an accident. None had a record of admitting anyone called Alice Grey, nor of anyone matching her description.

Relieved, but frustrated, he began a methodical search of the house. People didn't just vanish, especially with a four-year-old in tow. She had no car - she'd sold the Mini when they'd moved in, arguing they didn't need two cars - and none of her things appeared to be missing. If she had taken off, it had been in a hurry, which meant she'd been genuinely scared about Marcus Fenson returning to the house. But why?

He started at her old oak dresser, sifting through drawers of paperwork; utility bills, bank statements, and a wad of Lily's old drawings, not really sure what he was looking for. A diary? A newspaper clipping, or a magazine feature about a town or village that had caught her eye? All he found were old receipts, instruction manuals for electrical gadgets he didn't even know they owned, an assortment of batteries, keys, phone chargers and light bulbs, but nothing that remotely resembled a clue to where she'd gone.

He sorted through Alice's well-thumbed paperbacks on the shelf above the television, flicking through their pages and tossing them onto the sofa one by one. He tore through the magazines on the coffee table, and even checked down the back of the sofa, and in the cupboard under the sink.

In their bedroom, Jez turned out the stack of shoeboxes in Alice's wardrobe, heaping her high heels in a pile in the middle of the room. He shone a torch into every nook and cranny, and stood on a chair to peer onto the shelf above the rack of her clothes where she kept her suitcase. He swept under the bed, and searched for any loose floorboards. He went through the folded stacks of clothes in her chest of drawers, poked his head into the dingy attic, and even hunted through Lily's toys, dolls and teddies in her bedroom.

It was past eleven when Jez finally conceded defeat, having turned the house upside down, and not having come any closer to finding out what had happened to Alice. He collapsed on their bed, hungry and exhausted, his mood black.

He stared at the ceiling, and the ugly brown watermarks burning through the paintwork. Where could she have possibly gone? And why was she avoiding his calls? If something had happened to her, he'd never forgive himself. He should never have walked out. If only he'd called the police the night he'd heard an intruder in the house, instead of taking matters into his own hands.

Eventually, Jez fell into a fitful sleep, lying fully clothed on top of the duvet, his anxious mind keeping him from falling into a deep slumber. His dreams were plagued with images of Alice and Lily running towards a danger they couldn't see; edges of cliffs, wild animals and speeding cars. When he tried to shout a warning, the words stuck in his throat, and his legs turned to jelly.

A loud bang woke him with a start. He sat up, momentarily disorientated and his heart hammering.

More banging.

Someone at the front door.

He scrambled for his phone, and found it on the floor. He checked the time.

Six-thirty.

He immediately thought of Alice and Lily. Something had happened to them, he was sure.

He jumped off the bed, and raced down the stairs, tucking his crumpled shirt into his trousers as he went. He bounded down the hall, and threw open the door.

Two police officers with serious expressions were standing outside. A man with pockmarked skin, and a woman with thick-rimmed glasses. One tall. One short.

'Mr Jeremy Hook?' asked the male officer.

Jez took an involuntary step back. 'Yes,' he said.

At first, he thought they'd come to tell him they'd found Alice, except from the looks on their faces, it wasn't good news. Jez shivered, either from the cold, or the shock, or both.

'My name's PC Claire Sinclair, this is PC Rob

Pearce. We'd like to ask you a few questions. May we come in?' the woman asked.

'Have you found them?' Jez's voice was a hoarse whisper. He cleared his throat and tried again. 'Is this about Alice?'

The officers exchanged a puzzled glance. 'Better if we do this inside,' PC Pearce said.

Jez stood to one side, and let the officers in. As they filed down the hall, Jez pushed past, and ushered them into the lounge, trying to keep them from noticing the stain on the bottom of the stairs.

'Please, just tell me,' said Jez. His stomach tightened as he braced himself to hear the worst.

The two officers sat on the edge of the sofa without being asked. PC Sinclair took out a notebook and pen, and crossed her legs. 'We're investigating a serious allegation about an incident that's reported to have taken place on the recreation ground on Sunday,' she said. 'Can you tell us where you were at around eleven?'

'The recreation ground?' said Jez, confused. He rubbed his arms, noticing a chill in the room. 'What does that have to do with Alice?'

'Whose Alice, Sir?' said Pearce.

'My girlfriend, she's ...' Jez stopped himself. 'It doesn't matter.'

'Several witnesses say that a man matching your description tried to abduct a child from the play area. When some of the parents intervened, he became aggressive and ran off.' Sinclair raised an eyebrow, her pen poised.

'I didn't try to snatch a child,' Jez snapped. 'It was a misunderstanding.'

'So, you admit you were in the park on Sunday morning?'

'Yes, but it's not what it sounds like. You make me out to be some kind of child molester.'

Sinclair scribbled something in her book.

'Look, I can explain,' Jez continued, sitting on the arm of the chair in the corner. 'I'd gone to the park for a walk, to clear my head, and I thought I saw my girlfriend with her daughter by the swings. I went over to surprise them, but it wasn't them. That's it. There were some people who overreacted, and I got a bit scared, and ran off. There's nothing more to it than that.'

'If you'd done nothing wrong, why did you run away when you were confronted?' Sinclair asked.

'I told you, I was scared.'

'I see,' she said, jotting down another note.

'Your girlfriend, Alice is it, you said?' asked Pearce.

Jez nodded.

'And how old is her daughter?'

'Four.'

'And she lives here with you and Alice?'

'That's right.'

'Is she in? May we speak with her?' said Pearce, looking towards the stairs.

'No, she's not here right now.'

'Oh,' said Pearce, surprised. 'It's early to be out.'

Jez stared at the officer, trying to read his expression. Was it a casual observation, or did he suspect Jez was lying? He wanted to tell him the truth, that Alice and

Lily had gone missing, and that he had no idea what had happened to them. But they'd want to know why she'd left, and he'd have to tell them about the argument. How could he explain that away without telling them about Marcus Fenson?

'The truth is, I don't know where she is,' said Jez. He hung his head. He thought if they could see he was under emotional stress, it might buy him some sympathy.

In the silence that followed, Jez tuned into the early morning chorus of birds outside. He envied how carefree they sounded while his world was collapsing, mired in secrets and lies.

'When did you see her last?' asked Sinclair.

Jez looked up, and thought he detected a concern behind her thick glasses. It might not have been genuine, but he warmed to her for her gentle question.

'Saturday morning,' he said.

'And you've not seen her since?'

Careful, Jez.

'We had an argument.'

'What about?'

'It's silly, but I can't even remember. It seemed so important at the time. Stupid, isn't it?'

'You must have some recollection?' asked Pearce.

'Not really.'

'Have you tried calling?'

'Of course I've tried to call. She's not returning my messages or my texts.'

'But you've not reported her missing?'

Jez rubbed his eyes, and told himself to keep calm.

He was in dangerous territory with a fog clouding his tired mind.

Answer carefully.

'I didn't know she'd gone missing until last night. I've been staying with my parents.' A lump grew in Jez's throat, and he coughed to fight it back down. No point getting all emotional. It wasn't going to do him any good. 'I came home last night to talk to her, but she never turned up.'

'Are there friends or family she might be staying with?' asked Sinclair.

Jez shook his head.

'Any of her clothes missing?'

'No.'

Sinclair started scribbling again.

'I'm sure there's a simple explanation,' said Jez.

'Has she done this before?' Sinclair peered through her thick lenses.

'A couple of times,' Jez lied, seizing the lifeline she'd thrown him.

The female officer relaxed a little, her shoulders sagging. 'So it's not unusual for her to go missing?'

'Not really.'

'Do you want to file a missing person's report?'

'Oh, God, no,' said Jez. He jumped up, and moved into the kitchen to fill the kettle. 'Where are my manners. Would you like tea?'

'We're fine, thank you,' said Pearce, answering for both of them. 'Can we return to the incident in the park? Did you assault one of the mothers?'

'Of course not. Who told you that?'

'A number of witnesses say that you singled out the woman, and attacked her.'

'That's ludicrous,' said Jez. The kettle hissed and gurgled behind him.

'You deny it then?' said Pearce.

'Of course I deny it. Look, I've been under a lot of pressure lately. I saw a woman at the swings wearing a coat like Alice's, and I made an honest mistake. I'm sorry if I startled her, but I didn't attack her. That makes me sound like some kind of criminal.'

'Running off made you look like a criminal,' said Sinclair. Jez had thought she was the sympathetic one, but now he wasn't so sure.

'They were accusing me of all sorts of things.'

'They were going to call the police, weren't they?'

'Exactly.'

'And you could have explained your side of the story to us. Instead you ran away. Can you see how that looks?'

'Of course I can. But you don't believe me now. Why would it have been any different if I'd stayed? You'd have still taken their word over mine.'

'We deal only in facts, Mr Hook,' said Sinclair. 'We don't take sides.'

'What were you doing in the park?' asked Pearce.

'I needed some space. I'd spent the night at my parents', and they were doing my head in. I went out for coffee and some fresh air.'

'At the children's play area?' asked Pearce.

'No! I happened to be walking past when I saw the woman wearing Alice's coat.'

'Do you lose your temper easily?' Pearce's pock-marked face was a picture of innocence.

'What the hell does that mean?'

'Do you have anger issues?'

What was he fishing for?

'Not really,' said Jez.

'Sometimes then?'

'What's this got to do with anything?'

'When you argued with Alice, did you hit her?'

'What? No! Of course I didn't. What do you take me for?'

'Do you take pleasure in hitting women?' asked Sinclair.

'No, of course I don't. You're twisting everything.' Jez was bursting to tell them about Marcus Fenson. He was the one she was scared of. If anyone was responsible for her disappearance it was him. He was the one who broke into the house, not that he could tell them that now.

The two officers stared at Jez for much longer than felt comfortable, as if saying nothing would force him to fill the silence with a confession. But he resisted their cheap psychological game.

'What happens now?' Jez eventually asked. 'Are you going to arrest me?'

Sinclair closed her notebook, and slipped it back into a pocket in her stab vest. 'We have a few more inquiries to make, but we'll be back in touch soon. In the meantime, if there's anything else that occurs to you, don't hesitate to call.'

She gave him a business card. A flimsy rectangle of

white card embossed with a police force logo, and her name, mobile and email address printed in black.

'Is that it?' asked Jez, stuffing the card in his pocket, and standing as the two officers rose from the sofa.

'For now,' said Pearce.

They walked to the front door in silence, and let themselves out. Jez was about to close it behind them when Sinclair turned back towards him. 'I hope you find Alice soon,' she said.

19

Jez lost most of the next hour pacing up and down the lounge trying to straighten out everything in his head. Alice's mobile was still diverting straight to voicemail, but he'd given up leaving messages. Either she wasn't picking them up, or she was choosing to ignore him. Either way, another desperate message on top of all the others wasn't going to make any difference.

Instead, he called his boss.

'What do you mean she's missing?' asked Terry.

'She walked out a few days ago, and I don't know where she's gone. I could do with a few days to sort it out. I'm sorry it's short notice,' said Jez. 'I'll take it from my annual leave.'

'Is there anything I can do?' Terry sounded genuinely concerned.

'Not really. Thanks anyway.'

'Are the police involved?'

The image of the two young constables, Sinclair and Pearce, sitting on the edge of his sofa with their sneering accusations, popped into Jez's head, and he shuddered. 'Yeah, I've let them know. But there's not much they can do really. She's not considered to be high risk.'

'Right, that's a shame.' Terry hesitated, then asked, 'Any idea why she left?'

It wasn't like Terry to take such an interest in his private life, but he didn't want to get into the specifics. 'We had a bit of a row. Nothing serious, but she's taken Lily with her, and isn't answering her phone.'

'Ah,' said Terry, with the seasoned understanding of a marriage counsellor.

What the hell did he know about it, sitting at his breakfast table in his four-bedroomed new-build, slice of toast in one hand, his suit immaculately buttoned up, and his tie perfectly formed, with Mrs Neil opposite, straight-backed and neatly coiffured, pouring tea? They probably never argued about anything.

'Yeah,' said Jez.

'Well, good luck. Hopefully she'll be in touch soon, and you can work everything out. Take as long as you need.'

Jez hung up, and tossed his phone on the kitchen counter. The house felt like a soulless shell. He realised now how much he missed the noise and chaos of a four-year-old tearing up the place, the toys strewn around the floor, and cuddles on the sofa when she was sleepy. Most of all he missed Alice. Right now, he would have done anything to have her back.

He needed her back.

Whatever had happened in her past wasn't important. Their future was what mattered, and without her in his life, it didn't seem worth living. He'd been an idiot letting his petty jealousy drive them apart.

With the walls of the house closing in, Jez grabbed his coat, and headed out with fresh air and coffee on his mind.

He instinctively found himself heading for Alice's favourite coffee shop. He collapsed into one of the leather sofas in the window overlooking Preston Street, where a steady stream of commuters and school children filed past at the start of the new working day.

A waitress fussed around a gleaming locomotive of a coffee machine that took up most of the space behind the glass counter. She'd already lit the wood burning stove, but the room, with its wonky wooden floor, had yet to warm up, and Jez kept his coat on, watching the flames curl around a lump of firewood.

People didn't vanish into thin air. Alice must have left some clue. It was possible she'd sought solace with her family, but she'd never spoken about her parents, or any brothers or sisters, and Jez didn't know where to begin finding them. She didn't even have many friends. In fact, when he thought about it, he couldn't recall her mentioning any friends at all. The only names she ever talked about were people at work.

The waitress set his latte on the table with a polite smile, and retreated. Jez glanced at the clock on the wall above the fire.

Eight-thirty.

The time Alice usually left for work. Enough time to walk Lily to nursery, and be at her desk for nine.

And then it occurred to him. She must have spoken

to someone at the office, told them she was taking time off. Maybe she'd told them where she was going.

Jez excitedly found Alice's work number on his phone, and dialled, hoping the office was open.

'Good morning, Lambert and Steele Conveyancing Services, how may I help you?'

'Hi, it's Jez Hook. Alice's partner.'

'Jez?' The woman on the other end of the line sounded surprised. 'It's Tracey. Is everything okay?'

'Tracey, I was wondering if you'd heard from Alice?' said Jez. 'This might sound a bit strange, but has she been in this week?'

An awkward pause hung on the line. In the background, Jez heard the low hum of voices.

'We've not seen her since Monday. She took off early, and hasn't been in since.'

'Did she say why she had to leave?'

'A family emergency, she said. But it's not like Alice not to turn up for work, or at least not to let us know she's not coming in. Is everything okay? At home, I mean?'

The poor woman sounded genuinely concerned, and Jez didn't want to worry her any further. 'Everything's fine. I think she might be taking a bit of time out. I'll get her to call in when I see her,' he said. 'Thanks.'

Jez hung up, and bit his lip. What kind of family emergency could have called her away without letting him know? A health crisis? An elderly parent taken ill?

Because she'd never talked about her parents, he imagined they were already dead, or that they'd fallen out and lost contact. So, whatever had happened, it must be serious. Even so, the least she could have done was drop him a text to let him know.

Jez sank into the sofa as a gaggle of schoolgirls, laughing and giggling, stopped outside the window. He watched as one of the girls orchestrated the others into a tight group, then held up her phone to snap a picture. Each girl, full of the self-confidence of youth, put on a practiced pout, then they all gathered around to admire the finished shot. No doubt the image was destined to be shared on the web for everyone to see. Such was the way of the world. Almost everybody Jez knew had a social media profile these days. Everyone except Alice and his parents.

At first, he'd found Alice's resistance perplexing. She refused to have anything to do with Facebook, Twitter, or Instagram, and even banned Jez from sharing pictures of her or Lily on his own sites. He'd tried talking her around, but her view was immovable. She was painfully private, and insisted she had no desire to share anything of her life online.

It would make finding her difficult, but not impossible, Jez realised as the schoolgirls giggled off down the road. Alice may have shunned new technology, but it could still be the key to tracking her down.

He knew she'd grown up in Margate, and attended a local comprehensive school. They'd had a disagreement once about the merits of the county's selective education system. She'd called him a geek when she discovered he'd been a grammar school pupil, and he'd teased her about her intellectual shortcomings for failing the Eleven Plus exam.

It wasn't much, but it might be enough.

First, Jez searched on his phone for comprehensive schools in Margate. It turned out there was only one. Next, he found a Facebook page set up by former pupils of Hartsdown High School, and took a minute to scroll through a selection of old pictures of students in dark blue sweaters and stripy ties. He wasn't surprised that none of them appeared to be Alice.

It didn't matter.

He was looking for anyone who remembered her, and might know how to find her family.

He tapped out a post with his thumbs.

Hi - anyone remember Alice Grey? I lost contact with her a while back and would love to reach out again.

Jez made a quick calculation in his head, then continued typing.

She left Hartsdown in about 1994. Any former classmates remember her, or know where she is now?

It might take a while, but Jez immediately felt better for having done something positive. And wouldn't it be ironic if social media solved her disappearance.

Of course, there was another route to finding her. It wasn't one he wanted to confront, but with his options limited, it was a dark path Jez knew he would have to travel.

20

The discovery of an intruder in their home while they slept had shaken Jez to the core. It was one of the most frightening experiences of his life. But what remained terrifyingly vivid in his mind, was the moment he'd attacked Marcus Fenson, and almost killed him. He'd thought about little else, until Alice had disappeared.

He could recall in detail the exact colour of his hair, the spray of grey at his temples, and the moles on the back of his neck. He remembered all too clearly the precise angle he'd collapsed, with his arms twisted, and his legs splayed.

Sometimes Jez could still smell his aftershave, a woody fragrance with a hint of lavender, and recalled how it mingled nauseatingly with the metallic tang of his freshly spilled blood, and the chemical fug of alcohol on his breath.

It made Jez feel sick to the pit of his stomach, and provoked ugly questions that prowled his mind like monsters preying on his subconscious. What was his relationship to Alice? And why had he broken into the house to see her?

Her silence spoke volumes. It didn't take a genius to realise they were - or at least had been - lovers. So how had Alice, with such frighteningly cold detachment, been able to direct Jez to remove the body, and hide the evidence, while she stayed at home and scrubbed away all trace of Jez's brutality?

She'd even persuaded Jez there was nothing to link Marcus's death to either of them. But she must have known that if his body had been found, the finger of suspicion would have quickly pointed to them both. What better motive for murder than a cuckolded partner?

And yet, she had hardly shown a flicker of emotion that evening.

And now she'd disappeared.

If anyone had any idea what was going on, it was Marcus. He was the key to everything. And as unpalatable as the thought seemed, Jez knew he had to confront him again.

A sullen-looking woman with deep set wrinkles around her eyes appeared unimpressed by Jez's friendly smile.

'Can I help?' she said, flatly.

Jez leaned towards the glass screen at the reception desk. 'I was looking for a friend who was brought in on Saturday night,' he said.

The waiting area in the casualty department at the

William Harvey Hospital was packed with men, women, and children, some with bandaged limbs, others looking grey and pale. Polite coughs, low chatter, and the odd sniffle filled the room.

'His name's Marcus Fenson. He'd had a bang on the head.' Jez felt a pang of guilt as he recalled the ferocity of the attack that had left Marcus Fenson hanging to life by a thread.

The woman behind the counter tapped at a keyboard, and stared with vacant eyes at a computer screen. 'He was admitted to Cambridge Ward,' she said.

'Right,' said Jez. 'How do I find ...'

The woman pointed over his shoulder to a long corridor. 'Down there, third on the left, on the second floor.'

'Thanks.'

Jez eventually found Cambridge Ward at the end of a maze of busy corridors and staircases. At its entrance, two nurses were chatting at a semi-circular desk.

'I'm looking for a friend of mine. He was admitted to the ward at the weekend. He's called Marcus Fenson,' said Jez.

He held up a bunch of cheap carnations in a cellophane wrap he'd picked up as an afterthought from a petrol station on the way over, thinking it would make his visit appear more convincing.

'You can't bring those in here,' said one of the nurses, breaking off from the gossip she was sharing with her colleague. Her hair was an unnaturally dark red.

'Sorry,' said Jez, dropping the flowers to his side, and ruing the three pounds he'd wasted.

'Infection control,' said the second nurse, a young brunette with wide hips, and a full face. 'And besides, visiting isn't until two o'clock, after ward rounds.'

'Right,' said Jez. It hadn't occurred to him to check the visiting hours. Now he faced a three hour wait before he could see Marcus. 'I don't suppose I could pop in for just one minute? It's really important.'

'No,' said the red-haired nurse, crossing her arms. 'The patients need their rest.'

An elderly man shuffled out of the ward pushing a metal stand on wheels. A looping pipe attached a clear, saline bag to his arm. His pale skin was pulled so tautly over his skull he looked skeletal. The nurse with wide hips hurried over to help him.

'Are you okay there, Mr Rogers? Come on, let me give you a hand.'

The old man muttered something with ill-humour, and tried to push her away, but she took his free arm and steadied his sway.

'I need to ask him a question. Perhaps you could pass him a note?' said Jez.

'It's not really allowed,' said the nurse who'd remained behind the desk.

'Please?'

After a few seconds, her face softened. 'What's his name?'

'Thank you. It's Marcus Fenson.'

She tapped at her computer keyboard, and frowned

at the screen. 'I'm afraid Mr Fenson's already left us. He was discharged on Tuesday.'

'Really?'

'His wife signed the discharge papers against medical advice, but you know, it's not a prison. We can't hold people here against their will.' She gave Jez a knowing look.

'That's a shame, I made the journey specially to see him.' Jez feigned an abject look of disappointment. 'The thing is we'd lost touch in recent years, and I didn't get around to finding out where he's living now. I don't suppose you could ...?'

The nurse raised an eyebrow. 'Give you his address?'

'If you could.'

'No,' she said. She angled the screen away from Jez. 'You could be anyone.'

'Quite right. You can't be too careful.' Jez laughed nervously. 'I know he's in Thanet now, but ...'

'I can't give you his address.'

'Right.'

The nurse straightened up, and raised an eyebrow. 'Anything else?'

'No,' said Jez, 'that's all. Thank you.'

He turned wearily, fearing his best hope of finding Alice had been lost.

He remembered seeing Marcus's address on his driving licence when he'd checked his wallet, but couldn't recall the street. As far as he remembered, it was somewhere in Broadstairs, but that was it. Nothing else stuck in his mind.

'Actually, there is something,' Jez said, turning back

to the desk. 'Did Mr Fenson have any other visitors while he was here, I mean other than his wife?'

'Not that I recall,' said the nurse, 'but we don't monitor visitors in and out.'

'Of course, but what about a woman about my height? Long, dark hair, and light blue eyes? You'd remember if you saw her, I'm sure. She's quite distinctive looking. Attractive.'

'I'm sorry.'

'Right,' said Jez. 'Thanks for your help anyway.' He remembered he was still holding the limp carnations. 'You might as well have these then,' he said, dumping them on the desk.

'Thanks,' said the nurse.

As he turned to go, she picked them up, pulled a face, and dropped them in a bin.

21

A woman, dressed smartly in a three-quarter length charcoal overcoat and black knee-length boots, was loitering outside the house when Jez arrived home. Her face was pinched, and her hair pulled back in a bun. She seemed vaguely familiar, but Jez couldn't immediately place her.

'Jez? I work with Alice. We spoke on the phone this morning.'

'Of course. Tracey, right? Have you heard from her?' Jez felt a surge of anticipation.

The woman glanced at her feet, and scuffed a toe on the pavement. 'I'm afraid not. Listen, is there somewhere we can talk?'

'Sure, come in. I'll put the kettle on.'

'No, not here.'

Jez looked up and down the street. 'We could wander up to the quay? It'll be quiet at this time of day.'

'Perfect. I don't have long. I have to be back at the office by two.'

They walked the length of Abbey Street in silence, Jez desperate to ask questions, but sensing he was better waiting until she was ready to offer up the information in her own time.

He led her past the Anchor, and through the old wharf buildings now converted mostly into quirky independent antiques shops for the weekend tourists.

They found a bench on the quayside overlooking a flotilla of floating barges and houseboats lying lopsided in the mud left by the receding tide.

Tracey sat with her knees pressed together, her hands in her coat pockets, and a large handbag hanging off one arm. 'There's something I think you should know,' she said, staring across the creek, refusing to meet Jez's eye. 'I don't think you're going to like it, but you have a right to know.'

'Let me guess, she's having an affair,' said Jez, the bitter taste of jealousy rising from his stomach like bile.

'What? No, nothing like that.' Tracey looked shocked. 'Is that what you think's going on?'

Jez shrugged. 'I really don't know any more.'

Tracey shook her head resolutely. 'She'd never do that. She doesn't have it in her.'

'How can you be so sure?'

'I just know she wouldn't do it.'

A light breeze whipped in off the estuary, and Jez pulled the collar of his coat around his neck. 'What then?'

'If I tell you, you can't breathe a word of it to anyone. I could get sacked for telling you. Do you promise?'

'Yeah, yeah,' said Jez, beginning to suspect the woman was wasting his time.

'Are you aware she's using an assumed name? Her surname's Black, not Grey, but no one's supposed to know. It's a secret.'

'No, I didn't know,' said Jez, frowning. 'Why would she change her name?'

'For her own protection.'

'Look, Tracey, I appreciate ...'

'You don't believe me, do you? I knew this was a mistake.' She gathered up her handbag, and was about to stand, but Jez put a hand on her arm to stop her.

'I'm sorry, it's just, don't you think I would know if she was using a false name?'

'The point is, no one's supposed to know. I guess not even you, if she's not told you. I have access to all the personnel files. She had to change her name when she left her last job. Something to do with an ex-boyfriend who was trying to find her. God knows what he'd done to her. She had to let us know because her tax and bank details are still under her old name.'

Jez sucked in a gulp of air, and stared at Tracey, trying to work out whether she was being genuine. But then, what possible reason would she have to lie?

'And no one else knows?'

'A few of the senior managers are aware, but that's it.'

Suddenly, the image of Marcus Fenson was back in Jez's mind's eye, and everything started to make sense.

'I think I know who he is.'

'Who?'

'The ex-boyfriend,' said Jez. 'And it's too late. He's already found her.'

The colour drained from Tracey's face. 'Oh my God,' she said. 'Really?'

'And I think that's why she's run away. She's worried I can't protect her from him.'

'Why? Is he here, in the town?'

'Yes. At least he was.' Jez didn't want to tell her too much.

'How did he find her?'

'I don't know. It's not important. But I guess that's why Alice has disappeared. To get away from him again.'

Jez was struck by how deeply mired her past was in secrets and lies. He didn't know her at all. And how was that any kind of basis for a future together? He could count on the fingers of one hand the things he knew about her from before they were together. If she was being stalked by an ex-boyfriend, she should have told him. Didn't she trust him? At least he now understood her resistance to social media.

'So, what are you going to do?' asked Tracey.

Jez sighed. It was a good question. He should walk away. If Alice didn't want to be found, by him or anyone else, why should he waste his time and energy? She'd not been straight with him. She'd been quick to snare him as a father for Lily, but she'd not invested in the relationship.

Walk away.

But he couldn't. As much as he wanted to, he couldn't do it. Alice was in trouble. He'd made things worse by attacking Marcus, and then accusing her of having an affair, and walking out. He owed it to her to put things right, or at least give her a chance to explain. And then they could work out if they had any future.

'I'm going to find her,' said Jez. 'No matter what it takes, I'm going to find Alice and make sure she's okay.'

22

Jez couldn't remember how the evening had started, only that he was halfway drunk, and the pub was crowded, sweaty and noisy. After everything he'd been through in the last few days, it was invigorating to be letting off steam. The alcohol was already anaesthetising his worries, and he figured there was no point moping around the house with Alice gone.

'I was wrong about her,' Jez shouted over the din.

Mick slapped him so hard on the back he stumbled into a table, and slopped beer over his hand. 'So, you spoke to her?'

'No, I think she's still mad at me, but I found out something interesting about the guy who broke into the house.'

'Yeah?' said Mick, eyeing up a slim blonde who'd been poured into an impossibly tight dress.

'I thought maybe they were having an affair, but it turns out he's an abusive ex-boyfriend. Alice was hiding from him.'

Mick's attention returned to his friend as the blonde vanished into a throng at the bar. 'You're kidding?'

'I'm serious,' Jez slurred. 'I think she's scared he's going to find her again. That's why she's vanished.'

'And she's not been in touch?'

Jez shook his head. 'She's keeping a low profile, but at least now I can understand why.'

'Come on, drink up. Let's move on.' Mick downed his pint in one gulp, beer dribbling down his unshaven face, and staining his dirty grey t-shirt.

Finding another pub seemed an excellent idea, even though Jez's head was swimming. There was only an empty house waiting at home. He might as well stay and enjoy himself, now everything seemed a lot clearer in his head, the beer having brought clarity to his thoughts.

Alice hadn't been cheating on him at all. He wished she'd felt able to tell him about Marcus, but he could understand why she'd been so secretive. If Marcus had treated her so badly that she'd had to run away and change her identity, no wonder she'd been cautious. And who could blame her for trying to build a new life for herself and Lily?

Only now did Jez realise what a terrifying shock it must have been when Marcus not only tracked her down, but broke into the house in the middle of the night. It certainly explained why she had been so frigidly rational about getting rid of his body.

Except, Marcus was still alive. And what was worse, he now knew where Alice lived, and there was every chance he'd be back.

Perhaps if Alice had trusted Jez enough to tell him

about her past, things would have turned out differently. For a start, he'd have never have left her in the house alone with Lily if he'd known about Marcus. He could understand that she was angry with him for accusing her of having an affair, but why hadn't she returned any of his calls? He wanted to hear her voice, to tell her he was sorry, and that he would never let anyone hurt her again. But right now, she could be anywhere, and he was at a complete loss about how to find her.

It was standing room only in the new micropub at the top of Preston Street. Mick used his bulk to part a path through a packed crowd of bodies to the bar, and ordered two beers with foreign-sounding names drawn from a metal keg on a wooden rack.

'Thanks for dragging me out,' said Jez. 'I really needed this tonight.'

'No problem. I figured it would do you good after the week you've had. So, tell me, what's your plan for getting Alice back?'

'I don't know,' said Jez. 'She could be anywhere. I don't have a clue how to find her.'

'You must have some idea where she might have gone.'

'I know she grew up in Margate, but that's about it. I don't know whether she still has family there, or friends. I posted something on Facebook, and one woman did remember her when she was Alice Black.'

Jez had edited his message on the Hartsdown High school page after discovering Alice had changed her name. Almost immediately, a woman called Sarah had commented on his post, referring to her as the 'infamous

Alice' and wondering how anyone could have forgotten her after what she'd done.

Mick frowned. 'Black?'

'She changed her name when she went into hiding,' said Jez. 'Anyway, I've messaged this woman back, but she's not replied. Look, Alice is used to disappearing, so unless she chooses to get in touch, I don't know what more I can do.'

'Well, the Facebook contact is a solid lead, isn't it?'

'I guess,' said Jez.

'Get yourself up to Margate, and start sniffing around. You owe Alice that, surely? I'll come with you. We'll make a day of it.'

'Really?'

'Yeah, of course. It's the least I can do for a mate in his hour of need.'

'What about Donna and the kids?'

'She'll understand. And if you really love Alice, you owe it to her to make the effort. Come on, I can barely hear myself think in here, let's find somewhere else.'

They staggered out of the pub, and stumbled off the narrow pavement into the road between tightly parked cars. The air was chill and dry, but far from sobering him up, it only compounded Jez's drunkenness.

A three-minute walk took them to The Elephant at the top end of town, where it was much quieter. They found a window seat in the corner.

'What about this Marcus bloke? What are you going to do about him?' Mick's eyes had turned glassy, and his cheeks were glowing.

'What do you mean?'

'You can't let him get away with what he's done to Alice. Men like that, who hit women, need to be taught a lesson.'

'I nearly killed him,' whispered Jez, glancing around, nervous someone might overhear.

'Yeah, because he broke into the house. That's not what I'm talking about.'

'What then?'

'He needs to know he can't get away with being violent to women.'

'I don't know, Mick.'

'Where's he live?'

'Somewhere in Thanet.' Jez's ears were buzzing from shouting over the earlier noise, and he had a vague notion he was now speaking unnecessarily loudly to compensate. 'I went to the hospital to see him. I thought he might know what's happened to Alice, but he'd already been discharged, and they won't give me his address.'

Jez noticed a group of men at the bar. One was staring at him with cold, hard eyes.

'I bet he's not that difficult to find.' Mick peered into the bottom of his glass, lost in contemplation.

'Well, I never want to see him again.'

'We need to go and talk to him in language he understands. Give him a bit of a smack.'

'I already did that. Remember? Didn't turn out too well.'

The man at the bar put his glass down, and detached himself from the group. There was something familiar about his close-cropped hair, unshaven face, and crooked teeth. Maybe Jez had sold him a house, or perhaps they'd been at school together. Faversham was a small town. Except this guy didn't look too friendly.

Mick was saying something about gathering a few of the lads together, but Jez wasn't listening. He caught a glimpse of a tattoo on the hand of the man coming towards him, and remembered where he'd seen him.

One of the fathers from the playground.

'Mick, we've got a problem.'

His friend stopped mid-sentence, and glanced casually over his shoulder, following Jez's line of vision. The man with the tattooed hand was approaching their table, jabbing a finger at Jez.

'It's you,' he said, with a snarl. 'The pervert from the park.'

Jez jumped up, his heart in his mouth. His chair fell backwards, clattering on the floor, and attracting the attention of the whole pub. 'Now, listen ...' he said, but the man seemed in no mood to listen to anything he had to say.

'You dirty bastard. You might have blagged your way out of it with the police, but we all know what you are.'

'Look, it was a misunderstanding.'

'Misunderstanding my arse.'

'We're not looking for any trouble.' Mick had stayed seated. He spoke quietly but firmly. 'We're here for a quiet drink. So why don't you calm down, and go back to your friends before you make a fool of yourself.'

'I'm not talking to you, fat boy.'

'I'm sorry,' said Mick. 'What did you say?'

'I said, button it, fat boy. This is between me and him.'

Mick was out of his chair quicker than should have been possible for someone of his size. 'Who're you calling fat?' he asked, grabbing a handful of the man's t-shirt.

'All right, calm down.' The man held up his hands in submission. 'I've got no beef with you, mate. It's your pervert friend I want a word with.'

'Firstly, I'm not your mate and secondly he's not a pervert. He told you already, you've made a mistake. Now back off.' Mick pushed him square in the chest.

The man lost his balance, and was caught by one of his friends as he fell backwards. His eyes burned with anger and humiliation as he scrambled to his feet.

Jez glanced at the door. Maybe he could slip away unnoticed. He wasn't a bar brawler, or a fighter of any kind, and he was going to be no help to Mick in this situation. His instinct was to run. Running away had always been his solution to avoiding trouble.

The only time he'd ever been in a fight was when he was twelve, and Paul McGann had deliberately tripped him up in the corridor. In the heat of the moment, and sore with humiliation, he'd grabbed the boy in a head-lock, and spent the next minute or so grappling with him to the cheers of the other boys in his year, until they were separated by a passing prefect, and sent their separate ways.

But this was a proper fight. Real fists, and violence, and the intoxication of alcohol, with the possibility of blood and broken bones.

Before Jez could move, one of the other men at the bar, a stocky bruiser in a Chelsea football shirt launched himself at Mick, his fist wheeling in a wide arc. Mick stepped to one side, weaving, and jabbed the man in the face so hard he collapsed like a felled tree.

Behind the bar, the landlord was on the phone. He punched three numbers into a handset, and held it to his ear, waiting to be connected.

The man with the tattooed hand roared. He flew across the room, pinning one of Mick's arms to his side, grabbing him in a bear hug.

Jez edged around the table, closer to the door, trying to keep clear of flailing arms and legs.

The two men fell to the floor in a bundle of writhing limbs, the sweat and heat rising from their bodies, their faces taut and twisted.

Jez's hand reached for the brass handle.

From the shadows a third man appeared. He was stick thin, spindly, and undernourished, with a scrawny neck and prominent Adam's apple. He picked up a chair by its legs, shuffling closer to the two men fighting on the ground. He stood over them, legs planted slightly apart, the chair raised high, and Jez realised he was waiting for an opportunity to bring it down on Mick's head.

He pulled the door open an inch, letting in a dry blast of cold air.

On the floor, Mick was getting the better of the smaller man. He had his head pinned to the floor under one of his meaty hands, squashing his red face against the floorboards. He kicked a free leg over his opponent's thigh, and rolled his weight on top of him.

The man with the chair took aim.

Jez slammed the door shut.

He couldn't leave Mick when he was only trying to clean up his mess. He had to do something. He looked for a weapon, but saw only the two half-finished beer glasses on the table. He knew the damage a smashed glass could do to flesh, and immediately put the thought out of his mind. He was in enough trouble with the police.

Mick's wide back was now fully exposed to the man with the chair. Jez had no time to think. The adrenaline that spiked through his veins made him feel like Superman. He pushed the table to one side, and threw a wild punch at the scrawny man's exposed side, catching him square in the ribs under his arm. It wasn't the deadliest blow in the world, but the surprise did the trick. The man was thrown off balance, and the chair smashed harmlessly into the floor, splintering into three sections, and more importantly, missing Mick.

Jez staggered backwards, clutching his fist. The punch had hurt more than he'd imagined. The scrawny man turned on him, scowling with fury. He pulled back his shoulders, and formed tight fists with his hands.

Jez backed away, until his heels caught on the edge of the fireplace, and he was up against the mantelpiece. He had nowhere to go, and no idea what to do to protect himself.

But the punch that came his way was so slow and predictable he was easily able to duck under it, swaying at the waist, and dropping his shoulder.

Unfortunately, he didn't see the second punch

coming, a jarring uppercut that he bowed straight into, snapping his head backwards, and almost shattering his jaw.

His legs turned to jelly, unable to hold his weight, and the night stole into his vision. The last thing he remembered was a sensation of falling. And there was nothing he could do to stop himself.

23

The last thing Jez saw before he hit the ground was the wash of flashing blue lights. In the distance, the drone of sirens sounded pitiful and urgent.

A strong hand grabbed him under his arm, and pulled him to his feet.

'Get up. We've got to get out of here.' Mick's voice sounded dull, as if someone had stuffed wads of cotton wool in Jez's ears.

He had the loose sensation of being pulled across the floor, his feet dragging. A flimsy wooden door banged open, and they moved into a dark corridor.

Another door. A different light. The smell of stale urine and disinfectant. His head being shoved down roughly into a stainless-steel sink. Cold water on his face. On the back of his neck. Shocking his body into consciousness.

Jez bolted upright, bile rising from his stomach, and gasping for air like a drowning man breaking the surface of the ocean. Water dripped from his head, soaking his shirt.

'Wake up,' Mick shouted, his huge frame almost filling the room. 'The police are coming.'

Jez wiped a hand over his face, and winced as he touched his jaw, recalling the bone-shattering punch that had knocked him cold. His vision cleared, and he wondered why Mick had dragged him into the men's toilets. Three steel urinals. One sink. A metal hand drier screwed to the wall. And only one door in.

'We're trapped,' said Jez. 'There's no way out of here.'

'Up there.' Mick nodded at two long windows in the wall above the urinals, no more than a metre wide and only half as tall.

'We can't fit through there.' Jez looked at Mick as if he'd gone mad.

'Yes, you can. Hurry.' Mick reached for a latch, and pushed one of the windows out on a hinge that ran along its uppermost edge. 'We don't have time to argue.'

'Perhaps there's a back entrance or something?'

'Jez, trust me on this.'

Mick's dirty grey t-shirt was rucked, torn and stained with dark sweat patches. His breathing was still coming hard from the exertion of the fight, his fat stomach rising and falling over the top of his jeans.

'What about you?' said Jez. 'I'm not trying to be funny, but you'll never make it through there, mate.'

'Stop worrying about me. You're wasting time.'

'I can't leave you here.'

'Do I have to throw you out?'

'All right, all right, I'm going.'

Jez grabbed the edge of the window, and hoisted himself up using one of the urinals as a foothold. He shoved his head out first, and squeezed his shoulders through the narrow gap.

'Hurry!' said Mick, as a frantic banging began on the door.

'Police! Open up!'

Jez wiggled his hips, and kicked his feet, until his body slid out. He fell in an ungraceful heap on a patch of ground strewn with rocks and weeds.

'Open this door!' shouted the voice again, with a little more urgency.

Jez dusted himself down, and reached up on the tips of his toes to peer in through the window. Mick was leaning with his back to the door, his legs braced, using all his weight to stop someone on the other side forcing it open.

'Grab my hand,' said Jez, stretching his arm in.

'Run,' said Mick. 'I can't hold them off much longer.'

'I can't leave you.'

'Just go! Hurry!'

The door opened an inch, and slammed shut with a loud bang as Mick arched his back into it.

'Are you sure?'

'Of course I'm sure. I'll call you later.'

Jez gave his friend an apologetic smile. 'As long as you're okay. I owe you, Mick.'

'Just go.'

Jez scrambled along the narrow alley that ran

between the back of the pub and a row of houses behind, struggling in the dark not to turn his ankle on the uneven ground. His heart was racing, and he shivered in the chill of the night, wondering how the evening, that had started with so much promise, had descended into such chaos. He shouldn't have come out. Not with Alice missing. He should have stayed at home, and waited for her to call. What if she'd gone back to the house and he'd not been there?

The alley emerged into a deserted lane, lit by a single overhead street lamp. Jez clambered over a rusty wire fence, checked the way was clear, then straightened his shirt and combed a hand through his hair. As casually as he could manage with his heart in his mouth, he sauntered into the open. He turned into The Mall without looking back at the pub, and stole towards the railway station, a euphoria swelling inside him with every step.

With any luck, the thug with the tattooed hand, and his leery mates would be spending the rest of the night in a police cell. That would teach them.

And then he thought of Mick. He taken the fall for Jez again, and the chances were he'd also be spending the night behind bars. Jez determined he'd make it up to his friend, just as soon as he had the chance.

When he saw the entrance to the underpass below the railway station ahead, Jez's casual steps became more urgent, and soon he was running. A gentle jog at first, and then a full-on sprint, arms and legs pumping, the wind in his hair, and exhilaration in his veins.

He only slowed as the underpass drew near. He

risked a glance behind. Two police cars were parked haphazardly in the street outside the pub, headlights blazing and blue lights bubbling. Shadows emerged. Men in handcuffs being marched out, escorted into the back of a waiting van.

Jez laughed.

Then threw up, all over his trainers, his abdominal muscles cramping, and the bitter sting of stomach acid clawing at his throat and sinuses.

He spat out the worst of it, and tried to ignore the mess on his feet. He had to cling to the walls to negotiate the steep steps, and emerged unsteadily on the other side, spilling into the road without looking.

A taxi driver slammed on his brakes.

Jez bounced off the bonnet, and landed on his back with the wind knocked out of his lungs.

'Shit!' Jez gasped, rolling onto his side, his teeth gritted.

The driver stuck his head out of his window, his face drawn in shock and momentary concern. 'Bloody idiot! Why don't you look where you're going? You're going to get yourself killed,' he yelled.

Jez held up a hand in apology, pulled himself stiffly to his feet, and rolled his neck. He checked his hands and arms and was surprised to find he'd come off with nothing more than a few scratches and grazes. 'Sorry,' he said.

The taxi driver shook his head, and drove off.

Jez staggered onto the pavement, wondering where he was supposed to be headed. He hadn't anticipated the evening ending quite so abruptly or dramatically, and now he was at a loss. His head was swimming with booze and he was on his own. He thought about the house, hollow and silent without Alice and Lily. Without them it wasn't a home.

He sat on a bench under a tree, with his head in his hands. The tears boiled up from somewhere deep inside, and the more he tried to fight them, the faster they flowed. He felt bereft and alone. He'd ruined everything. All the good things he'd had with Alice were gone, and he had no one to blame but himself.

He wiped the snot from his nose, and looked up at the stars, unusually bright in the clear sky. He was marvelling at the enormity of the universe, and his minuscule role in it when his phone buzzed in his pocket, an unexpected distraction from his thoughts. He tugged it from his jeans pocket with a thumb and finger.

'Hello?' he said, his voice hoarse and weak. When he licked his lips, he tasted the metallic tang of blood. At first, he heard only shallow breathing. 'Dad, is that you?'

'Jeremy?'

'What is it? What's wrong?' It was unusual for his father to call, let alone so late in the evening. It could only be bad news. Jez braced himself for the worst.

'It's your mother.' His father's voice cracked. 'She's been taken to the hospital.'

24

Hawkish porters wheeled trolleys along corridors while tired-looking nurses drifted between wards under the harsh light of fluorescent bulbs. Even in the small hours, the hospital was alive with activity, and the air heavy with the aroma of the hydrogen peroxide they used to clean the floors.

Jez had jumped in a taxi, and headed straight for the hospital without a moment's hesitation. He found his father in a deserted waiting room populated with rows of empty plastic chairs. He was sitting looking dishevelled, with his head in his hands, and the collar of his shirt poking out of his sweater.

'Dad?' Jez couldn't remember a single occasion his father had shown any emotion, but now his eyes were sore with tears. 'What's happened?' He wanted to hug him, to hold him close and feel the protection of his father's arms. But he didn't know how.

'She collapsed,' he said.

'What? Where?'

'In the kitchen, clearing up after dinner.'

'My God.'

'They think she might have had a stroke.' His father's lip trembled.

'Is she going to be ...?'

'I don't know. It's too early to say.'

'That's not good enough. I'll find someone. Wait here.'

'Sit down, Jeremy.'

'But they have to tell us what's going on.'

'And they will. Leave them to do their jobs. Now sit down. She's in good hands.'

Jez sat reluctantly, his mouth parched, the alcohol working a slow route through his liver. 'You should have phoned me earlier.'

'I've been trying your phone all night.'

'Oh,' said Jez. Guilt burned his insides. 'I didn't hear my mobile.'

'Apparently not.'

'Have you seen her yet?'

'No,' his father said. 'They think it might have been brought on by stress.'

'What stress?'

His father said nothing.

'Oh, I get it,' said Jez. 'You think this is my fault.'

'That's not what I said.'

'But it's what you're thinking.'

'Don't be ridiculous. Your mother's had a lot on her plate recently, that's all.'

'Like what?'

'All this business with you and Alice for a start. She's been worried sick.'

'So, you do blame me.'

'I'm just saying she cares about you, about you both. Not that you'd notice.'

'What's that supposed to mean?'

'Nothing.'

Jez crossed his arms. 'Come on, let's hear it.'

'This isn't the time,' his father said.

'I thought you and Mum were pleased I'd moved back home?'

'This isn't about you. Your mother's lying in a hospital bed, lucky to be alive. It would be nice if you spared her a thought or two. The world doesn't revolve around you and your problems.'

A fearsome-looking nurse carrying a stack of ring binders appeared from the corridor. 'Shhh!' she hissed. 'People are trying to sleep.'

'Is there any news on my mother? Mrs Hook?' said Jez, standing.

'Wait here, and I'll see if I can find a doctor to see you,' the nurse said. 'In the meantime, why don't you get your dad a cup of tea. He looks like he could do with it.' She smiled at the old man sweetly. 'There's a machine along the hall.'

Jez didn't move. He wasn't here to wait on his father. He was quite capable of buying his own tea. And besides, his head was pounding, and he still felt nauseous.

The nurse stood with a hand on her hips, staring at Jez with wide eyes, waiting for him to go.

'Fine,' said Jez, his resistance crumbling. 'You want sugar?'

'Since when have I taken sugar in tea?'

'No, right.' Jez fished in his pocket for loose change, and slouched out of the waiting room.

The machine was halfway along the corridor. It spewed out two plastic cups of warm, pallid liquid that vaguely resembled tea, and tasted of nothing much at all.

'It's warm and wet,' said Jez, handing one of the cups to his father, 'but that's about the best it's got going for it.'

It wasn't the greatest peace offering, but his father seemed grateful for the gesture. Jez regretted snapping, but he couldn't fathom how he could possibly be held to blame for his mother's ill health. She was getting old. Old people fell ill. It didn't have to be anyone's fault.

'I wasn't blaming you,' said his father.

'I know.'

'I'm worried about your mum.'

'She'll be fine.' Jez tried to make himself comfortable in one of the hard, plastic chairs but found it virtually impossible.

'Have you heard from Alice?'

'Not yet.'

'Did you call her?'

'Yes, of course I've tried calling her.' Jez felt his ire rising. His father had such a knack of asking ridiculous questions that he wondered if sometimes he did it deliberately to wind him up. 'She's not answering her phone.'

'It must have been some row.'

'It was a silly misunderstanding. It's complicated. She'll come around.'

'Your mum and I have had our fair share of arguments over the years. It's only natural. But I never walked out,' his father said. 'You have to work at these things, not run away at the first sign of trouble.'

'Yeah, I know, I'm a crap son, and a worse boyfriend. Any more words of encouragement?'

'Don't be so touchy.'

'You're not exactly Mr Perfect, are you?' said Jez.

'Is that right?'

'Mum's been running around after you for years. It's no wonder she's stressed.'

'You don't know what you're talking about.'

'I have eyes, Dad. I can see what's going on.'

'Don't you dare talk to me like that. You stink of booze and vomit, and you can hardly stand up straight. You're a bloody mess, so I hardly think you're in a position to hand out the lectures.'

'At least I'm here.'

'Eventually.'

'Mr Hook?'

Jez hadn't noticed the bleary-eyed man with sleeves rolled up to his elbows appear.

'Yes,' said Jez and his father at the same time.

'I'm Doctor Nandamuri. I've been treating Mrs Hook.'

Jez's father jumped out of his seat. 'How is she? Can I see her?'

'Not at the moment. She's resting,' the doctor said. 'Please, sit.' He drew up a chair opposite the two men, and crossed his legs. 'We believe Mrs Hook has suffered a transient ischaemic stroke. It's sometimes called a mini stroke.'

'What does that mean?' said Jez.

'It happens when the blood flow to the brain is disrupted, often by a blood clot. But you did the right thing. You called an ambulance straightaway, and we were able to treat her quickly.' The doctor smiled. 'She's had a scan and we're treating her with drugs. All being well, there's no reason she won't make a full recovery.'

'You mean she's going to be all right?' said Jez.

'It will take time, and she'll need a lot of support from her family, but yes, all should be well.'

'Thank God,' said Jez's father.

'She's sedated for now, so you won't be able to see her until the morning, I'm afraid.'

'Can I stay with her?' Jez's father asked.

'Go home, Mr Hook. Get some sleep, and come back in the morning. We'll call if there's any development.'

'I'd rather stay. I don't want to go back to the house on my own.'

The doctor shrugged. 'That's up to you.' He stood, shook hands with both men, and sloped away.

They watched him go, each lost in their own thoughts, Jez hardly daring to believe the news had been so positive.

'He's right, Dad. We should go home and get some rest. We'll come back first thing.'

'I'm not going anywhere.'

'You can't stay here,' said Jez, glancing around the waiting room. 'Where are you going to sleep?'

'I can't leave her here on her own.'

'She's going to be fine. Come on, let's get a taxi.'

'No.'

His father could be an obstinate old bugger when he put his mind to it.

'Fine. You stay then. Want me to bring anything in the morning?'

His father shook his head. He looked old under the bright lights. His skin was lined and grey, his thinning hair now barely concealing his skull.

'Well, I'll be back at around nine then. I'll see you in the morning,' said Jez, turning to leave.

'Don't go.'

'What?'

'Stay. Please don't go home. I need you here with me.'

25

Jez woke with a dry mouth, and a crick in his neck. Bright lights in the ceiling burned his eyes, and his foot, propped up on a chair opposite, was numb.

He sat up too quickly, and the blood drained into his trainers. For a second, he thought he was going to pass out as his vision clouded and stars danced before his eyes.

He felt like he'd been run over by a train. His muscles ached, and his hands stung where he'd scuffed off the skin on his palms. Worse was his head which throbbed and pulsed with the beginnings of a killer hangover.

'How did you sleep?' His father was already awake, and looking remarkably fresh. He'd combed his hair flat with some water.

'Not great.'

'I could tell from the way you spent most of the night snoring.'

'Did I?'

'You look a state. Go and wash your face. You'll feel better for it.'

Jez stood and stretched, feeling a painful pang in his ribs. 'Any news on Mum?'

'Not yet. It's still early.'

'I need a coffee. Want anything?'

His father shook his head. 'I'm fine.'

The coffee from the machine in the corridor was little better than the tea. Darker in colour but equally tasteless.

Jez sat cradling the cup, sitting on the sill of a low window overlooking an enclosed courtyard behind the main hospital building where two cleaners were chatting over a cigarette. The wind was picking up again, ruffling the branches of a tree planted in the centre of a circular paved patio.

When Jez returned to the waiting room, his father was reading the posters taped to the walls, his hands in his pockets, shoulders back. Stop smoking. Give blood. The danger signs of diabetes.

His father lingered over one advising how to spot the signs of a stroke. Act F.A.S.T, it said.

Fortunately, his father had done exactly that, and probably saved his mother's life.

Would Jez have done the same? It was difficult to know how he'd react in a crisis, especially a medical emergency. He'd wanted to call an ambulance when he'd attacked Marcus Fenson. But Alice had talked him out of it. She was the one who'd taken control. So calm and unflappable under pressure, even when they thought Marcus was dead.

A matronly nurse with an easy manner and a uniform a size too small for her corpulent frame emerged from the corridor, and greeted them with a smile.

'Mr Hook?' she said, looking between the two men. 'Your wife's been asking for you. You can see her now, if you like.'

Jez and his father followed her onto a stuffy ward thick with the smell of soap and antiseptic. Jez tried to ignore the thousand-yard stares from the ghoulish geriatric patients, moaning and muttering, propped up in their beds.

His mother was laid up at the far end of the room. The sheets had been folded back neatly over her chest, and her frail arms rested on top of the covers. Her hair was lank and loose, and the dark green gown they'd dressed her in drained her of colour. She'd always taken a pride in her appearance, and never chose green. She said it didn't suit her. Now it emphasised how washed out and pale she looked.

'She's had a good night, but she's a little confused this morning,' said the nurse. She pulled a curtain around the bed to give Jez and his father some privacy. 'You can spend a few minutes with her, but she needs to rest, so don't tire her out too much.'

Jez took his mother's bony hand, and noticed the sparkle in her eyes had gone, along with the strength on one side of her face. Her left eye, cheek and the side of her mouth drooped as if being tugged by an imaginary thread.

'How are you feeling, Mum?'

A dribble of spittle rolled down her chin as she muttered an inaudible response. Jez's father jumped up and pulled a tissue from a box by her bed to wipe away the drool.

When she tried to speak again, he leaned closer and kissed her tenderly on the forehead. 'No, love, you'll have to stay a few more days until the doctors say you're well enough to go home. You need to build up your strength,' he said.

His mother had always been a fiercely strong, independent woman, running the kitchens at the nearby primary school until they'd made her redundant when they brought in outside caterers. But now she looked pathetically frail. Her skin was papery thin, almost translucent.

Nothing had ever fazed her before. Even when she lost her job, she simply refocused, and concentrated on running the house with the same dedicated efficiency as she'd run the school kitchens. And when she found that wasn't enough to fully occupy her time, she'd joined the Women's Institute, throwing herself into meetings, coffee mornings, baking and jam-making.

By contrast, his father had settled into retired life with ease, whiling away his days pottering in the garden and watching test match cricket on the television.

Now though, it seemed as if a little bit of his mother had died.

'Where's Alice?' she asked, trying to sit up, her words slurred.

Was she querying why Alice hadn't come to visit, or

had she remembered she was missing? Jez didn't want to say anything to upset her.

'She's looking after Lily,' he said. 'But she sends her love.' Strictly speaking it wasn't a lie.

His mother seemed placated, and collapsed back onto her pillow, her tongue darting between her lips.

'Are you thirsty, love?' His father jumped out of his seat again, filling up a plastic cup from a jug. He pressed it to her lips, and held a tissue under her chin.

'So, we talked to your doctor last night,' Jez said. 'It was lucky Dad called an ambulance straightaway, otherwise …' He stopped himself before he said it, not that his mother seemed to notice. She was staring at the ceiling with her breath coming in slow, shallow gasps. 'Anyway, he thinks you'll make a good recovery.'

Suddenly her hand snatched Jez's wrist, and her eyes opened wide as if something of dreadful importance had occurred to her. 'Food,' she said, the effort of speaking almost too much for her.

'Are you hungry, Mum?' said Jez, not understanding what she was trying to tell him.

His father put his ear to her mouth, then smiled for the first time since Jez had arrived at the hospital.

'She's worried there's no food in the house for us,' he said, grinning. 'She wants us to stop on the way home and pick something up.'

Jez laughed. A welcome release of tension. It was typical of his mother to be worried about them when she was the one who'd been taken ill.

'Don't worry,' he said. 'Concentrate on getting better.'

'That's right,' his father added. 'Jeremy and I will cope. We'll survive perfectly well until you get home.'

His father had never cooked a meal in his life. He'd been a butcher for the best part of forty years, and could tell you a dozen ways to cook a fillet of beef, but had never had to cater for himself.

'I'll make sure he doesn't burn down the house,' said Jez. 'And I promise you we won't starve.'

His mother relaxed, and a crooked smile appeared on her face. 'You're a good boy, Jeremy,' she said, struggling to pronounce his name with a mouth that no longer worked properly.

'You rest now, and make sure you get better soon.'

His mother patted his hand, and her eyes fluttered closed.

The nurse poked her head through the curtains. 'How are you getting on?' she said, then noticed Jez's mother had fallen asleep. 'Ah, you've exhausted her out. It's been a long night. Why don't you leave her to rest now.'

26

Hot, steaming jets pounded Jez's body, easing his aching muscles. He watched the water pool and swirl around his feet, gurgling down the plughole with a scummy froth of soap suds. When he finally felt a little revived, he grabbed a towel and rubbed himself dry.

Stepping out of the shower, he caught his image in the misted mirror over the sink.

He was officially a wreck.

A bruise spread from his shoulder to his bicep. A wide red mark crept around his ribs under his arm, and his hands were swollen, grazed and sore.

He thought about Alice, and whether they were the sort of injuries she'd suffered at Marcus's spiteful hands. His stomach tightened. Did she have to cover her bruises with make-up, scarves and long-sleeved tops?

Jez had no doubt what Mick had in mind when he talked of gathering some of the lads together to hunt Marcus down, and that he needed to pay for what he'd done. But in his heart, Jez knew it wasn't the answer.

Mick was a good friend, and he meant well, but he could be impetuous and hot-headed at times.

And then he remembered abandoning his friend at the pub.

He'd not given it a second thought with everything that had happened with his mother. He didn't even know if they'd charged him, or if he'd been released from custody yet. He knew he should call, but his head was throbbing, and all he wanted to do was sleep.

Jez drifted into the bedroom, threw on some old clothes, and checked his phone. It had become an unconscious tick. But still no word from Alice.

He went through the motions of dialling her number, listening to the familiar dead air and the click as it diverted to voicemail. He didn't leave a message. What was the point? He'd only be wasting his breath.

The knock on the front door was as loud as it was unexpected, startling Jez as he threw the phone on the bed. Someone hammering with a clenched fist. Not a polite knock, but a determined, confident banging. He froze, and listened hard, isolating noises outside. A distant hum of traffic. Wind rustling leaves. A blackbird's warning cry.

Another three knocks came in close succession.

Urgent.

Persistent.

Impatient.

When had Jez become so jumpy about anyone calling at the house?

It was probably the postman with a parcel for Alice.

Jez opened the door cautiously, peering around the

frame. Two men in cheap suits and serious expressions were standing on the doorstep. Police officers, for sure, with an unmistakable don't-give-a-shit superiority.

'Mr Jeremy Hook?' asked the older of the two men, his head combed neatly into a side parting. 'DC Alan Fox, Kent Police.' He held up a warrant card in a black wallet.

Jez gave it only a cursory glance.

'This is my colleague, DC Gerry O'Hare. Can we have a word?'

Fox and O'Hare? Were these guys for real? 'It's not convenient right now. And I already told your colleagues it was a misunderstanding. Can you come back another time?' With the hangover he had brewing, it was the last thing Jez needed.

'It won't take long, but better if we do this inside, Sir, unless you want your neighbours gossiping?' said the second officer, O'Hare.

'All right, all right, come in.' Jez backed up into the hall, and thought about the old crone next door, her net curtains twitching.

They convened in the lounge and stood in an awkward huddle.

'We're looking for Alice Grey.' Fox lifted his chin with a haughty arrogance.

'Yes?'

'Is she here?'

'Not at the moment. Can I help?'

'Do you know when she'll be back?'

'I'm not sure.'

'I see,' said Fox. He shot his partner a glance. 'And when was the last time you saw her?'

A chill ran through Jez's veins. 'What do you want with Alice?'

'Just answer the question.'

Jez scratched his head, and swallowed hard. 'Err, Saturday morning I think.'

'You've not seen her since Saturday morning?'

'That's right.'

'Do you know where she is?' asked O'Hare.

'Look, I'll be honest with you,' said Jez. 'She kicked me out after we had a bit of a row at the weekend. I went back to my parents' for a few days, but when I tried calling she wouldn't answer. I came back to the house to speak to her, but she wasn't here. She'd gone.'

'Gone?'

'Yeah, vanished. Disappeared. Gone. Understand?'

'No need to take that tone, Sir,' said O'Hare.

'Mind if I take a look around?' asked his colleague.

'Actually, I do, unless you can tell me what's going on,' said Jez.

O'Hare shoved his hands in his pockets, and sighed. 'One of your neighbours was worried about Miss Grey's welfare. She said she'd heard screaming and shouting coming from the house, and was concerned she'd not seen Miss Grey for a few days.'

'It hardly sounds like a police matter.'

'It's our job to investigate complaints of this nature,' said O'Hare. 'We sent a patrol around to the house a couple of times, but no one was in. So, tell me about this row.'

'It was nothing. We had a disagreement, but I don't remember that we were that loud.'

Fox drifted towards Alice's oak dresser and studied the framed photographs. 'This her?' he said, picking up the same picture of Alice and Lily that Marcus Fenson had found.

'Yes,' said Jez. 'That's her daughter, Lily.'

'She's a good-looking woman.' Fox put the photo back and wandered casually into the kitchen.

'Did you report her missing?' asked O'Hare.

'No.'

'Why not?'

'Well, she's sulking with me, that's all. She'll be back when she's ready.'

'I see.'

'What happened to the door?' Fox called from the kitchen.

Shit. The back door. He'd not had time to arrange a repair since Marcus had broken in.

'It's been like that for a while,' said Jez, weakly.

'Looks like someone's forced the lock.'

'I forgot my key a few weeks ago,' said Jez. 'I've been meaning to get it fixed.'

Fox shot him a look. 'Is that right?'

'Yeah. It's on my list to get a locksmith out.'

'You want to be careful leaving the house unsecured. Anyone could get in.' Fox prodded at the splintered wood, then apparently losing interest, turned away.

'Yeah, thanks for the advice,' said Jez, not meaning it to sound as sarcastic as it came out.

'Do you have any idea where she might be?' said O'Hare.

'Um, no, not really.'

'And you've checked with friends? Family?'

'Of course.'

'And nobody's heard from her?'

'No.'

'Are you not worried about what might have happened to her?'

'Of course I am. But I said some stupid things, and she's still angry with me. She'll be back when she's ready to forgive me. Look, I appreciate your concern, but I'm sure you have far more important things to be doing.'

Fox had wandered back into the lounge, his eyes scanning every surface. He prodded around the paperbacks on the shelf over the TV, flicked through the magazines on the coffee table, and picked up a handful of Xbox games in their plastic boxes scattered across the floor.

'You like to play games?' Fox said, raising an eyebrow.

'It helps me to relax,' said Jez.

Fox flipped over one of the boxes, glanced at the pictures on the back and frowned. 'I thought this stuff was just for kids.'

Jez ignored the jibe.

Fox wandered into the hall. Jez watched him out of the corner of his eye, his heart cantering as he thought about Alice cleaning the blood out of the carpet. Had she missed any?

'This argument, what did you say that upset Miss Grey so much?' said O'Hare.

Jez heard Fox hesitate at the bottom of the stairs. What was he doing? He edged casually to his right to see what he was up to.

'Honestly I can't really remember. You know, we both said things we probably regret.'

'Like what?'

Jez tilted his head as if he was thinking, and saw Fox on his haunches scratching the carpet on the bottom stair.

'I might have suggested she was seeing someone behind my back.'

Fox's attention shifted to the banister. He shuffled closer, and stared intently at one of the upright spindles.

'Why would you say something like that?' O'Hare asked.

Jez shrugged. 'God, I'm being so rude,' he said loudly, turning animatedly for the kitchen. 'Where are my manners. I should put the kettle on. Would you like a drink? Either of you?'

'Thank you, but we're not staying,' said O'Hare.

Fox stood slowly, and started up the stairs. Jez let out a long, silent sigh of relief.

'What's he looking for?' He asked.

O'Hare glanced over his shoulder, and back at Jez. 'He's just checking everything is as it should be.'

'Right,' said Jez, his mind racing to remember if there was any incriminating evidence upstairs that might connect them to Marcus Fenson.

The floorboard outside the bedroom creaked, and Jez heard the door swing open, banging against the wall.

'I'd like the names and numbers of any family and friends Miss Grey might have been in touch with, so we can double check with them,' said O'Hare, producing a notebook and pen from his jacket.

'I told you, no one's seen Alice.'

'They might be covering for her, if she didn't want you to know where she's gone. Let's start with family members. Parents? Brothers or sisters? Aunts or uncles?'

Jez shook his head sadly. 'I don't think she has any family.'

'You don't think?'

'She's never mentioned any.'

'Isn't that a little odd?'

'She's a private person. She never talked about them.'

'What about friends?'

Jez gave an apologetic smile. 'It's going to sound strange, but she doesn't really have any friends either.'

'No friends.' O'Hare scribbled something in his notebook. 'Did Miss Grey keep a diary at all?'

Jez shook his head. 'Not that I know of.' He didn't like to mention that he'd turned the house upside down looking for one.

'What about her computer or laptop? Can I take a look at those?'

'She doesn't have one.'

'No computer?'

'She uses her phone for everything she needs,' said Jez. 'Which isn't very much. And before you ask, she doesn't have social media accounts. She hates the idea of sharing anything about her life online.'

'I see.'

The creaky floorboard upstairs groaned, and Fox thudded down the stairs. He appeared in the door with a dark expression on his face.

O'Hare turned to him. 'Anything?' he asked.

Fox wet his lips with his tongue, and glowered at Jez. 'She doesn't appear to have taken any of her things. Her clothes are all still hanging in the wardrobe.'

'Interesting,' said O'Hare, who was also now staring at Jez.

'And there's blood on the stairs,' said Fox. 'A couple of tiny spots, but worth getting forensics to take a look, unless there's anything you'd like to tell us, Mr Hook?'

'What?' A lump was growing in Jez's throat that wouldn't go away no matter how hard he swallowed.

O'Hare slipped his notebook back into his jacket. 'Your neighbour, Mrs Dobson, says you told her you killed Alice.'

'Killed her?'

'You told her you buried her under the patio.'

'It was a joke! Christ, we don't even have a patio. Come on, you can't seriously think I've hurt Alice?'

'If you have anything you need to tell us, now would be a good time,' said O'Hare.

'This is crazy,' said Jez. 'You've got it all wrong.'

'Have we? So, tell us where we can find Alice.'

'I don't know where she's gone. You have to believe me.'

'Then perhaps we'd better continue this chat down at the station,' said Fox.

'No!' said Jez. 'This is madness. I've not done anything.'

'Don't make this any more difficult for yourself,' O'Hare continued. He hitched up his trousers, and stood with his hands on his hips.

'Why don't you believe me? Alice and I had a fight, I walked out, and she disappeared. How many times do I have to tell you?'

Fox sighed, and gave his partner a knowing look, as if they'd made a bet outside that this was the way it was going to go. 'In which case, Jeremy Hook, I'm arresting you on the suspicion of the murder of Alice Grey.'

27

The room was windowless and cold, with a tiled floor, bare walls, and a CCTV camera blinking in the corner. Jez had been left sitting at a rectangular table with only his thoughts and fears for company. Everything had happened so quickly, he could scarcely process what was going on. It was bad enough that Alice was missing, but to be accused of her murder was insane.

Almost an hour passed before Fox and O'Hare strode into the interview room. Announcing their names to invisible microphones, they pulled up chairs opposite Jez, and Fox laid a slim cardboard file on the table. O'Hare sat to his left with his legs crossed, and a notebook open on his knee.

'How long have you known Miss Grey?' asked Fox.

Jez chewed his lip, and considered how far he should co-operate with the detectives. If they thought he'd killed Alice, he ought to tell them everything to prove his innocence. Well, almost everything. Eventually, Alice would be found, and they'd realise they'd made a big mistake. In the meantime, he figured full co-operation was his best bet. 'Since the beginning of the year,' he said.

'How did you meet?'

'In a supermarket car park, of all places.' Jez smiled at the memory of how he'd chased after her with the bunch of sunflowers. 'I asked her out for a drink and it went on from there.'

'And you moved in together?'

'Yes, we moved into Abbey Street in the spring.'

'And that was with Alice and her daughter, Lily?' said O'Hare, checking his notes.

'That's right.'

'How was your relationship with Miss Grey's daughter?'

'Good. We got on well.'

Fox settled back in his chair, never taking his eyes off Jez. They bore into him like drills excavating for the truth. Jez couldn't hold his gaze. He picked at his finger nails, focusing on his hands in his lap.

'Tell me about the fight you had,' said Fox.

'I wouldn't describe it as a fight exactly,' said Jez. A fight sounded like two people throwing punches.

'How would you describe it?'

'An argument. A row. You know, couples do have them from time to time.'

'Let's not argue semantics. What was the argument about?'

'I told you all this at the house.'

'Tell me again,' said Fox, narrowing his eyes.

Jez sighed, and looked to the ceiling. 'I thought she was having an affair.'

O'Hare scribbled furiously in his notebook. 'And why did you think that?'

'I don't really know. Jealousy, maybe?'

'But something must have given you cause to think she was seeing someone behind your back?' said O'Hare.

The first tricky question. Jez needed to be careful. Or maybe it was time to tell them everything. Perhaps he should confess he'd attacked an intruder in their home, and that it had turned out to be Alice's abusive ex-boyfriend. If anything had happened to Alice, he was the one they should be questioning.

But if he confessed to the attack, and told them about Marcus Fenson, there was no turning back. He'd almost certainly be looking at an assault charge. Maybe even attempted murder.

'Nothing specific,' said Jez. 'A nagging feeling she'd not been totally honest with me.'

'How did the argument start?' asked Fox.

'What do you mean?'

'Well, something must have triggered it. Was it something she said, or did?'

'I don't remember.'

'That's convenient.'

'I'm trying to help here, but I honestly can't remember how it started.'

'But it ended with you accusing her of having an affair, and Miss Grey kicking you out?'

'Something like that.'

'Well, either it did or it didn't.'

'Yes,' said Jez. 'I said some mean things I regret. I know she's out of my league, and I guess I was feeling insecure.'

'Right,' said Fox. 'And does she have a history of being unfaithful? Has she seen other men behind your back before, to your knowledge?'

'No,' said Jez.

'In which case, I don't understand why you would accuse her of something like that out of the blue.'

'Neither do I,' said Jez.

'And when you walked out on Saturday morning, that was the last time you saw her?'

'Yes.'

'Did you ever hit her?'

'No,' said Jez. 'Never.'

'Maybe a little slap from time to time, to keep her in line?' said O'Hare, glancing up from his notes. 'I mean, who could blame you, if she was cheating on you.'

'You've got it all wrong. I've never laid a finger on Alice.'

'But she's disappeared, hiding from you because of your behaviour?'

Jez didn't like the way the interview was going. He sat up straight, and cleared his throat. 'Shouldn't I have a lawyer or something, if I'm under arrest?'

O'Hare sighed, and put his pen down. 'Well, we could call a duty solicitor for you. That's your right, of course. But it's going to take time, and will delay this interview. We'd have to put you in a cell in the meantime. The alternative is that we crack on, and iron this out as quickly as possible, especially if, as you say, you have nothing to hide.'

Jez shuddered at the thought of spending any time in a cell. O'Hare was right. It was better to get the interview over with. Straighten things out. 'Fine. Let's carry on,' he said.

'Good,' said O'Hare. 'Now tell me exactly how Miss Grey reacted when you accused her of cheating on you.'

Jez remembered her screams, and her refusal to explain how she knew Marcus Fenson. She'd thrown a mug at him, and missed. It had smashed against the wall, and shattered into sharp slithers. And that look she'd given him, of disbelief and disappointment. That was what hurt the most. He should have swallowed his pride, and apologised. Then none of this would be happening.

'She was angry. She shouted and yelled. I know now I was wrong, but at the time I was convinced she was hiding something from me.'

'And what made you come to that conclusion?'

'I don't know. The more I think about it, the more ridiculous it seems,' said Jez.

Fox leaned over the table, and put a hand on the cardboard file. 'Do you own a boat, Mr Hook?'

Jez's breath stuck in his throat for a second. They knew about the yacht. He said nothing trying to gather his thoughts. Sweat patches under his arms began to grow.

'The *Fare Winds*?' Fox persisted.

'Yes. That's my uncle's yacht. He left it to me when he died.'

'Can you explain the traces of blood we found in the cabin?' He flipped open the file, and pushed it across the table towards Jez.

On the top of a small stack of photographs was an image of a crimson smear across a vinyl floor. It looked like the floor of his yacht.

'Take a look through,' said Fox. 'There are more.'

With a trembling hand, Jez flipped through the pictures. More close-up shots of blood. On the striped seat covers. On the wooden uprights. A bloody thumb print on the hatch.

'In case you were wondering, it's human blood,' said Fox.

'When were these taken?' said Jez. 'Only I've not been on the boat for a while.'

'Yesterday afternoon. We were following up on information that you were spoken to by an officer near the boatyard in the early hours of Friday morning. What were you doing out that late?'

'I ... I ...' Jez stammered. 'I couldn't sleep. Like I told the officer, I thought a drive would clear my head.'

'Were you on the way to the boatyard?'

'No,' said Jez. 'Not at that time of the night. Anyway, shouldn't you have had a warrant or something before you started poking around my boat?'

'We had reason to believe a crime had been committed,' said O'Hare, with a look of self-satisfaction Jez wanted to knock off his face.

'You think this is Alice's blood, don't you?'

'Is it?' asked Fox.

'Of course not.'

'Then how do you explain it?'

Jez rocked back in his chair. Maybe he should tell them about Marcus Fenson, and get it off his chest. 'I know what you're thinking,' he said.

'And what's that?'

'That I killed Alice, that I drove her body to the boatyard, and hid it on the yacht.'

Fox's eyes opened wide. O'Hare's pen hovered over his notebook.

'But how would that be possible if I was arguing with Alice on Saturday morning? Mrs Dobson next door can vouch for that, if she heard us shouting.'

Fox looked momentarily deflated. 'She may have her days mixed up,' he said, without conviction.

'I didn't kill Alice,' said Jez. 'I don't even think she's dead. You need to stop wasting time talking to me, and get out there looking for her.'

'Believe me, we are looking, Mr Hook,' said Fox.

'What about her office? Have you spoken to them? She was at work on Monday morning, which proves I can't have killed her at the weekend.'

'That's a line of inquiry we are pursuing, but it doesn't explain the blood on your yacht.'

'I can't explain it either,' said Jez. 'But it's nothing to do with me.'

O'Hare folded his notebook closed, placed it on the table, and walked out of the room. He returned with a clear plastic bag. Jez immediately recognised the object it contained.

It thudded on the table when he put it down.

'For the purposes of the tape, DC O'Hare has returned to the room with exhibit 5F,' said Fox.

Jez stared at it with horror.

'Do you recognise it?' O'Hare picked up his notebook, and settled back in his chair. 'For the tape, Mr Hook is nodding his head. And can you tell us what it is, Jeremy?'

So, it was Jeremy now. No more Mr Hook.

'It looks like one of Alice's dumbbells,' said Jez.

'I noticed an identical one on the landing at your house earlier,' Fox said. 'The question is, what was this doing on your yacht?'

'I don't know,' said Jez, panic rising.

'Was it the weapon you used to kill Alice Grey?'

'No,' said Jez.

'Speak up.'

'No. I told you, I didn't kill Alice.'

Fox leaned forward, his face softening. 'I get it,' he said. 'She'd wound you up, hadn't she? You found out she'd been having an affair, but even when you confronted her she couldn't tell you the truth. You lashed out, grabbing the first thing that came to hand.'

'No,' said Jez, tears welling in his eyes.

'You were angry and humiliated. Who wouldn't have been in the same situation?'

'It's not what happened.'

'And when you realised the terrible thing you'd done, you bundled Alice's body into the boot of your car, and drove her to the boatyard. What happened next, Jeremy? Did you take the body out to sea, weigh it down with some chains, and throw it overboard? Come on, do yourself a favour. Tell me what happened. We all make mistakes, but you have a chance to put this right. If you keep lying, I can't help you. Tell me the truth, and we can sort this out.'

How could he tell them the truth?

Besides, without a confession they had no evidence he'd done anything wrong. And he wasn't about to hand it to them on a plate. He'd stick to his guns, and say nothing. If he waited long enough, they'd find Alice, and his nightmare would be over. He just had to hold his nerve, and keep his peace.

'I think I need that lawyer now,' said Jez.

28

The duty solicitor had a pleasant, avuncular face, with a drooping moustache and whiskery sideburns that wouldn't have been out of place in a Dickensian novel.

'The name's Mapp,' he said, as the cell door slammed closed. 'Peter Mapp. North Kent duty solicitor. Sorry it took so long to get here. It's been a hell of a day.'

Jez had been waiting for hours. They'd taken the laces from his shoes, and the belt from his trousers, checked behind his teeth with a torch, and stripped him of his watch. Dehumanised, and treated like a criminal.

Mapp took a seat on the edge of the bed, a thin plastic mattress on a concrete plinth attached to the wall. He placed a pile of papers on his lap, and shook Jez's hand with a firm grip.

'They think I killed my girlfriend,' said Jez.
'Did you?'
'No, of course not.'
'Then you have nothing to worry about.'

The tension lifted from Jez's shoulders. At last, someone who believed him. 'Do you think you can get me out of here?'

Mapp pulled a single sheet free from the bundle of papers, and squinted at the printed text through thick glasses. 'What did you tell them?'

'Nothing,' said Jez. 'Well, only the truth.'

'Which is?'

'Alice is missing, and I have no idea where she is.'

'Hmmm,' said Mapp. 'Did they ask if you wanted legal representation?'

'No.'

'Right, well from what I can see, their evidence is pretty flimsy, so no wonder they didn't want a lawyer in with you. It's a complete abuse of power, of course, but that will only strengthen our case.' He grabbed a pen from the briefcase he'd set down by his feet, and jotted down a note on the top of the sheet of paper. 'Nothing more than a fishing expedition. We should have you out in no time.'

'Thank God. I was beginning to lose my mind in here.'

'Mind you, you shouldn't have said anything to them without a solicitor in the room.'

'But I have nothing to hide.'

Mapp peered over his glasses, giving Jez the once over. 'That's immaterial. Now what we have here is all largely circumstantial. Nothing to indicate your involvement in the woman's disappearance at all.'

'Her name's Alice.'

'What?'

'My girlfriend. She's called Alice.'

'Of course. And when did you last see her?'

'Saturday morning. We had an argument. I walked out. I moved back in with my parents, and I've not heard from her since. She's been ignoring my calls and messages.'

'One of the detectives says he found blood on the stairs at the house, and that none of Miss Grey's belongings appear to have been taken.'

Jez stared at the solicitor blankly.

'So how do you explain that?' Mapp asked.

'I don't know about the blood. It could have come from any of us.'

'And why hasn't she taken any of her things with her? These are the sorts of questions a jury can attribute a great deal of significance to.'

'Maybe she was in a rush. It doesn't prove anything.'

Mapp ran his tongue over his teeth. 'What about this yacht, the *Fare Winds*?'

'It's my uncle's boat. Mine now, since he died.'

'And the blood stains they found on board?'

'I'm at a loss,' said Jez. 'I've not been to the boatyard for a long time.'

'Really?' Mapp frowned. 'But you were stopped in the early hours of Friday morning by the police near the entrance to the yard. A coincidence, or is there something you need to tell me?'

'I couldn't sleep. I went for a drive to clear my head. This has nothing to do with Alice disappearing. I know what they think, but it's not true.'

'What isn't?'

'That I killed Alice and dumped her body in the estuary. I can't even sail that boat.'

'And the dumbbell they found on board?'

'I don't know anything about it.'

'The police say they found an identical one at the house. They think they're a pair.'

'Nothing to do with me.'

Mapp slipped off his glasses, and drew a deep breath. 'I want you to understand that as the lawyer appointed to represent you tonight, anything you tell me is privileged. That means you should tell me the truth, no matter how prejudicial you think it might be, because it can't be used against you in a court of law. In other words, I need the truth. Not a sanitised version of what happened, but the warts-and-all facts. I need one hundred per cent honesty, or I can't help you.'

'You don't believe me,' said Jez, incredulous.

'That's not what I said. But it's important you understand the seriousness of what you've been accused of. I can help you, but you have to give me your full cooperation.'

'I am giving it to you.'

'Good. Because now would be the time to tell me about anything else pertinent to the case. It's not the time to be holding back.'

Jez put his hand on his heart. 'I swear to you, I've told you, and the police, everything I know.'

'Right, well then, let's get this mess sorted out. First and foremost, they've overstepped the mark, and they know it.' Mapp rubbed his eye with a finger, nudging his glasses off his nose. 'Questioning you without offering you any legal representation is unacceptable.'

'Do you think they'll charge me with anything?'

'I think that's unlikely with such a large hole in their case.'

'Hole?'

'No body,' said Mapp. 'They're after you for murder, but murder cases are notoriously difficult to prosecute without one.'

'I wish everyone would stop talking about bodies and murder,' said Jez. 'Nothing's happened to Alice. She's taking some time out. That's it. The police should be out looking for her, not hounding me.'

'That's the spirit.'

'If they don't have a case, why am I still here?'

'Because they're hoping for a confession.'

'They'll be waiting a long time,' said Jez.

Mapp shuffled his papers, and stuffed them in his briefcase. 'I'll start by making a complaint about the two arresting officers. That should rattle their cage. Police bail should be no problem. Everything else we can sort out in due course.' He hopped off the bed and straightened his tweed jacket.

'Will it take long?'

'Give me ten minutes,' said Mapp. He banged on the cell door with his fist, and was let out by a waiting officer. 'You'll be home soon enough.'

29

Headlights flashing past with a monotonous regularity scorched Jez's tired eyes. He'd thought the police would deliver him home when Peter Mapp had secured his release on bail, pending further inquiries. Instead, they'd called a cab, and kicked him out on the street. Too exhausted to complain, he was just grateful to be out of the claustrophobic cell.

Jez toyed with his mobile phone, delaying the inevitable phone call he knew he should make, watching the taxi driver hunched over the steering wheel, his unblinking eyes flicking between the road ahead and the speedometer. They were cruising at fifty, resolutely sticking to the slow lane, where even the heaviest articulated lorries were overtaking them.

Jez dialled the number and held the phone to his ear. 'How's Mum?' he asked, quietly.

'Where are you?' His father's tone was curt. It sounded as if he'd been dragged from sleep.

'I'm sorry,' said Jez. 'I know I said I would go back to

the hospital, but ...' He wanted to pour his heart out to his father, to tell him what had happened, and to hear his soothing words reassuring him that everything would be all right.

But how could he?

His father had his own worries. He didn't need to be burdened with Jez's problems.

'I've been with your mother on my own all day. She's been asking for you.'

'I know. Something cropped up.'

'Something more important than your mother?'

Jez was too tired to fight. 'I'm so sorry. I should have been there. How is she?'

'Sleeping. It's late.'

He glanced at the clock on the dashboard. 'Tell her when she wakes up that I'm sorry I wasn't there today, and that I love her.'

'You can tell her yourself.' The line clicked dead, and with a single press of a button his father managed to convey the depth of his disappointment. Jez had wanted him to shout and rage. But hanging up stung much worse.

'Where to?' asked the driver as they pulled off the motorway.

Jez was about to reel off directions home, but hesitated as he contemplated another lonely night without Alice. Instead, he gave an address on the northern edge of town, overlooking the old quay.

The three-storey townhouse, clad in blackened timber, was in darkness as Jez skipped up a short flight of steps and knocked lightly on the front door, fearful of waking the children. He stood back and waited.

When no one answered, he knocked again. Louder.

A light came on in a window on the first floor. A curtain twitched, and he heard heavy footsteps on the stairs.

When the door opened, the light from the hall silhouetted a gigantic figure. 'Jez? What the hell are you doing here? Do you know what time it is?'

Mick was wearing boxer shorts and a crumpled t-shirt which strained against his corpulent stomach.

'Sorry to turn up so late, but I had no one else I could turn to.'

'What is it?'

'Can I come in?'

'You'll have to be quiet, Donna and the kids are asleep.'

He led Jez through to a room at the back of the house, with wide patio doors that overlooked the quay. Jez collapsed on a black leather sofa opposite a wide screen TV, and kicked off his shoes.

'You won't believe the day I've had,' said Jez, rubbing his sore eyes.

Mick stood with his back against a wall, and his arms folded over his chest. 'Make yourself at home, why don't you, and yeah, I'm fine, thanks for asking. A slap on the wrist. No charges this time.'

'What?'

'The pub the other night? The fight? Remember?'

'Oh my God, I'm so sorry, Mick. I clean forgot. What happened? Did you get arrested?'

'A night in the cells, and a caution. I thought you might have phoned at least.'

'I don't know what to say. I've had a few things on my plate.'

'Donna blames you, you know. She'll be furious if she finds out you've been in the house.'

'Ah,' said Jez, picking at his fingers.

'What?'

'I was hoping I could stay the night.'

'Mate, I don't think that's such a good idea. She'll go crazy.'

'Mick, please? I can't go home, not with Alice missing.'

'Still no word?'

'No, and now Mum's in hospital too.'

'Christ, what happened?'

'They think she had a stroke.'

'I'm sorry.' Mick found two tumblers and a bottle of whisky in a cabinet, and poured a couple of large measures.

'She collapsed at home, but luckily Dad was around, and had the sense to call an ambulance straightaway.'

'Is she going to be okay?' asked Mick, handing Jez a glass.

'I don't know. The doctor said she should make a full recovery, but I guess you never know with these things.' The alcohol burned Jez's throat, and warmed his stomach. 'Then on top of that, I've spent most of the day in a police cell.'

'You too, huh?'

'They've got it in their heads I killed Alice.'

'What the hell?'

'They found blood on my uncle's yacht.'

Mick's face clouded with confusion.

'Remember Marcus Fenson?' said Jez.

'Alice's ex? The guy who broke into the house?'

Jez nodded. 'So, I was going to dump his body in the estuary, but now these two detectives have come up with a theory that it's Alice's blood on the boat, and that I killed her.'

'Did you tell them about Marcus?'

'How could I? I nearly killed him. It would have been as good as confessing to attempted murder.'

'You're going to let them think you killed Alice instead?'

'I just have to bide my time. She'll turn up when she's ready, and that will be an end to it.'

'And if she doesn't?'

'She will.'

'I'm not sure I'd have your confidence,' said Mick, topping up their glasses.

'What other option do I have?'

'You could try telling them the truth.'

Jez shook his head. 'It's too risky,' he said.

'And still no word from Alice?'

'Nothing. No one at work has heard from her, she's not been back to the house, and her phone is constantly switched off.'

'Do you think something might have happened to her?'

Jez swilled the whisky around his glass. 'I hope not. Otherwise I'm screwed.'

'What about her parents? If I know anything about women, the first sign of trouble they run to their mums.'

'I don't even know if her parents are alive, let alone where I'd find them. She never talked about them.' Jez sighed. 'To be honest, I know so little about Alice, it's scary. I can tell you the school she went to, and that she used to be called Alice Black, but that's about it.'

'Well, it's a start. We know she grew up in Margate, so the chances are her parents still live there.' Mick disappeared out of the room, and returned with a laptop computer under his arm. 'And there can't be that many Blacks in Thanet.'

'You think we can find them?'

Mick opened the computer, and prodded at the keyboard with two chubby fingers. 'Ah, there we go. Forty-five of them to be precise,' he said.

'Is that all?'

'And for a few quid we can download all the names and addresses from the electoral role. I reckon you could do that in a day.'

'What, turn up and knock on the doors?'

'Exactly. If they're still alive, it's your best hope of finding Alice, and getting yourself out of this mess.'

'I don't know, Mick. It's a lot of work.'

'Do you want to find her or not?'

'Of course I do, but -'

'But nothing. You have to do it.'

'Would you come with me?' Jez looked up hopefully. 'It's just I don't think I could do that on my own.'

'Sure. Why not,' said Mick.

'We could go first thing in the morning.'

'Hang on a minute. I promised to take Donna shopping.'

'I'll talk to her. I'll explain everything.'

Mick scratched his head. 'She's not forgiven you for getting me arrested.'

'Let me stay the night, and I'll talk to her first thing.'

'That might not be such a good idea.'

'Of course it is. I can't go home with Alice and Lily missing. We could get up early, and take your van. We could be there for breakfast.'

'What's wrong with your car?'

'The police impounded it.'

'Of course they have.' Mick stretched his arms above his head and yawned. 'Go on then. You can kip on the sofa. I'll grab a duvet. But you can talk to Donna.'

'Cheers, Mick. I don't know what I'd do without you.'

30

They arrived in Margate shortly after nine, just as the seafront shops were opening, and the first rays of a weak autumnal sun were breaking through a low cloud. They trundled along the front in Mick's box van, past the weather-bleached amusement arcades overlooking the sandy beach, and on towards the modernist Turner Contemporary gallery, all angular lines and frosted glass cutting through a wide, grey sky.

They parked on the harbour arm, and Mick handed over a wad of paper he'd folded into his pocket.

'Where do you want to start?' he asked, as Jez smoothed out the list of names and addresses on his thigh.

'I guess we start at the top and work our way down,' said Jez, overwhelmed by the length of the list they had to work through.

'We should group them by location, or we'll be back and forth all day. And if I'm not home by five, Donna will have had the locks changed,' said Mick.

Jez knew he was only half joking. Donna had been less than impressed when she found out her shopping trip was being jettisoned in favour of a boys' day out to Margate. It took all of Jez's persuasive powers and charm to convince her it was a genuine emergency, his last hope of finding Alice.

They started the search in the old part of town, but no one answered at the first two houses. At the third address, the door was answered by a vacant-looking man with sallow cheeks, nicotine-stained long, grey hair, and a crazed look in his eye. He was bare-chested, and so thin his ribs protruded through his skin. When Jez explained he was looking for a family called Black, he screamed like a banshee, and slammed the door in his face.

An elderly woman in a floral dress and a frilly apron at the fourth address was so deaf Jez had to shout in her ear, but even then, she couldn't comprehend what it was he wanted.

In Cliftonville, on the outskirts of Margate, they found two more empty houses. A polite, young Asian man who lived in a flat above a laundrette was desperate to help, but eventually conceded, apologetically, that he didn't know anyone called Black.

'This is impossible,' said Jez, as Mick pulled up outside a row of terraced houses near the sea. 'We're never going to find her.'

A seagull glided lazily on the breeze, and cack-cawed as it rose higher into the sky.

'Don't be so defeatist. We've barely started. We'll find her.'

'Right, well we'll try this one, and then I need a coffee.'

Jez hopped out of the van, and surveyed the street, checking the numbers on the doors against his list. Number twenty-seven was midway along the terrace. It had a green door with a tarnished brass knob.

He knocked and waited.

Eventually it was answered by a middle-aged woman with a shock of dyed orange hair, and hooped gold earrings. She looked far too young to be Alice's mother.

'Sorry to trouble you,' said Jez, forcing a false smile. 'I'm looking for the family of Alice Black.'

'Never heard of them. Think you've got the wrong house, love,' she said, folding her arms, and giving Jez the once over.

'Oh, right,' said Jez. 'Perhaps you might recognise her?' He showed the woman a photo of Alice and Lily on his phone.

'Sorry,' she said, shaking her head. She retreated inside, and Jez turned away as the door started to swing closed, another dead end.

'Hang on a minute. Did you say Black?'

Jez spun on his heel. 'Yes,' he said. 'Alice Black. She's my girlfriend. She's missing.'

'Now I think of it, I'm pretty sure the previous owner was called Black,' the woman said, screwing up her face as if she was trying to recall a distant memory. 'In fact, I'm sure it was. Don't know why I didn't think of it before.'

'Do you know where they are now?'

'No. It was years ago.'

'I see,' said Jez, his initial excitement evaporating.

'But I tell you what, Jean will remember.'

Before Jez could protest, the woman had pushed past, and was knocking at the house next door. He threw a glance at Mick, waiting in the van, and shook his head.

The door opened a crack, and the woman with the orange hair leaned close. 'Jean, you remember Mrs Black who used to live at our place, don't you? There's a man here trying to find her.'

A small figure, no bigger than a child, peeked out from the shadows.

Jez gave a shy smile, and waved a hand in greeting. 'I'm looking for Alice Black,' he said, raising his voice.

'There's no need to shout. I'm not deaf,' said the old lady, opening the door wide. She was stooped with age, and had rounded shoulders and thinning grey hair. But her eyes were pin sharp. 'I remember Alice.'

'You do?' said Jez, his heart fluttering.

'Jane's daughter.'

Jez tried not to get too carried away. 'How old was she when you knew her?'

'She was only a little girl back then.'

'She's in her thirties now, if it's the same person,' said Jez.

The old woman squinted, as if she was making a calculation in her head. 'That would be about right.'

'She's my girlfriend,' said Jez. 'But she's gone missing, and I'm desperately trying to find her. I thought she might have come home to see her mother. Do you know where she lives now?'

The old lady frowned. 'Jane left a long time ago. They took her into a home I'm afraid.'

'What home? Where?'

'It was a shame really. Poor old Jane didn't even know her own name in the end. The family had to sell the house to pay the fees.'

'Oh, that's so sad,' the woman with orange hair cooed.

'Please, which home did she go to?'

The old woman put her fingers to her lips. Her hand, speckled with liver spots, trembled as she tried to remember. 'I don't recall the name,' she said.

'Please try.'

'I know it was in Broadstairs. It began with a 'C'. Clover-something.'

'That's good,' said Jez, nudging the woman with orange hair to one side. 'Think really carefully. It's important.'

'Cloverdale.'

'Are you sure?'

'No, that's not it. Something like it.'

Jez checked his watch. This could take all day.

'I've got it!' said the old woman suddenly, holding a finger triumphantly in the air. 'Cloverfield. That was the name of the home.'

'You're positive?'

'Quite sure. Cloverfield.'

'That's brilliant.' Jez could have kissed her. 'Thank you so much.'

'That's quite all right. Mind you, it won't do you much good.'

'What do you mean?'

'If you're looking for Jane, I'm afraid she's not there anymore.'

31

'This is utterly hopeless,' said Jez. 'I knew we shouldn't have come. It was a bad idea.'

'You can't give up like that. It's a setback, but you still want to find Alice, don't you?' said Mick.

The weak sun, hanging over the horizon, glinted off the inky sea as they stared through the windscreen of Mick's van. It had been a stupid idea to come. A waste of time and effort, all for nothing.

'We should go home. If Alice's mother is dead, and there are no other relatives, how can I possibly find her? I should just wait until she's ready to get in touch.'

Mick picked through a pile of greasy chips in a paper wrap on his lap. He shoved one in his mouth, and licked his fingers. The smell of hot fat and vinegar filled the cab, but Jez had no appetite. 'What about the police? What are you going to tell them?'

Jez shrugged. 'Maybe I should tell them everything, and let them sort it out.'

'Including what you did to Marcus?'

'Why not? It's got to be better than this.'

'You give up too easily. There has to be another way.'

'There isn't,' said Jez.

'What about trying to find Marcus? Maybe he knows where we can find her.'

Jez shot his friend a withering look. 'I hardly think so. Anyway, I already tried that.'

Mick screwed up the empty chip wrapper, dropped it on the floor by Jez's feet, and wiped his fingers on his jeans. 'What about that woman from Facebook?'

'What woman?'

'The one who said she remembered Alice from school.'

'She never messaged me back,' said Jez.

'So what? Let's go and find her. See what she knows.'

'How?'

'Show me her message.'

'Why? It's not going to do any good.'

'Just show me,' said Mick, gulping from a bottle of Coke. 'It's worth a try while we're here.'

Jez sighed, and reluctantly found the post he'd drafted on the Hartsdown High School memories Facebook page, and located the one response he'd had to his plea for information about Alice. 'Here,' he said, handing his phone over.

'Right, this shouldn't be too difficult,' said Mick, studying the post. 'So, we know she's called Sarah Flannigan. Let's see what else we can find out about her.'

Jez craned his neck to watch Mick call up the stranger's personal profile. He tutted as he scrolled.

'What is it?'

'Luckily for us, almost everything on her profile is public.'

'Really,' said Jez, his interest suddenly piqued.

'Yeah,' said Mick. 'Updates, photos, friends. It's all here.' He flashed the phone at Jez who caught a brief image of a heavily made-up woman, in a low-cut top, pouting at the camera. 'And would you know it, she's a hairdresser in Margate.'

'Show me,' said Jez, snatching Mick's thick wrist, and twisting his hand so he could see the phone.

'She's even given us the name of the salon where she works. *Live and Let Dye*.' Mick tapped the screen, and called up a website for the business. 'Here you go, it's based in the old town. That's about a five-minute walk from here.'

'I don't know, Mick. We can't just turn up unannounced.'

'Why not?'

'I don't know. It doesn't seem right. Perhaps we should call first.'

'Stop being a pussy. Come on, let's go.' Mick checked his watch. 'It's only around the corner.'

'I'm really not sure about this,' said Jez, but Mick was already half out of the van, the icy wind whistling around the cab.

'Fine, I'll go on my own.' Mick wasn't taking no for an answer.

'Let's think about this for a minute. What are we going to say?'

'Come on, do you want to find Alice or not?'

The van door slammed shut, leaving Jez sitting on his own. 'Mick!' he shouted, but it was too late. His friend was walking away, hitching up his jeans, head down against the wind. He never looked back.

32

The hairdressing salon, housed in an old brick property at the end of Lombard Street, was painted a vivid, cobalt blue, with two vast plate glass windows revealing a minimalist white interior lit brightly from within.

A bell sounded above the door as Mick and Jez walked in. Two stylists, busy with a couple of middle-aged women, glanced up.

'Be right with you,' said one of the stylists, as she worked skilfully with a pair of scissors in one hand, and a comb in the other.

Mick and Jez stood patiently by a reception desk.

'What can I do for you, gents?' said one of the stylists, pulling away from her client. She had a severe bob and thick make-up. She approached the reception desk with a bright red lipstick smile.

Mick glanced at Jez. The hairstyle was new, but there was no mistaking the woman's face.

'Sarah?' said Jez.

'Yes,' she said, the smile locked in place.

'Sarah Flannigan?'

The smile slipped a little. 'That's right. What can I do for you?'

Jez was momentarily lost for words. He'd had no time to plan what he was going to say, and now that the woman who'd replied to his Facebook message was standing in front of him, he panicked.

'The thing is…' he said, shuffling from one foot to the other.

Mick nudged him in the back.

'What it is —'

'My friend thinks you might be able to help him find his girlfriend,' said Mick, cutting in.

Jez shot him a filthy look. 'You replied to one of my posts on Facebook. My name's Jez?'

Her smile faded a little, but Jez persisted.

'On the Hartsdown High School page? Do you remember? I'm looking for Alice Grey, although you remembered her as Alice Black. She's gone missing.'

He should have read the alarm in her expression, but in his nervous excitement, he was blind to her reaction. She backed away a little.

'I guess you might have been in the same class, or at least in the same year. Are you still in touch with her by any chance?'

'I'm sorry, I don't —'

'Or maybe you know some of her friends? I'd be grateful for any information at all really. I'm at a complete loss. You see, we had an argument, and well, you know how it is. Anyway, I just need to know she's safe.' Jez sensed he was babbling, but he couldn't stop himself. The words were tumbling out, unabated and unfiltered.

On the far side of the salon, the second stylist was watching with a concerned interest, a pair of scissors poised mid-air.

'I don't know who you are, but I think you'd better leave,' said Sarah abruptly. 'I'm sorry, I can't help you.'

Jez didn't register her objection.

'If there's anything you can tell me, I'd be so grateful.' He reached for her arm, but she swatted his hand away.

'Get off me!'

'Don't be like that, love,' said Mick, stepping forward.

Sarah's eyes opened wide as Mick bore down on her, like a grizzly bear sizing up its lunch. She squealed. 'Get out! Or I'll call the police.'

'Mick, you're not helping. Go back to the van. I'll see you back there in a bit,' said Jez.

'You sure?'

'Yes, just go.'

Mick shrugged, and turned for the door. The plate glass windows rocked in their frames as it slammed shut behind him.

'I'm sorry about him,' said Jez. 'We didn't mean to scare you.'

Sarah's eyes were red. She looked as if she was about to cry. 'Please, could you go?'

'Of course. We shouldn't have come. I'm sorry,' said Jez, finally sensing he was getting nowhere. 'But you might be my only hope of finding Alice.'

'Leave me alone.'

A single tear ran down Sarah's cheek, drawing a tract through her foundation.

'Anything —'

'Get out.'

Jez sighed. It had been another pointless exercise. He should have known better. They should have cut their losses, and headed for home. It had been a stupid idea to come to the town in the first place.

Jez reached for the door, defeated. 'It's only that I'm worried about her,' he said. 'She's been gone almost a week and I've not heard a word from her. I thought - it doesn't matter. I'm sorry to have bothered you.'

A blast of cold air rushed in as he pulled the door open.

'How long have you been together?' Sarah asked softly, almost under her breath.

Jez glanced over his shoulder. 'The best part of a year. We've been living together since the spring, with her little girl, Lily. She's missing too.'

Sarah wiped her eyes dry with the corner of a tissue. 'A daughter? How old is she?'

'Four.'

Sarah swallowed hard. 'Oh, God,' she said. 'I had no idea. Is she yours?'

'No.'

An uncomfortable silence hung between them for an

awkward moment, as Sarah seemed to be weighing up options in her mind.

Eventually, she said, 'You'd better shut the door. You're letting the cold air in. Let me finish up out here and I can give you five minutes, that's all. But I don't think you'll like what I have to say.'

33

Sarah grabbed a packet of cigarettes from a worktop next to a sink filled with dirty mugs and teaspoons in the narrow kitchen at the rear of the salon. She stepped out into a tiny courtyard garden. Jez watched in the doorway as she lit up, hunched against the cold.

'It's serious then, between you and Alice?' she said, blowing smoke from the corner of her mouth.

Jez watched it swirl and evaporate into the air. 'Yeah, it is. Or at least, it was,' he said.

'So, what happened?'

A seagull rose above the rooftops with its wings angled back, buffeted by the wind. Jez shrugged. 'We had a row over something stupid. I said some things, and walked out. I've not heard from her since.'

'Bummer.'

'Yeah,' said Jez. 'I thought she might have come back to Margate, but now I'm not so sure.'

Sarah snorted. 'I doubt it,' she said.

'Why?'

'It's a long story.'

'I'm in no rush,' said Jez. 'Tell me.'

Sarah took a long drag on the cigarette. Its tip glowed brightly. She held the smoke in her lungs for a few seconds, then blew it out between tightly-pursed lips. 'You don't know much about her, do you?'

'She never talked much about her past.' Jez thought about Marcus, and what life must have been like for Alice, locked in a brutal, violent relationship. 'But you were friends, right?'

Sarah laughed, which brought on a throaty, smoker's cough. 'Not friends, exactly. I knew her from school.'

'Did you stay in touch?'

'There was no reason. We were never that close.'

'Oh,' said Jez. 'So, what made you answer my Facebook post?'

Sarah took a final drag on the cigarette, and ground out the stub with her toe. She looked up, and studied Jez's face, as if she was weighing up whether to trust him. 'I don't know. I probably shouldn't have.'

'But you know something. You said I wouldn't like what you had to say.'

'We never really got on at school. Alice was pretty choosy when it came to friends. I guess my face didn't fit. Maybe I never had the right clothes, or the right hair.'

'Doesn't sound like her,' said Jez. It wasn't like Alice to be so superficial.

'I think most of the girls were secretly envious of her, and how popular she was. If they couldn't be her, they wanted to be with her. She was like a magnet. They couldn't leave her alone.'

'But not you?'

Sarah shook her head. Her fringe flicked across her forehead. 'No,' she said. 'And of course, she only had to flutter those big, blue eyes, and all the boys were putty in her hands.'

'You didn't like her much?'

'I don't think she liked me.' She ushered Jez inside, out of the cold, and locked the door.

'What about her friends? Are you still in touch with any of them? Anyone who might know where I can find her?'

'No.' Sarah filled a kettle, and set it to boil. She reached for three cups from a cupboard over the sink, and dropped a teabag in each one. 'So how did you two meet?'

'We had a disagreement over a bunch of flowers.'

Sarah raised an eyebrow.

'It's a long story,' said Jez.

'I'm in no rush.'

'You said you only had five minutes.'

Sarah checked her watch as the kettle gurgled and popped. 'I have another appointment at half past,' she said, slopping hot water into the mugs.

'I got lucky, I guess. I never thought she'd see anything in me, but we kind of hit it off. It helped we're in the same line of business. We have common ground.'

'Oh yeah?'

'I'm an estate agent. Alice is a legal secretary at a conveyancing firm.'

Sarah was about to pour milk into the mugs, but hesitated. 'Legal secretary? I never knew she had it in her.'

'Meaning?'

'Well, she might have been popular at school, but she was never the brightest.'

Sarah handed Jez a mug of tea, and called through to the salon. 'Karen, there's a cuppa here if you want one.'

The other stylist popped her head into the kitchen. 'Everything all right in here?' she asked.

Sarah gave her a reassuring smile. 'Everything's fine.'

'Well, I'm right outside if you need me.'

Jez waited for her to leave. 'Alice is actually very good at her job.'

'Good for her.' There was no disguising the contempt in Sarah's voice.

'Why do you have such a low opinion of her?'

'Who says I do?'

'You've not had a good word to say about her.'

'Maybe I know her better than you,' Sarah said, sipping her tea, and eyeing Jez over her mug. 'So, what was your row about?'

'I accused her of having an affair.'

'Why?'

'I don't know. Jealousy? I said some things I regret, and now she won't even return my calls. I have to find her, to tell her I'm sorry. Are you sure you don't know anyone who might still be in touch with her?'

'Positive.'

'But you don't think she's come back to Margate?'

'Not after everything that happened. She'd be a fool to show her face around here again.'

'I don't understand,' said Jez.

'The problem is, you don't know the first thing about her, do you? She's sucked you in just like she sucked in everyone else she ever met. I bet she never told you who the father of her child is.'

'It's not important.'

'Is that what she said?'

'No.'

'What did you say she's called?'

'Lily.'

'Well, I'm staggered they let her keep her.'

'What's that supposed to mean?'

'It doesn't matter,' said Sarah, turning away. She threw the remnants of her tea into the sink, and busied herself with tidying away some dishes left on the side to dry.

'No, come on. If you've got something to say, I want to hear it.'

'Really?' she said, spinning on her heel, and coming nose-to-nose with Jez. 'You really want to know what she's like? What she's capable of?'

Jez noticed a rosy flush rise from her chest and spread to her neck. 'Tell me.'

Sarah lowered her gaze. 'I have to get back to work.'

'Not until you explain what you meant.' Jez grabbed her arm.

'Ow, you're hurting me,' she squealed.

'Why did you say you were surprised they let her keep Lily?'

'You don't want to know.'

'I have to know, Sarah. This isn't a game. This is important.'

Sarah snatched her arm back, and rubbed the skin. She looked him defiantly in the eye. 'Because she's a murderer. She killed a little girl, and I'll never be able to forgive her for that.'

34

Jez blinked hard, not sure he'd heard right. Blood rushed in his ears, and the strains of an indistinct pop tune carried through from the salon.

'She's a killer,' said Sarah. 'She murdered a child in cold blood, and never showed a scrap of remorse.'

Jez felt his world falling apart. 'What are you talking about? What child? Why are you saying these things? Alice isn't capable of anything like that.'

'Yeah, well, like I said, you don't really know her then, do you?' Sarah's voice sounded strained as if she was battling her emotions. She lowered her head, letting her fringe conceal her eyes. When she looked up mascara streaked her face.

'I think I know her better than you,' said Jez, his anger rising. How could anyone accuse Alice of something so wicked? It was obvious Sarah wasn't her biggest fan, but to suggest Alice had killed anyone, let alone a child, was an extraordinary allegation to make.

'It was in all the papers,' said Sarah, sniffing. 'That poor little thing.'

'Who?'

'Her name was Ellie. I can remember her face, even now. She was such a sweet, innocent little thing. And Alice ran her down. She didn't stand a chance.'

Jez stared at Sarah in disbelief. She must have been mistaken.

'She bled to death with her head cracked wide open on the road,' Sarah continued. 'It was awful.'

'An accident?' Jez croaked.

'No. She did it deliberately. Cool as you like. She knew exactly what she was doing.'

'Impossible,' Jez gasped. He was struggling to breathe, like his chest had been gripped in a giant vice.

'It happened all right.' Sarah stood straight, composing herself. She wiped her nose with a tissue, and cleared her throat. 'When the police investigated, they didn't find skid marks or any evidence that she tried to brake. There was no doubt she meant to kill that girl.'

'But - it makes no sense. Why would she do it?'

'Spite?'

Jez shook his head. It seemed such a wildly implausible story, and yet, Sarah's grief was raw, and real. 'Who was she?'

'That's the saddest thing. Ellie was the daughter of one of her best friends. She found out Alice was having an affair with her husband, and was furious. But when she confronted Alice about it, Alice went crazy. She wouldn't accept it was over, and so she went after the one thing she knew her friend loved more than anything else; her daughter. She planned it all. So cold and calculating.'

'How do you know all this?'

'Everyone was talking about it. She was only four years old, with her whole life to live. It wasn't fair. They should have locked Alice away and thrown away the key.'

Four years old. The same age as Lily. A rising nausea swelled in Jez's stomach. He couldn't imagine Alice doing it. He tried picturing her in a car, hands gripping the wheel, and her foot on the accelerator, deliberately driving at an innocent child.

'I had no idea,' he said. 'How long ago did it happen?'

'A few years back.'

The implications crowded Jez's mind. He had so many questions, but one kept coming to the fore. 'What happened to Alice?' he asked. 'Was she arrested?'

'I don't know. She vanished,' said Sarah. 'The next time I heard her name was when you put that message on Facebook, and it brought it all back.'

'You must know if she went to jail.'

Sarah brushed her fringe from her eyes, and frowned. She fixed her gaze on a spot over Jez's shoulder, as if she was trying to remember. 'I don't know,' she said at last, frowning. 'I suppose she must have done. You can't get away with something like that. But I'm surprised they let her out.'

No wonder Alice had been so cagey about her past

life. It certainly explained why she'd moved away from Margate, changed her name, and kept a wide berth of social media. She'd clearly been terrified of the past catching up with her. Not for the first time, Jez felt as though he'd been played for a fool.

'I can see it's a bit of a shock. I'm sorry to be the one to tell you,' said Sarah.

'I feel so stupid.'

'Don't be. She's always been manipulative. You weren't to know.'

'What am I going to do?' said Jez.

'Move on. Forget her. She's poison.' Sarah reached out, and stroked Jez's arm with a tender touch.

'I can't,' said Jez. 'I still love her, despite everything.'

Sarah pulled back her hand, as if she'd been bitten. 'Then you deserve each other.'

Somewhere in the distance, the bell over the door chimed, but Jez hardly noticed. From the salon, raised voices clashed, urgent and threatening.

'I can't help how I feel. If I could just talk to her, maybe I could —'

'What? Forgive her? I'd never be able to forgive anyone who could do that.'

'Hey, Sarah, Steve's here!' There was an unmistakable note of alarm in Karen's call from the salon.

A warning shout.

Sarah tensed, and the colour drained from her face. 'You've got to go,' she said, terror in her eyes. 'He can't find you here.' She charged for the back door, and fumbled with the key in the lock.

'Who? What's going on?'

'Come on, hurry!' Sarah hissed. 'It's my boyfriend. He'll kill us both if he finds you here.' She pulled Jez by his hand into the courtyard out the back. 'You can get out over the back wall.'

'What's wrong?' said Jez, perplexed. 'We've not done anything.'

'He won't understand. I'm begging you, please go.'

Sarah slammed the door closed, leaving Jez standing forlornly in the cold, feeling like he'd been caught up in the middle of a bedroom farce.

Through the glass, he saw the hulk of a man appear in the kitchen. He had the look of a bodybuilder with wide gym-bulked shoulders, a pumped-up chest, and biceps that threatened to rip the sleeves of his figure-hugging t-shirt. Wild, furtive eyes scanned left and right.

Jez ducked out of view, cowering behind a scrawny potted conifer. He peered through its branches, watching as Sarah attempted a timid kiss, reaching up on tiptoes for her boyfriend's cheek. A moment before she'd been a bright, confident young woman. Now she was cowed and afraid; a wilted flower.

'Who was in here?' The man's voice, dripping with menace, carried out into the courtyard.

'No one,' Sarah said.

'Then whose tea is this?'

He picked up the mug Jez had hurriedly left on the counter.

'I made an extra one for Karen.'

'Liar!' He hurled the mug across the kitchen. It smashed against the wall, narrowly missing Sarah's head. It left a dark stain of tea running down the paintwork.

Sarah screamed.

The wall at the end of the garden was less than ten metres away, and the only feasible way out given that Jez didn't fancy trying to stay and reason with Sarah's crazy boyfriend. He sized up its height, wondering if he would be able to find a foothold on the weather-worn bricks.

Decision made, he waited until Sarah's boyfriend had turned his back, then made a bolt for it, legs pumping. He counted every step, adjusting his stride like an athlete sizing up a long jump, aiming to land his right foot on a jagged edge of brick so he could launch himself towards the top.

Behind him, the kitchen door swung open.

'Oi! Stop! Get back here!'

In his panic, Jez mistimed his jump, leaping too close to the wall, which allowed his knee to tuck up under his chest. With his arm fully stretched, he reached for the top of the brickwork, and hooked his fingers over the crown of the wall. His feet scrambled and slipped over the greasy bricks, his legs flailing.

The pounding of feet on the paving slabs sounded desperately close, and Jez imagined Sarah's boyfriend breaking into a sprint, his muscled arms pumping.

With adrenaline flooding his veins, and using all his strength, Jez hauled his body up and over, bruising his knees, and scraping the skin off his fingers. He landed in a narrow alley, but fell awkwardly, twisting his knee. He yelled in agony, pain shooting up his leg, but had no time to worry about the damage he'd done. A pair of enormous hands appeared over the wall, followed by a head, and a face twisted in anger.

Jez picked himself off the floor, and winced as he put weight on his leg.

'I'll teach you to try it on with my woman.'

Hobbling on his injured leg, Jez hustled to the end of the alley where crowds of people were milling about. He emerged into a small market square surrounded by tall buildings, and heaving with casual shoppers and tourists who drifted between a dozen or so stalls set up under heavy duty awnings.

Jez aimed for a horseshoe of tables groaning with fruit and vegetables, where a woman wrapped up in a brightly-coloured scarf was distracted taking money from a customer. With her back to him, Jez dived for a stack of cardboard boxes, and hid.

A moment later, Sarah's boyfriend, fists clenched tightly, charged out of the alley. He pulled up when he saw the crowds, and approached the market slowly, checking every face. Jez held his breath as the man passed within a few feet, and carried on walking.

He reached the edge of the market, and turned left along Lombard Street, disappearing back towards the hair salon.

Jez let out the breath he'd been holding, and pulled himself gingerly to his feet, testing out his knee. The woman with the bright scarf gave him an odd look, but said nothing as he emerged from behind the boxes.

Jez gave her an apologetic smile, and limped away.

Mick was waiting in the van on the harbour arm.

'Come on, let's go,' said Jez, pulling his door shut.

'Find out anything useful?' The van's engine spat and coughed as Mick turned the key in the ignition.

'Only that my life with Alice has been a complete and utter sham,' said Jez, slumping in his seat. 'Let's get out of here.'

35

'So that's it? You're giving up on finding Alice?' asked Mick, killing the engine.

'Alice doesn't want to be found,' said Jez. 'So, what's the point being here?'

The wind whipped a fine mist of sand across the beach, and battered the aluminium skin of the van. A mother struggled with a pushchair along the esplanade, her hair blowing wildly around her face.

'What exactly did Sarah say?'

Jez sighed. 'That Alice killed a young girl, the same age as Lily.'

'Killed her? How?'

'She ran her down in her car.'

'You mean an accident?'

Jez shook his head. 'Not according to Sarah. She says she did it after the girl's mother found out Alice was having an affair with her husband.'

Mick blew the air from his cheeks. 'Wow,' he said. 'I don't know what to say.'

'You don't have to say anything. Just take me home.'

'Is it true?'

'Why would she lie?'

'I don't know,' said Mick, lifting his cap, and scratching his head. 'It just seems so unlikely.'

'Yeah, well I'm done with all of this. I don't know what to believe anymore. I'm fed up with the secrets and lies. Whatever happened, Alice never trusted me to tell me, so what hope is there for us? Sarah's right, I should forget her and move on.'

'What about Lily?'

Jez rubbed his eyes with the balls of his hands. Lily was collateral damage, the one who was going to suffer the most. He was sorry she'd been caught up in Alice's charade, but it wasn't his fault, and not his problem. She wasn't even his child.

Jez's phone vibrated in his pocket. 'She's with her mother. It's the best place for her,' he said, pulling out his mobile, and groaning inwardly when he saw who was calling. 'Dad? What's up?'

'Jeremy, there's a bit of a problem.' His father sounded breathless. 'Can you come over?'

'Can it wait? I'm in Margate at the moment.'

'The electricity's gone off.'

'Have you checked the trip switch? It's in the cupboard under the stairs.'

'What cupboard?' Jez could hear the frustration in his father's voice.

'Under the stairs, by the meter. Remember I showed you?'

'Nothing's coming on. Should I call the electricity

company?'

'Not until you've checked the trip switch, Dad.' Jez rolled his eyes. 'Listen, I'll come over and sort it out. Sit tight. I'll be there as soon as I can.'

'Would you?'

'I'll be an hour or so.'

'Right-o,' his father said. 'I tried putting the kettle on, but that's not working either.'

'No, okay, Dad. Be there soon.' Jez hung up and threw the phone onto the dashboard.

'Problem?' said Mick.

'It's Dad. He's at a complete loss without Mum. He can't do anything on his own.'

'You want to go home?'

'Yeah, I'm done here anyway. Let's get back. He needs me.'

His father was sitting in the gathering gloom, huddled in his favourite chair, with his coat buttoned up to his neck, and a chill in the air.

'It's freezing in here,' said Jez.

'Nothing's working.'

Jez felt a pang of guilt. 'I'm sorry, Dad. I should have been here.'

Jez located the meter under the stairs using the torch on his phone. He flicked the trip switch, and light immediately flooded the hall. Throughout the house, electronic beeps and alarms sounded from various items of electrical equipment as the power was restored.

Jez checked the boiler, and heard the reassuring whoosh of gas igniting. He filled the kettle, corrected the clock on the oven, and as he waited for the water to boil, leaned against one of the cupboards and ran a hand over his face. It had been a ten second job to fix, and yet his father didn't have a clue.

Was this what it was going to be like? A reversal of roles, where his father was now the one who needed full time care? He'd managed to run his own butchery business for the best part of forty years, but he'd been mollycoddled by Jez's mother for too long. She'd done everything for him, and now, without her, he was lost.

Jez's irritation quickly faded when he saw his father hunched up in his coat, his nose red from the cold, and he felt only sadness.

'Here, drink this,' he said, handing his father a mug of tea. 'How's Mum?'

'She's been asking for you. We thought you might have visited today.'

Jez winced. 'Sorry, I've had a lot on my plate, what with Alice missing, and the break-in at the house.'

It was out before he realised what he was saying. He'd not meant to tell his father about the intruder, but it tumbled from his mouth before he could stop himself.

'Break-in?'

'It was nothing. Don't worry about it. Is there anything in to eat?' said Jez, trying to change the subject.

'Only some of those ready meals your mother made me buy.'

Jez found a stack of pre-packaged meals in the

fridge. 'Lasagne or shepherd's pie?' he said, holding up two plastic cartons.

'Lasagne.'

They ate at the table, sharing a bottle of wine, conscious of the aching space where Jez's mother should have been.

'Have the doctors said when she might be able to come home?' asked Jez.

'Hopefully in the next few days.'

'Really?' Jez said, with his mouth full. 'That's good.'

'I don't know, Jezza,' said his father. 'She can hardly do anything for herself. She can barely stand, let alone walk, and she's struggling to speak. She'll have to have a physiotherapist, they reckon.'

With everything else on his mind, Jez hadn't really thought much about his mother's recovery. He'd assumed she'd be back to her old self within a few weeks. After all, the doctor had said she'd make a full recovery.

'You know how stubborn Mum is. She'll be back on her feet, and bossing us both around before you know it,' said Jez. It brought a faint smile to his father's face, but he knew neither of them believed it.

'It's unlikely she'll be able to make it up the stairs. We're going to have to think about making up a bed down here.'

'We'll do whatever it takes.'

After they'd eaten, and Jez had cleared away, they sat in silence watching a succession of his mother's favourite soap operas on the television, but which neither of them really had any interest in.

Jez missed being able to sprawl out on his own sofa, and with so much racing around in his head, he couldn't settle. Eventually, he offered to make more tea, and when he returned to the room with mugs his father was sitting quietly with the television off.

'There's something on your mind,' his father said.

'I'm worried about Mum, that's all,' said Jez, tucking his feet under his legs.

'If you were that worried, you'd have visited today.'

'That's not fair.' But his father was right. He'd been too focused on his own problems to be there for his mother in her moment of need.

'What was more important?'

'I was looking for Alice.'

His father raised his eyebrows. 'Did you find her?'

'No, but I found out a few things about her I wish I hadn't.'

'Want to talk about it?'

Ordinarily, his father would have been the last person on earth he would have confided in. They'd never shared much of a bond. His father held a traditional view of his role, providing food for the table, and a roof over their heads. Jez's mother was the one left to deal with the grazed knees and broken hearts.

But tonight was different.

Jez took a sip of tea, and scalded the tip of his tongue. 'She's been lying to me since the day we met,' he said. 'I found out today that she killed her friend's daughter.'

'How?'

'She ran her down, on purpose, apparently.'

'Who told you that?'

'Someone who knew her from school.'

'You know, people say things for all sorts of reasons, Jeremy. Sometimes they don't even mean to get their facts wrong, but somehow it gets mixed up in the telling. Do you know for a fact she was telling the truth?'

'Why would she make something like that up?' asked Jez.

'I'm not suggesting she did. All I'm saying is it sounds like gossip, and in my experience, tittle tattle like that is rarely based on truth.'

'Yeah, but it's not only that. There have been other things too.'

'Such as?'

Jez ran his numb tongue over the roof of his mouth, debating how much to tell his father. 'One of her ex-boyfriends broke into the house in the middle of the night,' he said.

'Broke in?'

'I found him in the lounge ranting about Alice and Lily, and when he went for the stairs, I hit him.'

'Jeremy ...' His father looked aghast.

'At first I thought I'd killed him. I was going to call the police, but Alice talked me out of it. She said they wouldn't believe it was self-defence, and that I should get rid of the body.'

His father's eyes widened.

'It's okay, he wasn't actually dead. I took him to hospital. But later, Alice let it slip she knew the guy, and I accused her of seeing him behind my back. That's why I walked out.' Jez watched the swirls of vapour rising from the surface of his tea. 'But I got it wrong. It was an ex-boyfriend, who'd been hitting her, and she was hiding from him, or at least that's what I thought, until I found out about the little girl she killed in Margate. And now I'm more confused than ever. The thing is, I want to wash my hands of her, but I can't. I think about her all the time. I wonder where she is, and what she's doing. Stupid, isn't it?'

'Only because you still care about her.'

'But look how she's treated me.'

'You need to talk to her.'

'What good's that going to do?'

His father steepled his fingers under his chin. 'If you don't, you'll always be wondering, and you'll never move on with your life. A relationship can't be based on secrets, so find out what's really going on, because it strikes me you don't know the truth about anything. And until you're satisfied you know the facts, how can you make any decisions about your future? Do you have any idea where she might be?'

'None. I turned the house upside down looking for clues. She could be anywhere,' said Jez.

'You need to look harder.'

'I've tried everything. And what if she doesn't want to be found?'

'Why not talk to the mother of the girl she's supposed to have killed?'

'I couldn't do that,' said Jez, horrified at the thought.

'Well, you want the truth, and if anyone can shed light on that, surely it's the mother of that little girl.'

36

Jez slipped into the house, and for the first time since Alice had disappeared, didn't check for signs she might have returned home. He hung his coat on a hook in the hall and kicked off his trainers, not bothering to set them straight with no one to nag him about keeping the house tidy.

He'd left his father asleep on the sofa, tucked up under a blanket, and walked home with a plan racing through his head. The fresh air and exercise had cleared his mind. He grabbed a bottle of beer from the fridge and opened his laptop at the breakfast bar. If he wanted closure, he needed to discover the truth for himself.

The story of the little girl's death wasn't difficult to find. After only a few minutes trawling the internet, he discovered a local newspaper had covered the incident, and posted a series of articles over several weeks.

The first story made only five brief paragraphs. Hardly any detail. Not even a name, but it seemed to match with the details Sarah had described.

The story was accompanied by a photograph of a nondescript tree-lined street where the incident had taken place.

He read the story three times.

Police have confirmed a four-year-old girl has been killed after a collision with a vehicle in Broadstairs.

The incident happened shortly before 5pm yesterday at what is believed to be the girl's home.

The girl, who has not been named, was pronounced dead at the scene.

Kent Police has issued an appeal for witnesses, but has released no further details at this stage.

Three people are helping police with their inquiries.

Two days later, the paper had posted an update. Not much more information about what had happened, apart from one significant fact.

Police say they will not be bringing any charges following the death of a four-year-old girl in Broadstairs earlier this week.

The victim, named locally as Ellie Fenson, died when she was in collision with a vehicle at her home in the town.

Three people who had been helping police with their inquiries have been released without charge.

A spokeswoman for Kent Police said the death was being treated as a tragic accident.

Jez jerked his hand away from the keyboard, the words swimming across the page like tadpoles in a pond.

He re-read the girl's name, hardly able to believe it.

Ellie Fenson. Could she be Marcus's daughter?

The coincidence seemed too great to dismiss. And then another revelation hit him, something that had been bubbling under the surface for days, but which he'd refused to acknowledge.

If Alice had fallen pregnant by Marcus during their affair, it was likely he was also Lily's father.

Jez rocked back on his stool, his mind a fog as he tried to fit the pieces together. Everything he thought he knew was disintegrating like snowflakes in his palm. So many lies and secrets he didn't know what to believe.

He returned to his computer and continued to search, unable to resist the draw of finding out the truth, no matter how unpleasant it might be.

A third article, posted a day later, included a photograph of Ellie; a beautiful, fresh-faced little girl with a sparkle in her eyes and freckles that peppered her nose.

The parents of a four-year-old girl killed when she was in collision with a vehicle at her home in Broadstairs have paid tribute to their 'little angel'.

Ellie Fenson died at the scene of the incident despite the efforts of two ambulance crews.

Her mother, Anna Fenson, said their lives had been ripped apart by her daughter's death.

'She was our little angel, full of hope, happiness and fun. Words cannot express how much she will be missed.'

Ellie's father, Marcus, described his daughter as the 'light of his life'.

'We would like to thank people for their kind words, but we would ask now to be left alone to grieve in peace,' he added.

Three people who had been held in connection with the death have been released without charge.

Details of how the little girl died are still unclear.

A funeral for Ellie will take place on Friday at the Thanet Crematorium.

Jez swallowed hard as he scrolled back up to the image of Ellie, imagining the horror of her last few moments. Such a tragic waste of a young life. He pushed the thought away, hoping she'd not suffered, that death had come quickly. It was almost too hard to think about.

He thought again of Alice behind the wheel, fury in her eyes. But as much as he tried to imagine the scene, he simply couldn't reconcile it with something Alice was capable of.

Jez re-read the article, examining every word, looking for something he'd missed. But the report didn't seem to add up to what Sarah Flannigan had told him.

Three people had been held in connection with Ellie's death, but subsequently released. He assumed that must be Marcus, his wife, Anna, and Alice.

But if Alice had driven the car deliberately at Ellie, why hadn't the police charged her? Did Marcus lie to protect her? Or maybe there were no other witnesses, and Alice told the police it was an accident? Then it would be the Fensons' word against hers.

Sarah had told him the police had found no evidence that Alice had tried to brake in the seconds before she hit the little girl. Wouldn't that be sufficient evidence to prove her intent?

The final article on the website reported Ellie Fenson's funeral. There were several pictures of a tiny white coffin on a horse-drawn carriage, alongside the photo of her they'd previously used.

Thousands of people had apparently turned out to watch the funeral procession, the headline describing a town brought together in mourning. People had lined the streets, and thrown flowers into the path of the cortège. It was standing room only in the crematorium chapel.

Ellie's parents had led the mourners. A picture, taken on a long lens, showed the little girl's mother dressed in black, clutching a teddy bear to her chest, her face crumpled in grief. At her side, a younger, slimmer-looking Marcus dressed in a black suit, his face ashen and emotionless.

But curiously, the article made no further reference to Alice, nor the police investigation. If the police had concluded it was a tragic accident, why had Sarah told him that Alice had deliberately killed Ellie Fenson? Salacious rumours maybe?

Jez was left with more questions than answers. He needed to hear the truth from Alice, but he was no closer to finding her. He shut the lid of the laptop and finished his beer. As much as he hated the thought of it, he realised his father was right. If he wanted to find Alice, and the truth of the little girl's death, he had to speak to Anna Fenson.

37

The street was as Jez had imagined from the picture on the newspaper website. A wide, tree-lined boulevard with generous detached houses at the end of long, sweeping drives in an affluent part of Broadstairs. Only a short taxi ride from the railway station, it nonetheless felt a million miles from Margate's kiss-me-quick arcades and nostalgic seaside charm.

Jez had the driver drop him at the end of the road so he could gather his thoughts. He'd rehearsed some lines on the train, but as he approached the Fensons' house, his mind went blank, and his fears stole all the moisture from his mouth.

He was going to ask a stranger to tell him what she knew about the woman who'd not only stolen her husband, but killed her child. It had seemed an excellent idea the previous evening. Now he was actually in the street, it seemed a ludicrous flight of fancy. He could only imagine Anna Fenson's reaction.

Jez slowed to an amble, and steeled himself as he approached the house.

The property was partially hidden behind a towering conifer hedge, interrupted by a set of wrought-iron gates at the end of a gravel drive. Jez peered through the bars, and recognised the house from the satellite image he'd studied on his laptop. A grand red-brick Victorian villa with spired turrets and mullioned windows, a red Volvo parked in front of a garage adjacent to the main building. The archetypal image of middle-class affluence and respectability.

Jez raised his hand to try the gates, but lost his nerve.

He couldn't do it.

He ducked past the house and kept walking, along the conifer hedge and beyond for another hundred metres, only slowing up when he'd put a safe distance between himself and the property.

All his fears and concerns came rushing into his head in a chaotic maelstrom, talking him out of what needed to be done. How could he turn up uninvited at Anna Fenson's house and bring all that grief back for the poor woman? Would she scream at him? Shout? Burst into tears?

He couldn't put her through it again, raking off the scars and opening up old wounds.

And yet, he'd come all this way. If he really wanted to find out the truth about Alice, he knew he had to confront Anna. If she wouldn't tell him, well, at least he'd have tried. He could move on, knowing he'd done his best to untangle the truth from the lies. He'd accept Alice was gone and didn't want to be found.

With renewed determination, Jez strode back to the gates. They opened with a gentle push, swinging on well-oiled hinges, and before he knew it, he was crunching up the gravel drive with the grand house looming ahead.

What about Marcus?

He'd been so focused on confronting Anna, he'd not even considered what might happen if Marcus was at home. What if he answered the door? Would he recognise Jez, remember the attack, and how he'd abandoned him in the boatyard?

Too late now. No turning back. He'd have to deal with that problem if it occurred.

As he trudged up the drive, Jez glanced at the Volvo, a gleaming, four-wheeled drive with a high bonnet, enormous tyres, and a personalised number plate. He noticed the driver's window was open a fist's width. No doubt it had been left unlocked too. It was the sort of neighbourhood you didn't have to worry about your car being pinched from outside your house.

He reached a flight of steps leading to an open porch, and felt his legs turn soft and his feet become as heavy as lead weights. He dragged himself up the stairs, and with a deep breath, hammered on a brass knocker.

The three sharp bangs echoed around the lawned garden, intruding on the suburban silence and sending a foraging blackbird hurrying for cover with a cry of alarm.

Jez counted to ten in his head, only remembering to breathe when he reached five, in through his nose and out through his mouth, trying to control his nerves. The seconds ticked by, and when no one answered, he knocked again.

Nothing.

Thank God.

No one home.

He sighed with relief. He'd come back another time.

He bounded down the steps, tasting the salt in the air on his lips, and feeling invigorated. He'd got himself all worked up for nothing.

And then he heard the clunk of a latch and the sound of the front door scraping open.

'Hello?'

Jez froze.

'Can I help you?' A woman stood in the doorway, hands on her hips. She pushed a pair of glasses up the bridge of a squat nose, and raised both eyebrows.

'I was looking for Anna Fenson,' said Jez, a tremor in his voice.

'That's me,' the woman said, with a goofy smile. 'Is it about the windows? Can you do the front and back? There's quite a few, I'm afraid.' She hesitated, looking beyond Jez towards the main road. 'Do you have a van or something? You can park on the drive, if you like.'

'No,' said Jez, not sure what to say, so he said the first thing that came into his head. 'I'm looking for my girlfriend. She's missing.'

'Oh.'

'Her name's …' He hesitated.

He thought he heard a child crying. Anna glanced over her shoulder, and with a tight-lipped smile, pulled the door closed.

'Yes?'

'She's called Alice Grey, but I think you know her as Alice Black.'

Like a storm rolling in to spoil a sunny summer's day, Anna's face darkened. Her jaw tightened, and the smile fell from her lips.

'Look, I know what happened here, and I'm so sorry about your daughter, but the thing is —'

'Who the hell are you?' Anna hissed. 'A reporter? How dare you turn up here like this. Clear off, before I call the police.'

'You don't understand. It's nothing like that. Alice is my girlfriend, or at least she was, but she's gone missing, and I only just found out about what happened with your daughter. Please, I need your help.'

Anna's eyes widened, and her body tensed.

Jez pressed on, shooting from the hip, his carefully-planned script forgotten. 'I know you were friends, once. You must have an idea where she might be now. Anything you can tell me might help.'

Anna snorted. 'Friends? Maybe once. A long time ago. If you know what she did, you'll understand why I've had nothing to do with her since. I'm sorry, I can't help. Goodbye.'

'Wait!' Jez jogged up the stairs, and grabbed Anna's arm. 'If you don't know where she is, at least tell me what happened with your daughter. They said Alice killed her out of spite, but that's not the Alice I know, and as far as I can tell, she was never charged by the police or taken to court. Please, I need to know who she really is, and if there's any truth to the story.'

Anna shrugged off Jez's hand. 'Story?'

'I don't mean it was made up, only that I've heard different things, and it would help to hear it from someone who was there.'

'You want to know the truth?' Anna folded her arms over her chest, and straightened her back, which only served to emphasise her diminutive frame. Jez wasn't tall, but her head barely reached his chest.

'More than anything. I have to know,' he said. 'Please tell me, and I'll go away. I promise.'

38

Anna squinted, studying Jez, loose strands of hair blowing around her face. She looked at him as if she was contemplating her next words carefully.

'You really want to know the truth?'

'I *have* to know. Can you understand that?'

'Forget her. She's trouble, and you're best off without her.'

'You're not the first person to tell me that,' said Jez. 'But I can't, not until I know for certain what she did. The Alice I know isn't capable of the things I've heard her accused of. I mean, she'd do anything to help anybody. I can't believe she meant to kill your daughter. It seems so unlikely, so out of character. Maybe it was an accident? Did you ever consider that?'

'An accident? You clearly have no idea how dark her heart really is.'

'Tell me,' said Jez. 'Two minutes of your time. That's all, and I'll be gone.'

'I said goodbye. This conversation is over, and don't

think about coming back. I meant what I said. Next time I'll call the police.' Anna stole back inside, and slammed the door so hard the knocker thudded against its strike plate.

Jez was left standing alone and confused on the porch. At least he'd tried, in his own ham-fisted style. It had always been unlikely that Anna would welcome his approach, and he could understand her reluctance to talk about the death of her daughter. The loss of a child, especially one so young, must be the worst kind of hurt. He imagined how he would react if anything had happened to Lily. The thought was unbearable, and he wasn't even her biological father.

Jez sloped off down the drive and pulled the iron gates closed quietly behind him. He turned left along the street, with a vague sense it would lead him back to Margate. He guessed it was a good three or four-mile march back to the station, but the exercise would help clear his head.

He set off at a quick pace with his hands shoved in his pockets and his head down, contemplating a future without Alice and Lily.

He decided in that moment to end the tenancy on the house, maybe move back with his parents, at least in the short term, and perhaps even look for a new job. A new start. A clean sheet.

At the end of the road, where the houses were packed more tightly into smaller plots, Jez turned towards the sea, following a maritime breeze carrying the lure of the ocean.

He slowed his pace, and found the meeting with

Anna was replaying in his mind. He didn't want to think about it, but the memory forced itself on him like a petulant child tugging at his coat tails. Every time he pushed it away, it came back to him, until finally he understood the reason why.

Something was bugging him. There was something out of kilter which had stirred an unease deep in his subconscious. Maybe it was the flicker of recognition he'd noticed when he'd introduced himself, or the sounds he'd heard from the house. Or maybe he was reading too much into the situation. He'd turned up at the house brimming with expectation, and it was entirely possible his mind was playing tricks. But the niggling feeling of all not being right wouldn't go away.

A seagull swooped low over Jez's head, and circled high into the sky with an angry ca-caw. Jez watched it soar on the breeze with its hoary wings angled back, and then with alarm realised it was lining up for a second pass at him.

It dived hard and fast, and as Jez instinctively ducked, he saw a flash of yellow and red from a vicious-looking bill. He felt a rush of air ruffle his hair, and shooed the bird away, figuring he must have strayed too close to a nest or intruded on its territory.

The buzz of his phone was a welcome distraction. He tugged it from his pocket and glanced at the screen expecting to see a message from his father or Mick.

Instead it was from a mobile number he didn't recognise.

Sorry if I was a bit harsh. You caught me by surprise. Anna x

Jez shuddered, then typed a brief reply.

How did you get my number?

He waited a few seconds, staring at his phone, until it chimed again. Another message flashed up from the same number.

Forgive me if I came across as rude. It was the shock of hearing Alice's name again after all this time. Can I make it up to you? A x

How could she possibly have his number, unless she'd spoken to Alice, or his parents? Jez stopped mid-step and typed with his thumbs.

Where's Alice? Do you know where she is?

The wait for a response was excruciating. Jez watched the seconds tick by with a mixture of dread and anticipation. The message that finally came through caught him entirely by surprise.

Can I buy you dinner to say sorry? It's not your fault what Alice did. Shouldn't have blamed you. Meet me tonight at the Sands Hotel at 7? I'll tell you what I can. A x

Dinner? Twenty minutes before, Anna couldn't get rid of him quickly enough. So why the sudden change of heart? The message did nothing to quell his unease. But on the other hand, she was offering to tell him everything he wanted to know.

Jez chewed his lip in concentration as he typed a brief reply, and hit send. He guessed there was only one way to find out what was on her mind.

39

The Sands Hotel, an imposing Victorian relic, overlooked the sweeping, golden beach on the seafront in Margate. It had been built in the tourism boom of the late 19th century, and returned to its original splendour on the back of a modern renaissance of the town, and now decorated in sophisticated shades of taupe and white by its new owners. The restaurant, on the first floor, remained its piece de resistance. Elegant and airy, its focal point a wide expanse of glass giving uninterrupted views across the bay.

Jez arrived early, and instantly felt under-dressed in the jeans and scruffy anorak he'd been wearing all day.

After a long walk back from Broadstairs, he'd spent the afternoon avoiding the lure of the town's many pubs and bars. It would have been easy to while away the hours drinking, kidding himself he needed some Dutch courage. Anna was as slippery as an eel, and he'd need his wits about him to face her again. So instead of the bars, he'd hit the arcades on the seafront, and when he'd run out of loose change, visited an exhibition at the modern Turner art gallery by the harbour. For the last two hours, he'd been holed up in a café on the seafront, reading the papers and drinking coffee until he was jittery and anxious, and only left when the owner wanted to close up for the evening.

Jez perched on a stool at the restaurant bar and ordered a pint of lager, feeling like a teenager on a first date.

Anna arrived on the dot of seven, almost unrecognisable from the woman who'd answered the door at the house earlier. Her glasses were gone, and she'd styled her hair like a Hollywood starlet. A delicate touch of make-up accentuated her eyes, cheeks and lips. She looked a million dollars, sweeping into the room with an assured confidence, turning heads, and greeting the staff with a serene smile.

'I wasn't sure you'd come.' She kissed Jez on both cheeks and wiped away the residual lipstick marks with her thumb.

'I was surprised to be asked,' said Jez. 'You weren't exactly pleased to see me earlier.'

Anna shrugged off a faux-fur coat and ordered a dry martini. Jez caught a waft of her perfume. Citrus and sandalwood. Not dissimilar to Alice's favourite scent. She wore an expensive-looking strapless dress with a daring slit up one side, and which showed off her freckled shoulders and a little too much cleavage.

Alice had an almost identical dress, but carried the look off with a little more style and grace. Anna came across a touch tarty, and when she crossed her legs, her skirt rode up, revealing a pair of stockinged thighs.

'You caught me at a bad moment. I shouldn't have been so rude, nor blamed you for what Alice did.' Anna smiled, coldly.

'I'm intrigued how you found my number.'

Anna sipped her drink and plucked an olive off a cocktail stick with her teeth. 'We should eat,' she said. 'I don't know about you, but I'm famished.'

'Did you get it from Alice? I'm begging you, if you know where she is, you have to tell me.'

'Begging?'

'It's not like her to vanish.'

'Isn't it?' Anna slipped off her stool, and rearranged her dress as a waiter took their coats. Jez reluctantly handed over his dirty anorak.

Anna had reserved a table in the window with spectacular views of the seafront, lit up like Christmas in the gathering early evening gloom. Lights twinkled across the bay, like stars in a cloudless sky. A waiter offered them menus, but Anna waved him away.

'We'll have oysters to start, and the venison loin to follow,' she said.

'Very good, madam.' The waiter gave an obsequious bow of his head. 'And to drink?'

'A bottle of Moët.' Anna glanced at Jez, almost as an afterthought. 'You do like champagne, don't you?'

'What are we celebrating?'

'I don't believe you need an excuse for drinking Moët. Don't you agree?'

Jez shrugged. He'd have preferred a beer, but if

Anna was determined to take control of the evening, he was happy to go with the flow, if it meant he'd finally have his questions answered.

'I'm sorry about your daughter,' he said.

'Thank you.' Anna fiddled with the hem of her napkin. 'No one should ever have to bury their child.'

Jez watched her carefully from across the table. 'I saw the pictures from the funeral.'

'Did you?'

'It looked like the whole town turned out. It must have been quite something.'

Anna shot him a wan smile. 'I suppose so.'

Suddenly, Jez felt bad for bringing up the subject so abruptly. 'I'm sorry. I shouldn't have mentioned it.'

'It's okay. Do you have children?'

Jez thought of Lily with her cheeky smile and wild hair. 'No,' he said. 'At least, none of my own.'

'Then you can't even begin to imagine what it's like.'

The only bereavement in Jez's family had been the death of his Uncle Tony. But while his demise had been unexpected, he'd lived an active life, fulfilled by the pursuit of doing whatever he damn well liked. Ellie's life, on the other hand, had ended before it had properly begun.

'Could you ever forgive Alice?' Jez instantly regretted the question. It was a stupid thing to say. He grabbed his glass for something to do with his hands, and sipped the champagne. The bubbles popped at the back of his throat.

'She killed my baby. And what made it worse, she knew exactly what she was doing. She wasn't satisfied with taking my husband, she stole my reason for living, and I can never forgive her for that.'

Jez shuffled in his seat, feeling warm. He wiped his brow with his napkin. 'And you're quite sure, I mean one hundred per cent sure, that Alice did it intentionally? Is there any doubt in your mind it might have been an accident? Because I have to know for sure.'

Anna answered without hesitation. 'No,' she said. 'No doubt. Alice knew exactly what she was doing. You see, I found her out for the lying, cheating slut she truly is, and she made me pay for it in the cruellest way.'

'But it seems so extreme. I just can't imagine her doing it,' said Jez, slumping in his chair.

'I couldn't imagine her screwing my husband behind my back either, but she did it.' Anna finished her glass of champagne in one, and poured herself another.

'But murder?' The word fell heavily from Jez's mouth.

'Trust me, I never thought for one minute she had it in her. But I guess, you never truly know people, do you?'

'You used to be good friends.'

'She was my best friend. We'd known each other for years, actually from when we were knee high, and all the way through secondary school. We lost touch for a while after that, but she came back into our lives after Marcus and I were married, and we moved back to Kent.'

Jez averted his gaze as Anna mentioned Marcus' name, fearful she might read the guilt on his face.

'We were inseparable,' Anna continued. 'She was like family, the sister I never had. She was always around at our house, coming and going as she pleased. I was even stupid enough to give her a key. God knows what they were getting up to when I wasn't there, mind you, probably even in our bed. And when they diagnosed her mother with dementia, we were the ones there for her, helping her through it.

'The day her mother died, I'd taken Ellie to the beach. It was the most glorious day, with a beautiful cloudless sky. We built sandcastles and paddled in the sea. But Marcus had a job to finish, and stayed at home in his workshop. That's where I found them when we got back, screwing over a French reproduction oak sideboard.' Anna spat out the words like they were poison.

Jez hung his head and swallowed his rising bile as he imagined Alice with Marcus, naked and sweaty. Hot with breathless passion. His stomach tightened and his fists clenched.

A waiter arrived with two plates of oysters. Anna tapped her foot furiously on the floor as he fussed around the table.

When he'd retreated, she continued. 'I found him with his trousers around his ankles, while she was clutching a glass of white wine, head thrown back —'

'Please, spare me the details,' said Jez. 'I get the picture.' He pushed his plate to one side, no longer hungry.

'I should have spotted the signs earlier, I suppose, but I trusted her. I trusted them both.'

'How long had it been going on?'

Anna poured more champagne. 'I don't know. He tried to tell me it was the first time.'

'But you didn't believe him?'

'Why would I?'

'So how did your daughter ...?'

Anna cleared her throat, and glanced out of the window. A stream of car headlights was snaking around the bay. 'Of course, Alice begged for forgiveness, but I never wanted to see her again. How can you forgive a betrayal like that? She called me all the names under the sun, but in that moment, I felt a sudden calm. I'd seen her for what she truly was. I threw her out, of course, but she had this fury in her eyes, like she was so angry and wanted to punish me, as if she thought I was in the wrong.

'I screamed at her to get out, and she ran. I suppose she must have seen Ellie playing on the drive where I'd left her.' Anna hesitated as if the memory of what happened next was too painful to contemplate. She pinched her lips between a thumb and forefinger. Eventually, she took a breath through her nose, and carried on. 'Alice jumped in my car and drove straight at my poor baby. I don't know if Ellie even saw it coming. She didn't stand a chance. By the time I reached her, it was too late. She died in my arms.' A solitary tear rolled down Anna's cheek. She wiped it away with her napkin. 'There was nothing I could do.'

40

Jez bit so hard on his lip he tasted blood. He struggled to picture Alice being so calculating and ruthless. He could understand her humiliation, her anger even, but to kill an innocent child in cold blood?

'What happened to her?' he asked.

'The police investigated, of course, but she told them it was an accident, that she never meant to do it. But I know what I saw.'

'And the police never charged her?'

'No.'

'I can't believe she got away with it.'

'I told the police everything, about how I'd found her with Marcus, and how angry she'd been. But in the end, they thought I was being vindictive, that I was trying to punish her for the affair by making it all up.'

'Were you?'

Anna raised an eyebrow. 'You asked me what happened. It's up to you what you believe.'

'And you never saw her again?'

'She vanished from the town, and frankly, good riddance.'

'I'm sorry,' said Jez, fiddling with his fork. 'I can see how painful this is for you.'

'And I'm sorry you had to hear the truth from me. It's shocking to find out the person you loved isn't the person you thought they were. Trust me, I get it.' Anna reached across the table for Jez's hand. 'I can see now that Alice had been jealous of my life for a long time. She wanted to destroy what I'd worked so hard for. She resented that I'd made a success of my business, and when she couldn't have my husband, she took away my daughter. That's not the sort of woman you want to be involved with.'

'I guess not,' said Jez, pulling his hand away.

'I hope she's learned her lesson, but I doubt she's changed. She's damaged. I trusted her as a friend, but in the end, that counted for nothing. Sooner or later, she'd have hurt you too. Be grateful you found out before it was too late.'

'Yes, I suppose.'

'Had you been together long?' Anna asked.

'Since the beginning of the year.'

'Were you happy?'

'Yes, for a while. I was flattered when she agreed to a date, and I got swept up in the euphoria of it all,' Jez said, thinking back to those early, heady days. 'We moved in together pretty quickly, but in retrospect, it was a mistake. We never really got to know each other properly.'

'Well, they say love is blind. What went wrong?'

'I accused her of cheating on me.' The image of Marcus sprawled out, bleeding in their hallway sprang into Jez's mind from nowhere. Not that he could tell Anna. She'd been through enough already, without finding out Marcus had tried to re-establish contact with Alice.

'You shouldn't feel bad,' said Anna, lowering her voice, and tucking a strand of hair behind her ear. 'Some women are like that. They can't help themselves. They're users. Alice might have tried to change, but infidelity is in her DNA. When I found out she'd been screwing Marcus, I thought for a long time it must somehow be my fault, that I was responsible for allowing my husband to stray. But I realise now it's not true.'

'I'm not convinced now she was cheating,' said Jez. 'I think I made a mistake, but I need to hear it from her.'

'Look, we all make mistakes. You'll find someone else. It hurts right now, but someone better will come along before you know it.'

Anna's foot brushed Jez's shin as she crossed her legs under the table.

'No, I jumped to conclusions without finding out the facts. And now she's gone. And no matter what she's done in the past, I'm worried about her.'

'Don't make excuses. I've told you what she's like. Count yourself lucky you got away unscathed.'

'I know there's no future for us anymore, but I still need to know she's safe. If you have any idea where she might be, I really need to know.'

A waiter floated towards their table to clear away

their plates. His lips turned up in a nasty sneer as he noticed how little they'd eaten.

A second waiter followed with their main course, venison served with fancy potatoes and a thick, velvety sauce. But neither Jez nor Anna had much of an appetite. Jez watched Anna poke her food from one side of the plate to the other, making no attempt to eat.

'I did wonder if she might have returned to Margate to be with her mother, but that was before I found out she'd died,' said Jez. 'Do you know if she has any other family?'

'She never told you about them, did she?' said Anna, with a curious smile, as if the idea of Alice keeping secrets from him was faintly ridiculous.

'No.'

'Well, I doubt very much she'd ever come back here. Too many people know what she did, and they don't forget something like that easily.'

'Come on, you must know something. Otherwise why agree to meet me?'

'What do you want from me, Jez?'

'I want your help to find Alice.'

'I'm sorry, I can't.'

'In which case, I'm wasting my time.' Jez dropped his cutlery on his plate with a noisy clatter, and scrunched his napkin into a ball. 'I thought…'

'What?'

'I don't know. I shouldn't have come.' Jez pushed his chair back and stood.

'Don't go.' Anna reached for his arm. 'Please?'

'What am I doing here, Anna?'

A heavy silence hung between them as Anna dabbed her mouth with her napkin. She folded it neatly, and leaned across the table. 'Okay, look, I wasn't going to tell you this, but it's probably best you know.'

'What is it? You can tell me.'

'I promised I wouldn't say anything, but I can see now how much you care about Alice, and as much as I hate her, you deserve to know.'

'You've heard from her, haven't you?'

Anna gave an almost imperceptible nod. 'Yes,' she whispered. 'She called me a few days ago, out of the blue. There was something she wanted to tell me, something you probably need to know.'

41

Jez lowered himself back into his chair. 'Why didn't you tell me earlier?' He couldn't believe Anna wasn't going to mention she'd heard from Alice.

'I promised not to say anything,' she said.

'Where is she? Is she all right?'

'She rang asking for my forgiveness. I told her I could never forget what she'd done, but that I forgave her.'

'You said you'd never forgive her for killing Ellie.'

'I know, but what was I supposed to say? It doesn't mean I feel it in my heart. There's not a day goes past I don't think about my little angel, what she'd be like now, what she would have done with her life. But Alice sounded so desperate. I never expected to hear from her again, and I said it before I could stop myself.'

'You're playing games.'

'Why would I lie to you?'

'What else did she say? Did she say where she's gone?' Jez asked.

Anna sighed. She rubbed at an oily stain on the tablecloth with her thumb. 'Only that she was going away.' She spoke so softly, Jez struggled to hear over the hum of the restaurant.

'Going away where?'

'You were right, she did give me your number. She said, in time, I should call, and let you know she was safe, but that she didn't want to be found. It wasn't supposed to be so soon, but then you turned up at the house, and I didn't know what to do. I panicked, and I was rude. That's why I invited you to dinner. I needed to work out what to do.'

'Where is she, Anna?'

She pushed her untouched plate to one side, and finished the last of the champagne. 'Come on, there's something I want to show you,' she said, standing.

'Tell me.'

Anna called for a waitress to fetch their coats, then picked her way through the restaurant, beckoning Jez to follow.

He snatched his anorak and reluctantly trudged after Anna. 'Wait,' he called, as he caught up with her on a wide, carpeted staircase that wound up through the heart of the hotel.

Anna checked over her shoulder with a coquettish glance, and began to climb the stairs, teetering on her high heels.

On the third floor, the stairs opened up into a long corridor lined with numbered rooms. Anna walked to the end of the hall, and produced an electronic key card from her clutch-bag.

'What are you playing at, Anna? What's going on?'

She put her finger to her lips with an impish smile, and let herself into a room. 'I told you, there's something I want to show you.'

The room was in darkness, with only a faint light coming from a window overlooking the beach.

Anna threw her coat on a chair. 'Leave the lights off,' she said. 'Come and see the stars. They're amazing tonight.'

She kicked off her heels, pulled back a thin net curtain, and pointed to the sky.

'Look, you can see Venus, and over there, that's Sirius.'

Jez moved closer. He had no idea what she was playing at, only that she had information about Alice that he needed to know. He followed the line of her finger, up to the cloudless sky flecked with more stars than he could ever remember seeing before. Tiny pin pricks of light clustered across the firmament.

'You know Turner used to love the light in Margate,' said Anna. 'But I think the sky is best at night, don't you? Where else can you see stars like this?'

'Where's Alice?'

Anna turned from the window, so close he could feel the heat radiating from her body, and taste her perfume on his lips. She took his hands, and coiled her fingers around his.

'I'm sorry,' she whispered, craning her neck to reach Jez's ear. 'She doesn't want to be found. Not by you. Not by anybody.' Her thumbs caressed the back of his hands.

'You can tell me,' said Jez.

'But she said I wasn't to tell anyone.' Anna pulled him closer, their bodies touching, her breath warm on his neck.

'Please, Anna.'

'I can't.'

'I need to know she's somewhere safe.'

Anna pulled away, and gripped his hands tighter. She gazed deeply into his eyes, as if she was trying to read his soul. 'I shouldn't say anything,' she said. 'But if you really must know, she's taken Lily to live in Spain.'

42

Her words hit Jez like a punch in the solar plexus. He untangled his fingers and pulled away.

'Spain? They might as well be on another planet,' he said. 'I can't believe she didn't tell me she was leaving the country. Are you sure?'

Anna's face softened. 'I'm sorry, I didn't want to tell you. I knew you'd be upset. She thought it would be for the best, and she specifically said to tell you not to try contacting her.'

'The best for who?'

'But I think you have a right to know, and now you should forget about her. I told you she's no good for you.'

Jez collapsed on the bed with his head in his hands. 'I don't want to forget about her. Don't you understand?'

'But she doesn't care about you, Jez. There's only one person Alice cares about. Open your eyes.'

'It's not true. You must have made a mistake. Maybe

she's been trying to call me.' Jez checked his phone for missed calls. Nothing.

'It's not right how she's treated you.'

'But I love her, and I'm sure, deep down, she loves me.'

'Come on, Jez, be serious. You had one argument and she walked out on the relationship, and moved abroad. That's not the behaviour of someone who loves you.'

Anna stood at the edge of the bed with her slim frame silhouetted against the window. 'Forget her.' As she spoke, she reached for a zip under her arm, and let her dress slip to the floor where it pooled in a silky heap at her feet.

'What are you doing?'

'She doesn't want you. She never wanted you,' said Anna. 'That's the truth.' Her body was lithe and toned. She grabbed Jez's hand, and pulled him from the bed.

He found his arm snaking around her body, his fingers on the small of her back. Her skin was warm and soft. She quivered at his touch.

'Stay with me tonight,' she breathed in his ear. 'I can help you get over her.'

Anna's lips brushed his mouth with the lightest of touches. Jez tried to fight his urges. It would be so easy to give in, and who could blame him?

He kissed her, slowly, tentatively at first, and she craned a hand around the back of his neck, running her fingers through his hair. He pulled her closer, and as she rose on the tips of her toes, their desire for each other became more intense. Desperate and needy. Animalistic.

His fingers roamed the length of her spine, and she moaned with pleasure.

'I want you,' she gasped, biting his bottom lip, and grinning when he flinched.

Her hands caressed his chest, her fingers exploring under his clothes, her nails scratching his skin.

He ached with desire, his whole body intoxicated with arousal. Sex had never felt so right and so wrong at the same time.

His fingers found the clasp of her bra, but as he fumbled with it like a teenager, he caught himself in a mirror on the wall.

No, it wasn't right. It wasn't what he wanted. It would solve nothing, and more importantly, he'd never be able to look Alice in the eye without burning with guilt.

He grasped Anna's shoulders and pushed her away. 'I can't do this,' he said, his breath coming hard and fast.

'Of course you can,' said Anna, lunging to kiss him again. 'Give in to your temptations. Don't fight them.'

'Anna, stop!' He pushed her away again, more forcefully.

She stumbled, and the expression on her face changed. What was it? Anger? Disappointment? He couldn't read it.

Jez smoothed down his t-shirt and jumper and, with the back of his hand, wiped away the taste of her lipstick on his mouth.

'You're making a big mistake.' Anna caressed a curl of hair behind her ear, and stood with her hands on her hips, flaunting her body like a cheap whore.

As if that would change his mind.

She was drunk on champagne, and had tried to take advantage of him, but he'd been strong. He'd almost let himself be seduced, but a night with Anna would put an end to any hope of rebuilding his life with Alice.

'I know you find this hard to accept, but I love Alice, and I can't do this to her,' Jez said.

'You think she loves you?' Tears pooled in Anna's eyes. 'You're nothing to her.'

'That might be true, but I have to find out for myself.'

'You're a fool.'

'Get dressed. I'm flattered, honestly, I am, but this isn't a good idea for either of us. I know your game, but I won't let you use me to take your revenge on Alice.'

'You think that's what this is?'

'Isn't it?'

'Screw you!' she screamed. 'You deserve each other. Run back to her then, like a pathetic puppy, but don't say I didn't warn you.'

'You're crazy,' said Jez, backing away. 'I'm sorry you lost your daughter, but you seriously need help.'

'She doesn't love you!'

'I'll take my chances.'

'Imagine what we could have together. I can love you better than she ever did.'

'But I couldn't love you.'

'Get out!'

'I do feel sorry for you, but I'm not the person who can help you. You need to do that yourself.'

Anna scooped up her dress, and pulled it on

awkwardly. 'I said get out!' She snatched a white china cup from the side and aimed it at Jez's head.

He ducked and it smashed against the wall, showering the floor with china shards.

Jez froze. The woman was deranged.

Her hand reached for a stainless-steel kettle and she lifted it above her head. Jez turned and scuttled for the door as the kettle crashed into a wardrobe behind him.

'You're insane!' he yelled, one hand on the door handle. 'One day you'll realise this isn't the solution to anything. In the meantime, get some help.'

Another cup soared through the air, but Jez ducked out into the corridor, and heard it shatter against the back of the door.

Anna screamed in frustration, a high-pitched banshee's howl that set the hairs on the back of Jez's neck on end.

He hesitated for a beat to check she wasn't going to come chasing after him, then threw on his anorak, and zipped it up to the neck.

'Crazy woman,' he muttered under his breath as he headed for the stairs.

43

Two technicians with jovial smiles and an infectious bonhomie lowered Jez's mother out of the back of an ambulance on a hydraulic ramp, while Jez and his father watched on. Propped up in a wheelchair, a blanket covering her legs, she looked a frail imitation of her former self. Her skin was papery grey, and she'd lost her usual vim and vigour. Her eyes were vacant and watery, her hair unbrushed.

'Nice to finally get you home, Mum,' said Jez, clutching her cold, bony hand.

She tried to smile, but one side of her face was still wilted, and it came out as more of a grimace.

Jez wheeled her into the lounge where they'd crowded the sofas into a corner, and shifted a sideboard into the hall to transform the space into a bedroom.

With his father's help, Jez lifted his mother into the bed they'd set up where the sideboard had been, and spent the next hour fussing around, checking pillows, arranging vases of flowers and cards, and discussing the practicalities of their new domestic arrangement.

That evening, Jez cooked, and his father helped to feed his mother, wiping her chin with a napkin when she dribbled bolognese sauce.

By eight, she was so exhausted she fell into a deep sleep, and Jez and his father retreated to the dining room to share a bottle of wine at the table.

'I don't know if I can cope with all of this,' his father said, running a finger around the rim of his glass.

'Of course you can, Dad. It's going to take some time to adjust, but you'll do great.'

'I don't have a clue what I'm doing. I've never had to do anything like this before.'

'I know, but you'll manage. The main thing is you're there for her.'

'I had no idea it was going to be like this. She can hardly do anything for herself. What kind of a life is that, for either of us?'

'Don't forget you'll have a carer in two days a week. The rest you'll make up as you go along.'

At first, his father had resisted bringing in any outside help, too proud to accept that he couldn't care for his wife on his own. He'd eventually been persuaded to take on limited help, but Jez wondered now whether it was going to be enough.

'What if I can't do it?' his father said.

'Then we'll bring in more help, or if you really can't cope, we can look at finding a nursing home close by.'

'No,' said his father, setting his glass down firmly on

the table. 'I'm not putting her in a home. She stays here with me. I'll do whatever it takes. I'm just saying I've never done anything like this before.' He hesitated a moment, then said, 'You know she's never going to get better, don't you?'

Jez shifted uncomfortably in his chair. 'I thought the doctor said she would make a full recovery.'

His father shook his head. 'In time, they say she should get her speech back, and with some physio, gain a little more movement, but that side of her body is always going to be weak, and she's going to need care for the rest of her life. And what do we do when I'm not around anymore?'

As far as Jez was concerned, his mother was going to bounce back to full health. It was only a matter of time. She'd been treated quickly, and the doctor they'd seen in the hospital had assured them there was nothing to worry about, hadn't he? 'Why didn't you tell me before?' he asked.

'If you'd been at the hospital, you'd have found out for yourself.' There was no anger in his father's voice. It wasn't an accusation. He was merely stating a fact.

Jez searched for something positive to say, but he could only think of his mother, crippled by an invisible clot on the brain, never getting better. 'But she's not going to be in that bed forever, is she?'

'I don't know.'

'Well, the doctors must have some idea.'

'Keep your voice down. You'll wake her,' his father said. 'It's a brain injury. It's unpredictable. No one knows for sure how she'll recover, but she's not going to be turning cartwheels any time soon.'

A wave of despondency washed over Jez. This was the sort of thing that happened to other people, not to people like them. And while he'd been entirely focused on his own problems, his father had been coping with it alone.

'I'm sorry I've not been around much,' Jez said, eventually, 'but everything's going to work out. And I'll be here to give you a hand. I promise.'

'That would be nice.'

The silence that followed was punctuated by a buzz from Jez's phone. He checked the screen, and dumped the call.

'Alice?' his father asked, a note of optimism in his voice. 'Your mother would love to see her.'

'I'm afraid not.' Jez laid the phone face down on the table so his father wouldn't see it was the latest in a long list of missed calls, all from the same number. Anna hadn't stopped calling since he'd run out on her at the hotel.

'The thing is ...' Jez began. He was about to explain that Alice and Lily had moved to Spain, and it was unlikely any of them would ever see them again. But his father had more than enough to worry about without taking on Jez's problems.

'What's that?'

'It doesn't matter.'

Jez finished his wine, and checked his watch. 'I'd better be making a move,' he said. 'It's getting late.'

'Are you not staying the night?' His father's face

crumpled with disappointment. 'I could really do with the moral support.'

Jez squeezed his father's arm. 'Not tonight, Dad. I need to get home. You'll be fine without me, and I promise I'll be back first thing.'

44

Jez immediately sensed something was wrong as he pushed open the front door and threw his keys on the shelf over the radiator. He ran straight up the stairs and crashed into the bedroom.

'Alice?'

A heavy scent of perfume lingered in the air. Delicate notes of citrus with a woody undertone that stirred a nostalgic sadness. He patted the wall to find the light switch, and a chill seeped into his bones.

The duvet was crumpled, although he was sure he'd made the bed before he'd left. He remembered smoothing out the sheet.

He stood motionless in the doorway, studying the room. He glanced at Alice's dressing table where her bottles of lotions were stacked up. Everything looked as it should, but it was impossible to tell for sure if anything had been touched or moved.

His eyes fell on the wardrobe. One of the doors was open a fraction. Only an inch or so, but he was convinced he'd left them shut. Or had he? The magnetic latch was temperamental, and the wooden doors slightly warped. They could have easily swung open on their own.

He crossed the room with a growing disquiet.

As he yanked the wardrobe door open, a shoebox tumbled out with a hollow clatter, and a pair of Alice's black high heels he'd never actually seen her wear spilled onto the floor.

Jez jumped two feet backwards, his heart exploding in his chest. He took a deep breath, scooped the shoes back up into the box and balanced it on top of the teetering pile he'd haphazardly constructed after going through Alice's belongings a few days before.

He scanned the tightly-packed rail of clothes, examining Alice's dresses, blouses, jumpers and skirts. He reached on the tip of his toes to feel for the suitcase on the high shelf, and found it exactly where he'd left it. If Alice had returned home, it certainly hadn't been to collect any of her belongings.

He crept out onto the landing and shouldered his way into Lily's room, not sure what he was looking for.

He hit the light switch, and recoiled in horror.

A row of soft toys and dolls had been lined up on Lily's bed, each of their heads ripped off and discarded on the floor, leaving stuffing spilling out of their necks like fluffy, white entrails.

'What the hell?' Jez muttered. Someone had been in the house, but it hardly seemed likely to have been something Alice or Lily would have done. Maybe

Marcus had come back. But what point was he trying to make?

Jez backed out of the room and pulled the door closed. If for some inexplicable reason Alice had come home and was responsible, why hadn't she taken any of her stuff? Surely, she would have filled a suitcase with a few of her things. At the very least, she would have needed a change of clothes, and their passports.

Passports!

Jez rushed back into their bedroom, dived under the bed, and rummaged around until his fingers fell on the hard edge of a clear plastic box where they kept all their important paperwork. He hauled it out with one hand and tipped it onto the bed. Birth certificates, bank statements, a rental agreement, insurance documents. And three passports.

Anna had been lying. Alice and Lily couldn't possibly have gone to Spain.

Jez raced down the stairs and bolted the front door before cautiously checking the lounge.

Everything was how he'd left it; an Xbox controller on the floor by the TV, a clutch of Lily's felt tip pens on the coffee table and a mug on the mantelpiece above the fire. All the framed photographs on Alice's oak dresser were in their places, and the cushions scattered haphazardly on the sofa.

He crept into the kitchen and inspected the back door, cursing that he'd still not had the lock replaced, but relieved to find no evidence it had been forced open again. The key was still in the lock, so whoever had been in the house must have come through the front. And that meant they had a key.

Jez vowed to call a locksmith first thing in the morning, and maybe even have him change the front door locks while he was at it. At least the house was secure for the night, and maybe everything would make more sense after a decent night's sleep.

Jez took a glass from one of the kitchen cupboards and was about to fill it with water, when he noticed a wine glass by the sink. He picked it up by its stem and held it to the light, noticing a puddle of red wine residue.

Alice always drank white. Never red.

Around the rim, the glass was smeared with bright, scarlet lipstick.

In the hallway, the phone rang. Jez dropped the glass and checked his watch. Only his parents ever called the landline, but it was late for his father, unless there'd been an emergency with his mother.

'Hello?'

At first there was only silence.

'Who's there?'

'You've not been returning my calls.' Anna's voice was husky with alcohol, or tiredness. Or both.

Jez pulled his mobile from his pocket. Forty-eight missed calls.

'I wanted to apologise for the other night,' she said. 'I came on too strong. I didn't mean to frighten you off.'

'How did you get this number? It's not listed. In fact, how did you get any of my numbers?'

'It's not important. All that matters is that we should be together.'

'We're never getting together, Anna. Who gave you my numbers?'

'Alice. Remember, she called me.'

'You're lying.'

'Of course I'm not. Why would I do that?'

'You told me Alice was in Spain.'

'That's right.'

'So how did she manage that without her passport?'

Anna paused a beat. 'I'm only telling you what she said.'

'You've not heard from her at all, have you? You made it all up. Why?'

'Don't be ridiculous. Look, she obviously doesn't want to be found, wherever she is. Perhaps she thought if you heard from me that she'd moved abroad, you'd be more likely to believe it, and that you'd stop looking.'

'Have you been snooping around the house?' said Jez.

'What?'

'Did you break in here, and go through Alice's things?'

'Darling, I've no idea what you're talking about. I've been at home all day. Look, let's meet up, and I can make everything better. And I promise not to come on to you so strongly.'

'Seriously, Anna, leave me alone.'

'What about a picnic on the beach? How are you fixed tomorrow?'

'Anna, get it into your thick head, I don't want anything to do with you. I just want to find Alice.'

'She can't love you like I can. And anyway, she doesn't want you anymore.'

'It's not true.'

'She abandoned you, Jez. I would never do that.'

'She just needs some time out. She'll be back.'

'You sound so sure,' said Anna. 'And yet you couldn't be more wrong.'

Jez swallowed hard, the realisation finally dawning on him. He listened to the hum of static, and Anna's light breathing. 'Anna, what have you done with Alice?'

No reply.

'Have you hurt her? Anna? Where are they? Have you done something to Alice and Lily?'

The line clicked dead.

'Anna! Anna!' Jez screamed into the phone. 'If you've done anything to them, I will kill you.'

But it was too late. She was gone.

45

Jez woke in a hot sweat, dreaming of decapitated dolls swimming in a sea of blood, their lifeless faces staring wild-eyed into the sky. Gasping for breath, he snatched his phone from the cabinet beside the bed and checked the time.

It was still early. He rolled over and pulled the duvet over his shoulders, but sleep eluded him. His mind was churning, and with a busy day ahead, he decided a prompt start would do him no harm. He threw his legs out of bed, and dragged his body to the bathroom. He ran the shower until the water turned hot, then stepped under the torrent of high pressure jets, letting the water ease his muscles. The room filled with steam, and his skin turned bright pink.

He was back in the bedroom, pulling on a clean pair of jeans, when the banging started at the front door. Loud and insistent, despite the early hour.

On the landing, Jez pulled back a sliver of net curtain at the window. A police patrol car had double parked outside the house. A uniformed officer sat behind the wheel, and another loitered on the pavement with his thumbs hooked in his belt.

A second vehicle, a dark-coloured saloon, was parked behind the patrol car. Jez recognised it as belonging to the two detectives, Fox and O'Hare. He could just make out the tops of their heads by the front door.

'Police! Open up!' one of the detectives shouted through the letterbox, making Jez jump.

He didn't have time for this.

He tugged on a pair of socks, grabbed a hooded top and stole down the stairs, crouching low to grab a pair of trainers from the hall. He slid through to the kitchen, and winced as he tried to silently unlock the back door. It opened with a noisy squeak on rusty hinges.

He was scooting across the back lawn when his phone buzzed. Too early for Anna to be calling, and when he checked, he didn't recognise the number.

'Hello?' he whispered.

The hammering at the door became more urgent. Maybe the two uniformed officers had been brought along to batter it open.

'Jeremy, it's Peter Mapp. Listen, the police are on their way around to take you in for further questioning.'

'Right,' said Jez. 'Why?'

'They say they've uncovered significant evidence against you. But don't worry, we can sort this out. Now, they'll probably take you to Medway nick again, but for Christ's sake, don't say anything until I get there. Is that clear?'

'What evidence? Is it Alice?' Jez asked tentatively, not sure he wanted to hear the answer.

'They won't say over the phone, but I think they would have confirmed if it was a body. Try to keep calm, and remember don't answer any questions until I get there.'

'I'm not at home right now,' said Jez. He glanced over his shoulder, half expecting to see the detectives come bursting through the back door.

'It's important you're not seen to be avoiding them,' said Mapp, an edge of concern in his tone. 'Where are you? My advice is to make yourself available to them. We don't want to do anything that could be construed as being obstructive.'

'That's going to be difficult right now, but I think I know how to find Alice. Can you stall them for me?'

'Jeremy, this is serious. If you don't co-operate, they'll take it as a sign of guilt.'

'But if I can find Alice, that would prove I didn't kill her, wouldn't it?'

'Well, obviously, but if you have any information about Alice's whereabouts you need to let the police know immediately. They'll take a very dim view of this.' Mapp sounded exasperated. Jez didn't care.

'Sorry, Peter, you're breaking up. I can't hear you.'

'Jeremy?'

Jez cut the call, and vaulted the brick wall at the end of the garden. He landed in the alley that ran behind the house, and ducked down low where the stench of urine made him gag. He waited until he'd caught his breath, then hurried towards the main road, heading for the train station.

He stopped only briefly, to withdraw cash. The most it would allow him to take out in one day was three hundred pounds, but that would be plenty. He certainly didn't want to be using his credit or debit cards, and give the police a chance to trace his movements. He shoved the wad of notes hastily into his wallet, and immediately felt like a walking magnet for every mugger in the vicinity.

He bought a ticket with a crisp, ten-pound note at a machine in the station concourse, keeping his head down to avoid the CCTV cameras. Then on the train, he slumped low in his seat and watched the countryside roll past. He'd been lucky to pick up the fast service from London, and rolled into Margate thirty minutes later. By then, he'd finalised his plan.

46

Margate station was crowded with bleary-eyed commuters heading west, their heads down over their mobile phones. Jez emerged from the concourse into a small car park overlooking the town's golden sands, and where a stream of white taxis formed a patient queue. He'd not anticipated arriving so early, but thanks to the morning call from the police, he had plenty of time to concentrate on the finer details of his plan.

With a grumbling stomach, he ambled towards the town and slipped into a greasy spoon café where condensation rolled down the windows and the air was thick with cooking fat and grease. A tinny radio competed to be heard over the sound of sausages and bacon hissing on a hotplate.

He ordered a full English breakfast, checked his mobile was fully charged, and killed any unnecessary apps which might drain the battery. It was too soon to make the call, but he didn't want anything to go wrong today.

A waitress in a dirty apron slid a plate across his table without so much as a smile. Jez ate slowly, flicking through the pages of a tabloid newspaper someone had left behind, and tried to ignore that the sausages tasted cheap, and his egg was overcooked.

When he was finished, he folded the paper in two and pushed the plate to one side.

Outside, the salty air was a welcome relief from the muggy atmosphere in the café. He zipped up his jacket and meandered towards the seafront with his mind clear and his stomach full.

Finding a guest house in Margate wasn't difficult. He chose one with lacy net curtains and a 'vacancies' sign hanging from a wooden post in an overgrown front garden. He paid up front in cash, and was shown to an attic room with mould on the ceiling by a brassy blonde landlady chewing gum.

The bed was soft, but comfortable enough, despite springs poking through the mattress in places. Jez folded a pillow under his head, and staring into space, began rehearsing his lines over and over, planning for every eventuality. What if she didn't answer? What if she refused to come?

Eventually, Jez's eyes fluttered closed, and he fell into a deep, dreamless sleep.

It was close to half eleven when he woke, his breakfast sitting heavily on his stomach. He sat up and rubbed his eyes. Somewhere in the building a vacuum cleaner droned with a low hum.

In a tiny bathroom, built into the corner of the room, Jez splashed cold water on his face. He patted his skin dry with a threadbare towel and studied his reflection in the cracked mirror. He took a deep breath.

It was time.

Anna's number had flashed up on his phone so many times, he knew it by heart. He dialled carefully, and waited as the call connected.

'Jez?' She sounded surprised, the buzz of a busy office in the background. 'How lovely to hear from you.'

'Sorry, are you at work? I can call back later…'

'No, it's fine,' Anna said. The background chatter went quiet, as she moved somewhere private.

'I've had some time to think about what you said about Alice, and I might have been a little hasty.'

'I should be the one apologising. I was too blunt.'

'No, you were right. I was being blind. Alice doesn't love me. I should have listened.' Jez sat on the edge of the bed and stared out of the window where a pigeon had perched on a length of guttering, its feathers plumped up, soaking up the rays of sunshine. 'And look, about the other night,' he continued. 'I reacted badly. My head was in a weird place.'

'I shouldn't have come on so strong.'

'No, I was flattered,' said Jez. 'Truly I was. It was just a little unexpected. You took me by surprise.'

He could tell she was smiling. She was buying every word.

'You don't have to apologise,' said Anna.

'Yes, I do,' said Jez. 'And I'd like to make it up to you, my way of saying sorry. Are you free today? I'm in Margate. I could meet you for lunch.'

At first Anna said nothing. He forced himself not to fill the silence.

'Why not? I'll juggle some appointments.'

'Great,' said Jez. 'We could go for that picnic you suggested.'

Anna laughed. 'You remembered?'

'Of course I remembered. I remember every word you said. I've thought about little else.'

'All right, then. Where shall I meet you?'

'Pick me up at the harbour arm, by the gallery, at one.'

'Can we make it two?'

Jez bit his lip. What the hell. He'd waited this long; another hour wasn't going to make much difference. 'Great,' he said. 'I'll see you then.'

He hung up, and collapsed on the bed, his pulse racing.

47

Anna's red Volvo swung through a set of traffic lights, and pulled up by the monolithic Turner Contemporary gallery. Jez waved cheerily, and threw open the passenger door.

'Hey,' he said, climbing in. He surprised her with a peck on the cheek, and elicited a coy smile.

He caught a faint trace of perfume as she nudged her glasses up the bridge of her nose, and ran a hand through her tightly curled hair.

'Hi,' she said. 'Fancy meeting you here.'

'I brought champagne.' Jez held up a bottle and two plastic glasses.

'On a school day?'

'It's Moët.'

'My favourite.'

'I know.'

'And I thought it was lunch you had in mind.' Anna put the car in gear, as Jez pulled on a seatbelt.

'We can eat later. Let's go somewhere we can talk.'

'My place?' Anna raised an eyebrow.

Jez inwardly shuddered at the thought of going back to the house. 'It's a nice day. Why don't we go to the beach?' He placed a hand lightly on Anna's knee, and felt her stiffen through the coarse fabric of her tweed suit.

'But it's freezing,' she said.

'I'm sure we can find a way to keep warm.'

Anna shot him a glance, a twinkle in her eye. 'Like what?'

'Come on, let's go.'

Anna swung the car around and took off, snatching through the gears too quickly so the engine struggled. 'I have to be back in the office later,' she said. 'I only have a couple of hours free.'

'Better than nothing.' Jez watched her carefully as she drove. Without her evening dress and make-up, she looked rather plain.

'I guess it's my turn to be surprised. Why the change of heart?' She giggled like a naughty schoolgirl.

Settling in his seat, Jez studied the sea stretching away as far as the horizon, rippling under a darkening sky. The day had started off with such promise, but now broiling dark clouds were gathering. 'I've not been able to stop thinking about you,' he said, as they rattled along, putting Margate behind them.

'Really?'

'Everything you said about Alice and how badly she's treated me, has been going around and round my head.' A weak sun, magnified through the windscreen, warmed Jez's face.

'So why did you ignore my calls?'

'I was confused. I suppose I was still in denial.'

'You said some pretty awful things,' said Anna. 'You know I'd never do anything to hurt you.'

'I know.'

Anna pulled up in a cliff-top car park overlooking a sandy cove, and yanked on the handbrake. As they stepped out of the car, a strengthening breeze ruffled their hair and tugged at their clothes.

'I love it here,' said Anna. 'The light is just perfect.'

Jez followed her gaze across the bay where the autumnal sunshine reflected off the chalky cliffs, and houses dotted along the headland.

'It's going to rain.' Anna nodded towards the horizon, as she tucked the ends of a thin chiffon scarf under the collar of her jacket.

'Not for a little while,' said Jez.

They picked their way down a steep set of concrete steps to the beach, their feet skidding on the fine sand.

At the bottom, Anna kicked off her heels and carried them in one hand. 'Where do you want to go?'

'Over there,' said Jez, grabbing Anna's free hand, and leading her to where the beach disappeared around a cliff face pitted and scarred by the wind and waves, out of sight of the main sands.

They found a spot protected from the worst of the breeze, tucked behind a rocky outcrop where Jez was confident they wouldn't be overlooked.

'What about here?'

Giggling, Anna sat down facing the sea with her

knees pulled up to her chest. 'What about that champagne?'

Jez popped the cork with his thumbs. It flew high into the air and landed in the water, where it was swamped by a wave and disappeared. He caught a fizzing eruption of champagne foam in a plastic glass, and Anna squealed with delight.

'To us,' he said.

'To us.'

Anna threw back her head, closed her eyes, and took a large gulp, as an unexpected gust of wind whipped in off the water. It tugged at her scarf, and before she could stop it, it was gone, yanked from her neck, sailing high into the sky.

'My scarf!' Anna howled. She tried to pluck it from the air, but it was well out of reach.

It danced and jigged as if being pulled on strings, then stuttered in mid-flight and plunged like Icarus into the sea. Jez jumped up, pulled off his trainers, and waded into the water up to his thighs. The cold took his breath away. Sharp rocks cut his feet.

'My hero!' said Anna when he returned holding the soaking scarf aloft like a prize trophy.

'I'm afraid it's a bit wet,' he said, shivering. 'But I'll hang it off a rock. It might dry.'

'So gallant for the lady,' said Anna, handing him his glass.

Jez took a sip and resisted the urge to pull a face. He still couldn't see what all the fuss was about. Maybe it was drinking on an empty stomach, but it tasted particularly bitter. Sour almost.

Anna knocked her own champagne back, then held up an empty glass. 'Is there any more?'

Jez topped her up from the bottle he'd stuck in a crevice in a rock.

'You're not angry about the other night?'

'No, of course not. I was an idiot.' Jez lay on his side and propped his head in his hand.

'I meant what I said, you deserve someone better than Alice.'

'Like you, you mean?'

Anna grinned. 'Maybe.' She lay on her back with her glass on her stomach, and an arm under her head. 'I'd never treat you like she did.'

'How can I be sure?'

'You could take a chance, and see what happens.'

With the lightest of touches, Jez traced the line of her cheekbone with the tip of his finger. 'I don't want to get hurt again,' he said.

'I won't hurt you. I promise.'

Anna curled an arm around Jez's neck, and pulled his head closer. Jez dropped his glass, and ran his fingers through her hair. He tasted the salt on her lips, and gave himself up to her hunger. He felt her body melting, as her leg twined around his wet thigh, her desire building.

'You're beautiful,' he said, studying her face like an artist admiring a portrait by a grand master.

'No, I'm not,' said Anna, turning away.

'Don't say that.' He turned her head back, and smudged what was left of her lipstick with his thumb.

She was right, of course. At best she could be described as handsome, but she was no beauty. Not like

Alice. Her nose was a little broad, her teeth crooked, and her eyes the colour of muddy puddles.

Jez's thumb drifted across her chin and along her throat until he reached the top of her blouse. He expertly teased open the buttons down to her navel, and ran a hand over her quivering stomach.

'Someone might see,' she said, putting up a pretence of protest.

'There's no one here,' said Jez, 'unless you count that seagull who's been watching for the last five minutes.'

'Where?' she said, sitting up.

'I'm kidding.'

'Oh.' She kissed him again.

Jez's fingers toyed with the strap of a lacy bra that had plenty of padding for a much-needed boost. She moaned with desire, grinding her hips against his body. He nibbled the lobe of her ear.

'Tell me what happened to Alice,' Jez whispered. She tensed, just a little, but tried to hide it. 'Do you know where she is?'

Anna brushed away his hand as it found its way to her breast, a flash of anger skittering across her face. She tried to get up, but Jez rolled on top of her, pinning her down.

'You're still obsessed with her, aren't you?' she hissed, struggling to break free of the grip around her wrists.

'Tell me what you've done with her.'

'Get off, or I'll scream.' She bucked and twisted, but Jez held her firm.

'Go ahead. There's no one to hear you. What have you done with Alice? Where is she, Anna?'

'How the hell should I know.'

'I thought she'd gone to Spain?'

'I was trying to save you from her.'

'That's noble.'

'It's so obvious she has no feelings for you.'

'We're meant for each other.'

'Ha! And that's why you're here with your hand up my blouse? And don't try telling me you're faking it. I can tell how much you want me.'

'Not if you were the last woman on earth,' said Jez. 'You think you compare to Alice? Well, try looking in the mirror.'

'Go to hell!'

'I understand what's going on now, Anna. You couldn't bear that Alice had everything you ever wanted, and can never have.'

'If she's so perfect, why did she leave you? Is it because you can't satisfy her needs? Not enough of a man? Maybe that's why she was screwing behind your back.'

'Shut up!' Jez gripped her wrists tighter.

'I wonder if she was doing it in your bed. What do you think?'

'I said shut your mouth!'

'Or what, Jez? What're you going to do?'

'I'll kill you,' he said, fury raging through his blood.

'I don't think you've got it in you.'

'You evil bitch.' His hands flew to her throat, and squeezed.

She snatched his wrists, and kicked wildly in the sand, as her eyes, stricken with panic, began to bulge, and her face turned red.

Jez thought of nothing in that moment but of how much he hated her. His thumbs pressed harder and harder, constricting muscle and sinewy cartilage until her breath stopped.

The fight quickly evaporated from her, and her eyes fluttered closed, her limbs losing their strength. Her hands dropped away, and her body fell limp. She was dying, but Jez couldn't stop himself.

Another minute, and it would all be over. And then, maybe, he'd never find Alice.

He relaxed his grip a little, and a rasping, wheezy breath slipped from Anna's throat.

It was too late by the time he saw her arm swinging towards his head, the empty champagne bottle in her hand. It caught him on the back of his skull with the force of a baseball player hitting a home run. His world exploded in a kaleidoscope of pain and colour. Darkness crowded his vision, and he slumped in a semi-conscious stupor with an acidic, bilious burn rising from his stomach.

Anna rolled out from under his slack body, and left him face down in the sand.

He coughed and spluttered, a searing pain splitting through his brain.

Bitch!

Jez lay motionless for a moment, catching his breath, and dragging himself back from the cusp of unconsciousness.

Unsteadily, he pulled himself to his feet, and checked his skull. His scalp was tender to the touch, but there was no blood. He blinked hard, willing his vision to come back into focus, scanning the length of the beach.

But Anna had vanished.

He pulled on his trainers, ignoring the pain from the cuts on the soles of his feet. Then he ran, half stumbling through the sand, back towards the car.

'Anna!' he yelled, his legs turning weak. 'Come back.'

Ahead, he saw a blurry figure, heading for the concrete stairs. Jez made a superhuman effort with legs pumping and his thighs burning. He reached Anna as she made it to the bottom step.

With one last effort, he lunged for her arm, and brought her down with a scream. They grappled in the sand, kicking and fumbling, until her elbow struck him across the temple, and a wave of nausea rushed from his stomach.

His head swam and his guts cramped, then his whole body convulsed with the effort of vomiting.

He tried to stand, but his stomach knotted again, and he collapsed to his knees. The last thing he remembered was seeing the waves crashing on the shore, leaving a foaming white residue on the sand.

48

Jez woke shivering so hard his teeth rattled in his head. He was curled in a tight ball, lying on a grassy bank. Above, the sky was heavy with thick, black cloud. A gusty wind blew across the bay.

He had a vague recollection of crawling across the beach and collapsing. He remembered chasing Anna, and the crippling pain in his stomach before he passed out. He sat up slowly with his nose and throat burning with the vile aftertaste of vomit. His head ached, and his brain was woolly, like the worst hangover he could imagine. And yet he'd barely touched any champagne.

He felt with his fingers for the tender spot on the back of his skull where Anna had hit him so hard with the bottle it had knocked the air from his lungs. He found a swollen lump, sore to the touch, then remembered his hands around Anna's neck, squeezing out her life with a terrifying, all-consuming rage. He had no doubt he fully intended to kill her.

He recalled chasing her along the beach, and pulling

her to the ground. He remembered the sickness in his stomach that came from nowhere, and the dizziness. And then nothing.

It must have been the bang to the head. But he'd been concussed once before, as a teenager playing football at school. Never the most able of sportsmen, he'd somehow run into a goalpost and knocked himself out cold. For the next hour he'd floated in limbo between dreams and reality.

But this was nothing like that. It was ten times worse, like his brain had been syphoned out of his skull and replaced with candyfloss. More like a chemical-induced soporific fugue, like when he'd taken those seasickness tablets he'd bought over the counter in Greece.

Jez licked his dry lips, and tasted a metallic tinge.

Anna had drugged him. It was the only explanation. He remembered racing into the sea to rescue her scarf. She must have dropped something into his glass while he was distracted.

He rolled onto his back and groaned, his tender stomach muscles protesting. He thought he'd had every eventuality covered, and yet Anna had still outmanoeuvred him. He'd been foolish to think she'd give up information about Alice so easily. And now he'd blown everything.

A heavy drop of rain hit him between the eyes, making him start. He wiped it away with the back of his hand, and felt a vibration in the back pocket of his jeans.

He turned onto his side, and with some effort, pulled out his phone. He glanced at the screen, and stopped breathing. He blinked twice, and rubbed his eyes, convinced the drugs Anna had dropped in his drink were still messing with his mind.

With a trembling hand, he answered the call, and slowly brought the phone to his ear.

'Alice?' he said.

49

'Hello,' said Alice. Her voice was subdued, almost as if she was holding back tears.

'Oh my God, Alice, I've been so worried about you. Where are you? Are you okay? Why didn't you call?' Jez's questions poured out in a torrent.

'I'm fine.'

'And Lily?'

'She's fine too.'

Jez hesitated, sensing something was wrong. 'That's it?'

'I'm sorry, Jez. I don't know what to say. Things have been…' She struggled for the right word. 'Difficult.'

'Where are you?'

'I can't tell you.' Alice spoke so quietly he struggled to hear over the surf crashing on the beach.

'Why not? I want to see you. I *need* to see you.'

'No. You can't.'

'Why not?'

She sighed. 'Look, things are complicated, okay? I can't see you again. You have to forget about us.'

'Alice, what's going on?'

'It's over, okay? It's time to move on with our lives.'

'I don't want to move on with my life,' said Jez, frowning. 'At least let's talk about it. I mean, if this has something to do with what I said, then I'm sorry. It was all in the heat of the moment. I didn't mean any of it. Give me the chance to make it up to you.'

'I have to go now, Jez. Don't try to contact me again, please.'

'Wait! Don't go.'

'Goodbye, Jez.'

A heavy silence hung between them. Jez listened to her breathing. He'd been desperate to hear Alice's voice - and now this?

'Are you in some sort of trouble? Whatever it is, we can work it out. I don't care what you've done, just don't cut me off. I love you.'

'If you love me, then let me go.' She was crying now.

'I know about Anna and Marcus. I spoke to her. She said you'd moved to Spain. Is it true?'

If she was surprised, she didn't show it. 'I have to go. I'm so sorry, for everything.'

'I'm begging you, don't do this.'

The line clicked dead. 'Alice?' Jez screamed. But she was gone.

He stared at the screen of his phone in disbelief. She'd hung up on him with no explanation. What could possibly have happened that meant she never wanted to see him again?

He dived into the call register, and hit redial. But it went straight to voicemail, an automated, digital message telling him Alice was unavailable. Disconnected and inhuman.

'Alice, it's me. Call me back. Please. I know we can work this out, whatever the problem is,' he said.

If only she'd agree to meet him, he could make her understand how much he loved her, and prove he was worthy of a second chance. He'd tell her how good they were together, how sorry he was for doubting her, and for walking out when he should have stayed and talked.

He dropped the phone in the sand, with tears rolling down his cheeks, and sobs rising from his chest. He stared out to sea, unable to determine where it ended and the horizon began. The wind had reached a tempestuous fury, whipping up the waves. Thick globules of rain began to fall, leaving dark marks in the sand, and as Jez looked up at the black blanket of cloud, he sensed the heavens were about to open.

50

Jez arrived back at the guest house late in the afternoon, drenched to the bone, and in a mood that could sour milk. He'd trudged through the rain with Alice's words echoing through his head, making less sense the more he pondered them.

He stole into the house, grateful to find it was deserted, and climbed the stairs wearily, leaving wet footprints on the carpet. He let himself into his room and locked the door.

If Alice hadn't wanted to be found, what was the point of calling? And why was she so insistent he forget her? There was something she wasn't telling him, but if she thought he was going to give up on her, she had another thing coming.

Jez peeled off his wet clothes, and draped them over the radiator under the window. He took a long, hot shower, and with only a towel around his waist, fell onto the bed listening to the rain hammer on the roof.

Rivulets ran down the window, and the wind rattled the glass.

He tried Alice's number once more, but it went straight to voicemail again. He didn't bother leaving another message. Next, he called his father. He'd meant to ring earlier, but had been so pre-occupied he'd clean forgotten.

'Dad, it's me,' he said, when his father eventually picked up.

'Where are you? I thought you were coming over this morning.'

'Sorry, Dad. I had to come back to Margate.'

'You promised.'

'Yeah, I know. I'll be there a little bit later, but there's something I need to sort out first.'

'Alice?'

'Yeah,' said Jez. 'How's Mum getting on?'

'She's in pretty good spirits. I think she's glad to be home.'

'And she had a good night?'

'Yes. What time will you be here? Your mother's worried.'

Jez peered out of the window at the grey skies. 'I don't know.' He was sure his father could cope on his own for a few more hours.

'Jeremy, come on. I need you here.'

'And I'll be there as soon as I can, Dad. It's just this thing with Alice.' He wanted to tell his father everything, to unburden, but it wasn't fair, not with his mother so ill. 'I'll tell you all about it later.'

'Hang on, your mother's calling.'

'I'll see you later, Dad.' Jez hung up, and blew out an exasperated puff of air from his cheeks.

He tapped his phone on his knee, thinking of his mother, and of Alice. The two most important women in his life, and how he was letting them both down.

He sat up and made one more call. From the background noise, it sounded as if Mick was in the pub already.

'I can't hear you. I'm just popping outside,' he shouted over the noise.

Jez rolled his eyes, and fell back on the bed.

'What's up, fella?'

'I've heard from Alice,' said Jez.

'That's great. What did she say?'

'That it's over between us. She doesn't want to see me again.'

'Oh, mate, I'm sorry. That sucks. Did she say why?'

'Not really. She said it was complicated, and wanted me to give up trying to find her.'

Jez heard Mick suck the air through his teeth. 'Ah,' he said.

'What?'

'Well, you know what that means.'

'Enlighten me.'

Mick paused a beat. 'I might be wrong, but it's what they usually say when there's someone else involved.'

'No, I don't think so, Mick. I think she's in trouble, but she's trying to protect me.'

'How do you figure that?'

'She sounded odd on the phone, like she was holding

back. She says she doesn't want me, but I can't shake this feeling that there's something not quite right.'

'What're you going to do?'

'I'm not sure. I spoke to Anna, the mother of the girl Alice killed, and she definitely knows more than she's letting on. I think she's involved. She hates Alice, and still blames her for what happened.'

'That's hardly a surprise.'

'Especially as she also discovered Alice was having an affair with her husband.'

'Christ.'

'Remember the guy, Marcus, who broke into our house?'

'That's her husband? You're kidding?'

'I wish I was.'

'What are you going to do?'

Jez stood, and wandered to the window. The rain was easing, but the skies were still leaden. 'I'm going to go back to Anna and Marcus's place. It's where this all started. I can't think what else I can do. I've run out of options. I need to confront Anna, one last time.'

51

With sea mist swirling around its spires and turrets, the Victorian villa at the end of the sweeping gravel drive looked like a setting from a horror movie. It stood partially in shadow, with the light from a waning moon bathing it in a silvery glow. Jez stood at the gates in the dark and shivered, his breath condensing in white vapours. The place gave him the creeps.

He looked past the red Volvo, parked in front of a single storey garage, to a spot where he imagined Anna's daughter had died, cradled in her mother's arms. He pushed the image away.

After speaking with Mick, he'd come up with a plan to break into the house as the only way to prove Anna knew more about Alice's disappearance than she was letting on. It had seemed like a perfectly rational idea while sitting in the comfort of the guest house, but now he wasn't so sure.

He darted through the gates, like a thief in the night, and dropped for cover behind the Volvo, his back against its bumper. He counted to thirty with his stomach twisting in knots. He didn't have a clue what he was looking for, only that he thought he would know it when he found it.

Keeping low, Jez tried the car's passenger door. To his surprise, it wasn't locked. It opened with a click that sounded unusually loud in the silence of the night. An owl screeched in a nearby tree, and a misfiring engine faded into the distance, but no one came to investigate.

Emboldened, Jez eased the door open wider, and the car flooded with light. He hopped into a soft leather seat, and sat with his hands on his knees, studying the interior. If Alice and Lily had been in the vehicle, maybe they'd have left a clue. A hair slide, or one of Lily's toys? But the car was immaculately clean. There was hardly a speck of dust or dirt. Even the dashboard had been polished to a high sheen, as if it had come straight off a showroom forecourt, and curiously, the key had been in the ignition. How trusting of Anna.

Jez felt around the footwell, running his hand over a cream coloured mat, but found nothing. He rummaged through the glovebox and poked around under the seats. He checked behind the sun visors and in the pockets in the door, but it was possibly the most sanitised vehicle he'd ever seen, a far cry from his own car which was usually littered with old sandwich wrappers, drinks cans, and Lily's toys.

The overhead lights faded and went out. Along the street, a dog barked. There was no avoiding it. He'd have to try the house. Maybe he should have called the detectives, Fox and O'Hare, as soon as he'd heard from

Alice. It was proof, of course, that she was still alive, and would clear him of murder. But he still didn't entirely trust them. And what exactly could he prove? He could show them he'd received a call from Alice's mobile, but it was hardly conclusive. He knew the way their minds worked. They'd accuse him of arranging the call himself to cover his tracks. No, it would be better to involve them later. His priority was finding Alice and Lily.

The car door closed with a hollow thud. Jez scanned the house. All the curtains were pulled, and only one light was on inside, behind a ground floor window. No way to tell if Anna or Marcus were home. He'd have to chance his luck, and thought his best bet might be trying around the back.

Jez hurried across the gravel towards the garage, and threw himself flat against the door. Suddenly, the outside space was illuminated with white light so bright it hurt his eyes. He threw an arm over his face and cursed. Squinting, he spotted the source. A security lamp mounted on the side of the house, lighting up the top end of the drive, and the steps leading up to the front porch.

He waited motionless for what seemed like an age, until eventually the light went out and he was plunged back into darkness. He tried the garage door. The latch lifted, but it wouldn't budge. He gave up trying, and with his night vision returning, slipped into a narrow alley that ran between the house and the garage.

Ahead, a featureless garden was fringed by tall trees, and to his right a set of steps led to the house. Another low building with a pitched roof sat adjacent to the villa. It had been constructed in a similar style, with matching roof tiles, and built from the same colour brick, although their pigmentation suggested it had been a more modern addition. A wooden, painted sign had been hung over a heavy oak door. Through the gloom of the night, Jez could just about make out the words:

Marcus Fenson. Furniture Maker.

It hit him like a hammer blow. The workshop where Anna had caught Alice and Marcus screwing over a French reproduction oak sideboard, to use her words. Her graphic description had stayed with Jez, and he found it difficult not to dwell on the thought. Two bodies entwined in a lustful embrace. Jez felt a pang of jealousy, as if it was a personal betrayal, even though it had happened long before he and Alice were together.

Two windows facing the house had been boarded up behind a steel grille, and when he tried the oak door he found it was secured with a substantial mortice lock. He rattled it in its frame, and almost missed the sound of a door opening and slamming shut.

Jez retreated into the shadows and crouched low as Anna, carrying a tray and two bowls balanced on one hand, emerged from the house. His jaw clamped tight as he watched her teeter down the steps. The last time he'd seen her, he'd had his hands around her throat, throttling her life away, unaware that she'd drugged him. The sight of her again filled him with loathing.

She stopped at the bottom of the stairs, selected a key from a small bunch, and unlocked the workshop door. She let herself in and locked the door behind her.

Jez hunkered down and waited, not daring to move.

Less than a minute later, Anna reappeared without the tray. She pulled the door closed, and carefully checked it was secure before vanishing back inside the house.

Jez stood slowly, imagining the worst. He pictured Alice and Lily held prisoner inside the building, fed on scraps, and with no hope of escape.

Anger simmered from a place deep inside him. He balled his fists, and ground his teeth, plotting the violent revenge he'd take on Anna and Marcus if they'd laid a finger on the two people he realised he cherished most dearly in the world.

Jez sprinted up the steps to the house and with clammy palms, eased open the back door. He stepped into a dark kitchen. From a faint light coming from the hall, he made out walls lined with Shaker-style cupboards facing a free-standing island with a deep sink sunk in its middle.

A floorboard creaked, and a pipe gurgled and popped. Jez's eyes swept through the darkness, over the worktops, until he spotted a bunch of keys tossed casually to one side, next to a potted plant with tumbling green foliage. He plucked them up and backed out of the room, stumbling down the steps in his haste to reach Alice and Lily.

At the workshop door, he fumbled with the keys, hunting for the one that would fit. He found it on the fifth attempt, relieved when he heard the lock spring open.

He stepped into a narrow hall, and was confronted

with a second door, perpendicular to the first. A light was on in the room beyond. He sorted through the keys again and had better luck, finding the correct one on only the second attempt.

The door rolled open. Bright light and the powerful aroma of polish and sawdust spilled out. The room was cluttered with wooden furniture; tables, dressers, chairs, and wardrobes. Sitting at the far end, hunched over a bowl, a man looked up. His hair was a scraggy mess and he needed a shave, but it was his cold, dead eyes that were the most disturbing feature of his face.

'Marcus?' said Jez. 'What are you doing in here?'

52

Marcus grunted a reply, before returning to his bowl, spooning at it with a fork clasped in a clawed hand. He shuffled into a corner, turning his back on Jez, as a bedraggled figure rose from the floor on the opposite side of the room. Her hair was matted and her clothes ripped and dirty.

'Alice?' said Jez. Her cheeks were sallow and pinched, her skin pale. 'What have they done?'

Alice squinted at him, either confused or in disbelief. He rushed to her, knocking over chairs and tables in his haste, and threw his arms around her slight shoulders. 'If they've hurt you, I'll kill them.'

Alice tensed as he hugged her. 'I'm fine,' she said.

He held her at arm's length, studying every inch of her face. 'I thought you'd left me.'

'Not intentionally,' she said with a weak smile.

'Have you been here all this time?'

'Anna took Lily. I had to come and get her back.'

Jez looked around the workshop, expecting to see Lily busy playing. 'Where is she?'

Alice gripped his arm so tightly, her nails cut into his skin. She tried to speak, but her words were lost in a torrent of tears.

'Is she in the house?' asked Jez.

'I don't know. She hasn't let me see her.' A choking sob stuck in Alice's throat. 'Please, we have to find her.'

'Okay, let me think for a minute.'

'There's no time to think. Come on.'

Jez shook his head, trying to make sense of what he'd walked into. 'And all this?' He waved a hand around the workshop. 'All because of what you did to Ellie?'

'I don't know!' Alice's face twisted in anguish. Her eyes darted over Jez's shoulder towards the open door.

He snatched her arm as she attempted to push past. 'No, I'll go. Wait for me,' he said.

'I'm coming with you.'

'No, you're not. Anna's car's parked on the drive. Get in, lock the doors, and call the police.' He handed Alice his mobile phone. She took it with both hands, as if she was receiving a precious gift. 'I'll be back as soon as I can.'

Alice glanced at Marcus, who was running a finger around the inside of his bowl, licking it clean. 'What about him? I can't leave him here,' she said.

'Hey, Marcus. Think you can help Alice to the car?'

He looked up briefly, and stared at Jez with vacant eyes.

'He doesn't speak much,' said Alice.

'Did I...?'

'Maybe, but you can't change the past. We can talk about it later. Please, just go and find Lily.' Alice pushed him towards the door.

As Jez left, he gave her an encouraging smile. 'I won't be long,' he said.

And then he was outside again, in the dark and the cold. He took the steps up to the house two at a time, pumped up on adrenaline and fury.

The kitchen door opened noiselessly. Whatever stupid game Anna was playing, it was over. He was finishing it, here and now.

Inside, the villa was almost completely in darkness, and in an instant, Jez's bravado failed him. He swallowed hard.

The weak light from the hallway came from a table lamp positioned on a narrow sideboard adjacent to an ancient grandfather clock ticking a metronomic beat. Jez moved with leaden feet, his heart racing. The floorboards in the hall creaked. A dusty mustiness, like the smell of antique books, filled the air. If the house looked creepy from the outside, it was ten times worse inside.

He edged towards the bottom of a wide mahogany staircase, and stared up into the gloom.

'Anna?' he called. 'Lily?' His voice wavered.

He brushed past a vase of faded fabric flowers on a stand next to the clock, and disturbed a cloud of dust. He pinched his nose to stop a sneeze, caught it in his throat, and for a second thought he'd heard a low keening. A child sobbing, faintly, from somewhere above.

'Lily!' he shouted, charging up the stairs into the

enveloping darkness. On the landing, he patted the wall until he found a light switch. 'Where are you?'

He had a choice of six doors to try, all pulled shut, but was drawn to the one with a silver key extending from its lock.

'Are you in there, Lily?' he said, trying the handle.

With a trembling hand, he turned the key, and shouldered his way in, stumbling into the dark. Vague shapes morphed into recognisable objects as his eyes adjusted. A wardrobe; a bed along one wall; a chest of drawers by the window. The door swung closed behind him, and Jez was plunged into the impenetrable treacle of night.

He flapped wildly for a switch. A naked bulb hanging from a thin electrical cable turned night into day, and he found he was in a young girl's room. The walls were painted pastel pink, and a wooden doll's house had been set up on the floor. A coral-coloured rug partially covered the carpet and, under the window a row of soft toys had been lined up on a chest, staring blankly into space.

A cold chill ran down Jez's spine as he realised it must be Ellie's room, untouched since the day she died, and left as a shrine to her memory.

He stumbled backwards, feeling for the door handle. He'd been in thousands of homes, measuring up and making valuations, but he'd never felt more intrusive, as if he'd lifted the lid on Anna and Marcus's private grief.

His eye was caught by three photographs on a bookshelf, each in a little white, carved frame, and each featuring the same three faces. Anna and Marcus looked younger and happier. The young girl with them had long, dark hair, and a devilish glint in her eye. Ellie's likeness to her mother was striking. She had the same nose and thin-lipped mouth.

Jez reached for the nearest picture, a shot captured on a beach under an azure summer sky. Three faces beamed with joy. Ellie was at the front. Her parents behind, and to one side. Marcus had more hair. Anna had less grey. The picture of a perfect family, who had no idea their lives were about to be torn apart.

Jez almost dropped the frame when the door creaked open behind him.

'What are you doing? Put that back,' Anna hissed.

Jez spun around. 'Anna, I…'

'Put it back!' She snatched the photograph and placed it back roughly on the shelf.

'I'm sorry, I didn't mean…'

'What are you doing here?' She raised a hand, pointing a knife at Jez's face. Its blade glinted, catching the light.

'Anna, take it easy. It's me. Jez,' he said, backing away with his hands up.

'Why are you here?'

'I've come to take Lily home,' he said, recovering his senses.

'Is that right?'

'Where is she?'

'I told you to forget them both.'

'I can't,' said Jez.

'Why? Alice doesn't love you. Why can't you understand that?'

'It may not be perfect between us, but we'll make it work, the three of us.'

Anna snorted a derisive laugh. 'While I'm left here with the shattered pieces of my broken life?'

'You can't keep blaming Alice.'

'Can't I? She took my husband, and killed my daughter.'

Jez watched the tip of the knife dancing through the air as Anna waved her arm wildly at him. 'But keeping Alice and Lily prisoner here isn't going to bring Ellie back.' He took a step forward, hoping to force Anna to lower the knife.

'Stay where you are,' she said. But rather than dropping the knife, she thrust it at Jez's neck, pressing the blade against his skin.

'Anna, stop it. Someone's going to get hurt.'

'Of course someone's going to get hurt. They always do.'

'I've called the police. They'll be here any minute, so put the knife down. We can sort this out.'

Anna's eyes shot to the window, but fell back on Jez before he could react. 'Sort it out? What're you going to do? Tell me my husband wasn't screwing your girlfriend behind my back?'

'Look, I know things got a bit messed up for you but -'

'Messed up? Alice murdered Ellie. She deserves everything she gets.'

'And Lily? She's an innocent victim in all this. Tell me where she is, and let me take her home.'

Anna shook her head, her lips pressed tightly closed.

'It's been four years, Anna.'

'And after four years that grubby little whore still couldn't keep her hands off my husband,' said Anna, shaking.

'That's not true.'

'Can you explain how he ended up in hospital with his head smashed in? I'm assuming that was your handiwork. What happened? Did you find them in your bed?'

The memory of Marcus sprawled out in the hall, his blood staining the carpet on the stairs flooded back to Jez. 'It was an accident. I didn't mean to hurt him,' he said.

'I bet it felt good though.'

'He was drunk and broke into the house.' Jez felt the blade at his throat nick his skin. 'He wouldn't leave.'

Anna frowned. 'I don't blame you. He was there to see her, wasn't he?'

'It's not what you think.'

'Face it, they were screwing behind our backs. You know it's true, even if you won't admit it to yourself.'

'No.'

'I warned him,' said Anna. 'I took him back once, but he couldn't keep away.'

'You're making a mistake.'

'I found Alice's address on his phone. He was still seeing her, even though I warned him.'

A trickle of blood rolled down Jez's neck, and ran under the collar of his t-shirt. 'Alice was hiding from Marcus. She didn't want anything to do with him. Ask Marcus.'

'Thanks to you, he hardly knows his own name, let alone what he was doing last week.'

'You're crazy,' said Jez.

'But as far as I'm concerned, they deserve each other. And if she wants him so badly, she can have him. Let her look after him. I'm not playing nursemaid.'

'So, you turned the workshop into a prison for them both.'

'I thought it had a certain irony.' The trace of a smile crept across Anna's lips.

'And you took Lily to lure Alice here. How could you do that? Lily's done nothing wrong.'

Anna shrugged. 'Alice should have been more careful with her childcare.'

Jez frowned as he remembered finding the nursery closed and staff cleaning up after vandals. 'Did you have something to do with what happened at the nursery?' he asked.

'It was so easy to persuade that nice woman who was looking after Lily that I was her auntie,' said Anna, with a smirk. 'That's the problem with people these days. Too trusting.'

'You're evil.'

'And Alice murdered my daughter. I guess that makes us even.'

'Well, I'm sorry to be the bearer of bad news, but Alice and Marcus are free,' said Jez, watching carefully for Anna's reaction.

To his surprise, she lowered the knife, blinked twice, and stepped away. Jez dabbed at the wound on his neck. He inspected the blood on his fingers, already turning sticky. 'Put down the knife, Anna, before you do something you'll regret.'

Anna drifted across the room, towards the row of soft toys on the chest under the window. She tilted her head, picked out a scruffy teddy with a lop-sided grin, and sniffed its head.

'Lily has nothing to do with this,' said Jez, pressing the advantage he thought he had. 'Why punish her?'

'Because she deserves better than that whore of a mother, someone who can take care of her properly.'

Jez shook his head slowly. 'I get it,' he said. 'In your eyes, Alice took everything from you. And so you thought you'd take Lily, and try to seduce me.'

'If you like. Why not?'

'You couldn't stand that your best friend betrayed you, and killed your daughter.'

'Best friend?' Anna turned suddenly, a flash of anger across her face. 'She resented everything I'd ever achieved. She couldn't stand that I was successful, that I had a caring husband, a beautiful house, and the most perfect baby girl. Alice had nothing. She was alone and miserable, and she took everything from me. I hate her.'

Anna paused, her expression momentarily softening. She stroked the ear of the teddy between the finger and thumb of one hand. 'When we were young, we were so alike that people used to mistake us for sisters.' She paused, focusing on the bear. 'Until high school, and she changed. She'd always been a bit awkward, all arms and legs, but suddenly she grew into her looks. And with it came all the attention, and she didn't need me anymore. After all those years, suddenly, I was nobody to her.'

Anna's grip on the bear tightened. She held it at arm's length and with a sudden, violent swipe of the knife, cut off its head. She let its body fall to the floor and roll under the bed with stuffing spilling out of its neck. Anna tossed the decapitated head to one side and picked up a doll with blonde hair and blue eyes.

'After we left school, I hardly thought about Alice, until one day, out of the blue, she was back in my life. I guess I have my mother to blame for that,' Anna said, with a snorted half-laugh.

'How?' said Jez.

'She invited Alice to our engagement party, and when Marcus and I moved back to Kent, we picked up as if we'd never been apart. It was the biggest mistake of my life. When Alice saw what I'd achieved, it opened her eyes to the failure she'd become, and I guess she must have started to resent me for it. But I was blind, and there was hardly a day went past when she wasn't at our house. I didn't see it, but all the time she must have been thinking of ways to bring me down.'

'Do you really believe that?' said Jez. It sounded so implausible, knowing Alice as he did.

Anna hacked at the neck of the doll with the knife until its body was hanging by a thin shred of pink plastic.

'My problem is I'm too trusting.' With a final vicious blow, Anna cut the doll's head from its body.

'But this isn't going to change anything,' said Jez. 'Where's Lily? She needs to go home.'

'No,' hissed Anna, rushing at him.

Instinctively, he side-stepped. As she lunged with the

knife, she stumbled harmlessly past, but regained her footing, and turned on him with a nasty snarl.

'We could have been so good together,' said Anna. 'I gave you a chance, but you threw it back in my face.'

She was going to kill him. Jez could see it in her eyes. All her anger, humiliation and despair now concentrated on him. 'Put the knife down, Anna.' Jez glanced at the door, only a few strides away.

'I'm sure the police would understand I was only acting in self-defence. After all, I found you creeping around my house in the dark. I was alone and scared.' She put on a lost, doleful look, the perfect picture of female vulnerability that Jez had no doubt would convince even the most hardened detective.

'You bitch.'

She threw herself at him again, thrashing wildly with the knife, the blade a blur as it cut through the air.

Jez backed away until his legs were up against the bed, and with nowhere to go, threw up an arm to protect his face. Cold steel sliced through his forearm. Jez gasped, and lashed out with his uninjured arm. He caught Anna across the face with his clenched fist, and she rocked backwards with a split lip.

For a moment, she looked dazed, but quickly recovered, and came at him again, with renewed passion and fury, the knife aimed deliberately at his chest.

Jez snatched a pillow from the bed, and used it to parry the blows, blood dripping from his arm, and pooling at his elbow. The knife shredded the pillow, cutting through it in a confetti of downy feathers. But like a woman possessed, Anna's energy was undiminished. She continued to slash and jab in a relentless assault.

'Anna, stop!' Jez yelled.

But his words only seemed to inspire her to further violence. The knife sailed past Jez's cheek, each swipe coming closer and closer to inflicting serious harm. He stumbled onto the bed, and grasped a pink knitted throw spread over the duvet.

Anna's eyes widened, and with a scream, she threw herself at him, landing on the bed as Jez rolled away.

He staggered to his feet, and twisted the throw around his hands. Anna bounced off the bed, roaring with a frustrated mania.

When she attacked him again, Jez snatched her wrist in the folds of the throw, isolating the blade, and jerking her arm awkwardly behind her back. Anna squealed as Jez yanked her shoulder against its natural rotation, and she dropped the knife.

He kicked it away, across the room. Anna struggled free, spun on the balls of her feet, and kicked hard, aiming for his groin.

The pain was excruciating. Jez lost balance, and smashed his head against the bookcase as he fell, knocking over the three framed photos. His knees bowed, and as he wavered on the cusp of unconsciousness, he collapsed to the floor, acid rising from his stomach.

He heard the thud of feet rushing from the room, and the sound of the door slamming shut. He rolled onto his back, and sucked in a gasp of air, as the key turned in the lock, trapping him inside.

53

Even as the pain in his groin subsided, sparks of light rose and fell behind Jez's eyes, and darkness clouded in. He was bleeding badly from the cut on his arm, and he was acutely aware that if he didn't staunch the flow, he'd most likely pass out within a few hours. He could even be dead by the morning. His energy had been sapped, and his will was fading. It would have been easy to close his eyes, and let sleep consume his body. But then Anna would have won, and he would have failed Alice and Lily. They deserved better. They needed him.

Using the bedstead for support, Jez dragged himself to his feet. A gruesome trail of blood had soaked into the carpet, and seeped into the fibres. He stumbled against a chest of drawers, and swallowed back a rising nausea. Inside a drawer, he found piles of neatly folded clothes, and grabbed a pink t-shirt embossed with a magical unicorn under an arcing rainbow that he assumed had belonged to Ellie. With a pang of guilt, he wrapped it around his arm as a makeshift bandage, and tied it tight with the belt from a white towelling dressing gown hanging from the back of the door.

He regretted now that he'd given his phone to Alice, as Anna had trapped him in the room and he had no means to call for help. But at least Alice was safe for the time being. He was more concerned for Lily. In Anna's current state of mind, she was capable of anything. The police should be on their way, but he had no idea how long they'd take to arrive. He had to find a way out of the room, and stop Anna.

He staggered to the door and tried the handle. Locked.

The window was the only other conceivable option for escape, but even without looking, Jez knew the drop would be impossible to survive without breaking a few bones at least.

He thumbed a metal catch, and rattled the window open, letting a chill breeze into the room. He swiped the teddies and dolls off the chest under the windowsill, and leaned out. In the dark, the drop seemed dizzyingly high. His legs turned to jelly, and he ducked back into the room with his heart thumping. Jumping was out of the question.

He took a calming breath. There was only one other way, but it filled him with terror.

Leaning out of the window again, he confirmed a second window, roughly two metres to the left. Reaching it, however, would require a superhuman feat of courage.

He found that courage with the sound of Lily's piercing scream echoing through the house. Jez took a deep breath, crawled out, and sat on the ledge, trying not to look down.

Clinging to the frame with his good arm, he stood, balancing precariously on the narrow stone ledge. The next window along was a short jump away, but it might as well have been a million miles. It seemed almost impossible that he could make it, and keep his balance.

He stretched his foot across the gap as far as his legs and his grip would allow, but his trainer flapped hopelessly in the air several inches short. Jez pulled himself back, steadied himself, and tried again. He came closer, his toe brushing the stone ledge, and for a fleeting moment he thought he was going to do it. But his foot slipped, and with all his weight held by his arms and shoulders, he felt his balance going.

With his remaining strength, he caught his fall, dragged his body back, and pressed himself up against the window pane with a euphoric buzz of relief. The gap was simply too wide. He'd never make it.

In the distance, came the wail of a siren, and Jez prayed it was the police on their way. Not that he intended waiting for them. Lily was in danger. He had to try one more time. His family needed him.

With his heart rate still thundering like a Gatling gun, Jez threw his body across the yawning gap between the two windows, committing everything to the jump. Do or die.

He let go of the frame, and for a split second floated in mid-air. His foot landed squarely on the adjacent ledge, his body carried across the chasm by his momentum. His fingers scrambled for a hold. Time slowed, and he hung neither balanced nor falling, sensing the grip of gravity closing in on him.

His fingers, slick with sweat, clawed and slipped on the frame. For a moment, he sensed he was plunging backwards, and all he could imagine was the hard ground below. But his instinct to survive kept his hands working, exploring for grip, until he found a tiny gap where the window's lower sash ran along a carved channel. The groove was less than a centimetre wide, but big enough to hook the tips of his fingers into. They latched on, and with every tendon in his hand and forearm screaming with the effort, pulled himself flat against the window, with his breath condensing on the glass.

On the other side of the pane he saw another bedroom in darkness, and beyond the reflection of his face, a few pieces of furniture, and a door, left slightly ajar, which appeared to open out onto the landing.

Turning his face away, and screwing his eyes tightly shut, Jez aimed his elbow at the window. He was afraid of swinging too hard in case he lost his balance again, and his arm glanced harmlessly off the glass. He tried again, with a little more force, and a hairline crack appeared. It took three more attempts to smash out a hole. Shards of glass fell into the room, and onto the concrete path below.

Jez removed the sharpest fragments left embedded in the frame, and eased himself inside. It was similar in size to Ellie's, with a double bed, and a tall chest of drawers. But what caught Jez's eye was a thin strip of light around a bookcase recessed into the wall. Its shelves were heavy with paperbacks. Trashy spy novels and romances mostly. Jez ran a hand along the bead of light along one side of the bookcase. His fingers bobbled over a metal lump. Barrel-shaped and grooved. A hinge. He found two more. One above and one below the first. His stomach tightened. A secret door.

The bookcase rolled easily on hidden casters, opening up a narrow entrance into a windowless room hardly large enough for the single bed that took up most of the floor. The rest of the space was piled high with old junk. A faded velvet chair worn thin on the arms, heaps of cardboard boxes, and a standard lamp missing a shade. Over a stained mattress on the pine bedstead, someone had draped some old clothes on metal hangers. But there was no sign of Lily.

He was about to back out of the room when he spotted a short flight of steps partially obscured behind an old exercise bike under a stack of dining chairs, precariously towering towards the ceiling. Curious, Jez carved a route through the clutter.

Three steps ascended into the roof space, and ended at a solid wooden door with a padlock dangling open.

Jez nudged the door, his throat dry. 'Lily?' he whispered.

The door creaked on its hinges. It opened into a squalid circular space, no bigger than a garden shed. A filthy mattress balanced on roughly-sawn joists. Strips of crusty wallpaper hung from the low walls, and ragged cobwebs stretched loosely between the rafters. A black bucket had been pushed into the eaves where the roof rose in a sharp pitch. A tangle of sheets and a coarse, pink blanket were screwed up on the bed. And between a gap in the rafters, at the end of the mattress, Jez spotted the matted fur of a soft toy. He recognised it at once. One of Lily's favourites. A sad-looking dog with floppy black ears and a missing eye that she took everywhere. She never went to sleep without it tucked under her arm.

Jez ran its grubby fur against his cheek. His gut twisted. If Anna had laid a finger on Lily, he'd finish the job he failed on the beach. The woman was crazy. No matter what had happened in the past, he could never forgive her for harming Lily.

With his anger simmering, Jez stomped back down the stairs, crashed through the junk in the room below, and navigated his way out onto the landing.

'Anna!' he yelled. 'What kind of sick bitch are you? She's an innocent child. I want her back, and so help me if you've laid a finger on her.'

He paused to listen, but heard only the sound of muted sobbing.

'Lily? Where are you?'

He peered over the banister, and was startled to see her sitting on a chair at the bottom of the stairs. Her head was bowed, and her feet dangled a few inches off the ground.

'Lily-Bear! It's me - Jez. I've come to take you home.'

She lifted her head, and looked up with red, puffed eyes. Jez forced a smile, hoping to reassure her that everything was going to be fine.

'I want Mummy,' Lily howled.

'It's okay, we're going to find Mummy,' said Jez, rushing to the top of the stairs.

He was consumed with an overwhelming urge to sweep her up in his arms, and hold her tight, but he hesitated. His gut told him something was wrong. Why was Lily sitting in a chair facing the stairs? It looked staged, as if someone had placed her there.

'Anna, what are you playing at?' Jez spoke loudly, but there was no mistaking the tremor in his voice. 'Honey, can you move your arms?' he called down to Lily.

She shook her head, staring up at him forlornly, her glasses perched on the end of her nose. It was hard to tell for sure, but it looked as if her wrists had been taped to the arms of the chair.

'Where's Anna, Lily?' said Jez, his foot hovering on the top step. 'Have you seen her?'

Lily stuck her bottom lip out in a sad pout. 'I want to go home,' she said, sobbing harder.

'I know, sweetie. We'll be going home soon. I just need to find Anna first.'

He couldn't shake the bad feeling that he was being set up. But he couldn't leave Lily. She needed him. He placed a tentative foot on the first step, transferring his weight slowly, gripping the handrail for support.

Lily sniffed. She watched him with her big, brown eyes the size of plates behind her glasses.

'I'm coming for you, Lily,' said Jez. 'But let's play a game. If you see Anna, you have to shout out really loudly, okay?'

Lily nodded, then craned her neck, peering down the hall towards the kitchen.

'See her yet?'

'No.'

'Well, keep looking, won't you?'

The stairs creaked and groaned as Jez made a slow descent. His senses alive, and his skin tingling.

'I'm coming for you, baby,' said Jez, testing the next step with his toes.

When he looked back at Lily, her eyes were filled with terror, and her mouth open wide as if she'd meant to scream, but the sound hadn't materialised.

Jez knew immediately.

He spun around, teetering on one foot. Above him, Anna loomed large, lunging with a knife, her eyes wild.

But she wasn't quick enough. Jez snatched her wrist, and using her momentum twisted it against the joint. She howled, and dropped the knife. It tumbled harmlessly away. Lily screamed, finally finding her voice.

Jez stepped back, manoeuvring out of Anna's grasp. She lost her footing, and plummeted with arms flailing. As she sailed past him, her face changed from anger and hatred to shock and fear as she realised she couldn't stop her fall.

Her head struck the banister with a sickening crunch, and she crumpled into a lifeless ball, tumbling head over heels, gravity tugging her down, crashing against wood and plaster and stone.

Jez watched in slow motion, frozen to the spot, as her body came to rest sprawled out at Lily's feet, her limbs twisted and bent.

Lily sucked in a shocked lungful of air, and finally let out a piercing scream.

Jez hurtled down the stairs, slipping and tumbling in his hurry to reach her. He stepped over Anna's body, and hugged Lily tightly, pulling her head into his shoulder. 'It's okay. It's all over. You're safe now,' he said.

Anna had wound thick tape so tightly around Lily's wrists and the arms of the chair that her hands were turning blue. He wiped the tears from Lily's cheeks with his thumbs, and stroked her hair until she'd calmed down a little.

Lily pulled away from Jez and looked at him with sad eyes.

'Is she dead?' she whimpered.

54

Jez picked at the tape around Lily's wrists with his nails, but it wouldn't come loose.

'Get me out! Get me out!' Lily screamed. But the more she struggled, the more difficult it became to peel the tape back.

After a few minutes trying, Jez pushed the chair back against a wall, away from Anna's lifeless body. He held Lily's head in his hands and made her look him in the eye.

'I need to find something to cut the tape,' he said. Her skin was cold, and her body stiff. He wanted to get her out of the house. 'I'll be right back, so be brave.'

'No, Jez. Stay here.'

'Keep your eyes closed, and don't look at Anna, okay?'

'Don't go!'

He kissed her cheek, and edged away. 'I'll be right here. There's nothing to be scared of.'

He skirted back up the stairs, looking for the knife

Anna had dropped. He tried to remember where it had fallen, but it was nowhere to be found.

'Jez, hurry,' squealed Lily, between sobs.

'Keep your eyes closed Lily-Bear.' When he glanced back down the stairs, Lily snapped her eyes shut, screwing up her face with the effort. 'I need to look in the kitchen. Why don't we sing a song together so we know we're both safe?'

Lily nodded enthusiastically. 'What shall we sing?'

'You can choose,' said Jez, hustling down the stairs into the hall. 'What about Ten Green Bottles?' he said, when he saw her agonising over the decision.

'Okay.'

'I'll start, and you join in, but remember to sing nice and loudly so I can hear you.' Jez crept down the hall, past the old grandfather clock, towards the kitchen. 'Ten green bottles, hanging on the wall,' he sang. 'Ten green bottles hanging on the wall, and if one green bottle should accidentally fall ...'

'There'll be nine green bottles hanging on the wall.' Jez waited for Lily to take a deep breath and begin the next verse, before continuing onwards. 'Nine green bottles ...' she sang.

A bank of spotlights on the ceiling illuminated the kitchen as Jez hit a light switch on the wall. He scanned the work surfaces for a knife block, but Anna obviously liked to keep the tops free of clutter. There wasn't so much as a toaster or kettle on view.

'... and if one green bottle should accidentally fall,' Lily's voice carried through from the hall.

Jez frantically threw open cupboards and drawers,

noisily rooting through pots and pans, plates and mugs, looking for a knife or scissors. Anything he could use to cut the tape from Lily's tiny wrists.

He circled the central island, but found only a fridge, a well-stocked wine rack, and a set of vegetable baskets, full of onions and potatoes.

'... there'd be eight green bottles ...'

In his hurry, he'd missed a set of drawers full of cutlery, next to an integrated dishwasher. He dived into a tray of knives, forks and spoons, the noise drowning out the sound of Lily's voice. In the second drawer down he found a vegetable knife with a black plastic handle. He ran a thumb across its blade, and was relieved to find it was sharp.

'Lily?' he shouted, standing straight, and cocking an ear to the door. 'I can't hear you. Keep singing for me.'

An uneasiness formed in the pit of his stomach, but it was the sound of the front door slamming shut that galvanised him into action.

'Lily?' he shouted, racing into the hallway.

The chair Lily had been strapped to had been knocked over, and Lily was gone. No sign of Anna's body either.

Jez's skin prickled with a hot flush of panic. He sprinted to the front door, and reached for the latch. He took a breath and eased the door open, half expecting to find Anna waiting for him, knife in hand.

But there was no one there.

55

When Jez emerged into the porch, Anna was already halfway down the gravel drive, with Lily on her hip.

'Anna! Stop!' he yelled, his voice drowned out by the rain thundering on the roof.

Anna hesitated at the gates, and threw a glance back at the house. Wet clothes clung to her body, her hair a matted mess. Lily kicked and screamed, but Anna held her tight.

The wail of a siren sounded close. No flashing blue lights, but a promise that their nightmare would soon be over.

Anna reached the gates at the end of the drive, and shot Jez a cruel, arrogant smile. He had no idea what she was up to, or where she was going. His only concern was for Lily. Rain instantly seeped through his jacket as he charged down the steps in pursuit. It soaked into his jeans and rubbed his thighs raw as he ran.

Anna hauled open the gates, and turned with a knife she'd produced as if from thin air. 'Come any closer and

I'll cut her throat,' she said, holding the blade to Lily's neck, her hand shaking.

Jez skidded to a halt. 'Don't be stupid, Anna,' he said, peeling off the t-shirt he'd used as a bandage around his arm, and tossing it to one side. 'Give Lily to me.'

'Why wouldn't you leave us alone?' Anna screamed. 'You ruined everything.'

'You're scaring her, Anna. Stop this. She's just a little girl, cold and afraid. No different than Ellie.'

'Except Ellie's dead.' Anna shivered uncontrollably in the cold.

'But that's not Lily's fault. Please let her go.'

'I can't.'

'Yes, you can. All you have to do is hand her to me, and drop the knife.'

'She's all I have left.' Lines of mascara streaked Anna's face, her inky tears like dark rivers smudging her cheeks.

'But you're not her mother,' said Jez.

'I'm a better mother than Alice could ever be.'

'You can't use Lily as a weapon to get back at Alice. It's not fair. She's only a child. Look at her.'

The holler of sirens drew nearer, a little louder, as the rain eased.

'I should have killed them both while I had the chance,' said Anna, the blade of the knife perilously close to the milky skin under Lily's chin.

'I understand that you're hurt, and you're angry, but you're not a killer,' said Jez, inching closer.

'You know she's their daughter, don't you? A bastard

child conceived in a sleazy fumble in the backroom of a dusty workshop.'

'Anna, stop. Not in front of Lily.' He wanted to cover her ears. She had a right not to hear it. God knows what lasting psychological damage she'd suffered in the past few days. She certainly didn't need to hear the details of her inglorious conception. And neither did Jez. Not again.

'The irony that she was probably conceived on the day Ellie died would be funny if it wasn't so tragic,' Anna continued.

'She doesn't know her dad,' said Jez. 'I'm the best she's got, and I want her back.' He reached out a hand for Lily, but Anna backed away, through the gates and onto the pavement.

'Jez!' Lily cried.

'Sit still!' Anna snapped, clutching the little girl's thigh tightly.

Lily screwed up her face in a pitiful howl of anguish. All the colour from her cheeks had gone, and rain dripped from the ends of her sodden hair.

Jez forced a smile. 'It's okay Lily-Bear. I'm right here. We'll be going home soon.' He noticed the blade twitch at Lily's throat. 'Just sit still a few minutes more.'

'I want Mummy! I want to go home!' Lily screamed, as the first pulse of blue swamped the street.

Anna threw a desperate glance over her shoulder as a police car honed into view, its headlights bobbing, approaching at speed.

At last, help was on its way.

56

Jez didn't hear the car door open and slam shut, nor the crunch of feet on the gravel. He saw only Lily's eyes open wide with wonder and delight.

'Mummy!' she shouted.

'Get back in the car,' said Jez, taking his gaze momentarily off Anna when Alice appeared by his side.

'It's okay, Baby, I'm here,' Alice said, in the sing-song voice she only used when she talked to Lily.

'Want to go home.' Lily strained to reach her mother, but was yanked violently away by Anna, which provoked another distraught howl from the little girl.

'Please, Anna, don't hurt her.'

'Keep back.' The knife wavered in Anna's hand.

'I'm pleading with you.'

Anna's face was a picture of pure hate and anger. 'It's a bit late for that now.'

'Just stop it.'

'You're the one who couldn't keep your hands off my husband,' Anna screeched.

'I don't know how many more times I can say sorry before you stop punishing me. I never meant to hurt you,' said Alice. 'I regret it every day. You were my best friend, and I ruined everything.' She took a deep breath. 'But I can't change what happened.'

Jez took Alice's hand, and gave it a squeeze.

'You're only sorry you were caught,' said Anna.

'What I did was unforgivable, but it wasn't Lily's fault. I wish I could turn back time, and change how things turned out, but I can't.'

As Jez watched Lily struggling to get free, he recognised Alice in the shape of her face, the angle of her nose, and the hue of her hair. In her character too. Sassy, but timid, and still awkward in her young body. At times wickedly funny, and always as sharp as a needle. And for the first time, he saw a reflection of Marcus too, in the thrust of her jaw, and the colour of her eyes, like molten pools of chocolate.

Jez was convinced Alice regretted the pain and suffering she'd caused, but he was equally certain she had no regrets about the birth of her daughter. Lily was her life, and her soul. He doubted whether she would turn back the clock if it meant losing her.

'I wish I'd never met you,' said Anna, without a hint of emotion.

'Don't say that,' said Alice.

'It's true. Even when we were kids, I was always in your shadow, never good enough, even for my own parents. When you came back into my life I thought you'd changed, but I was wrong. All you wanted was to steal everything from me.'

'Stop it,' said Alice.

'I won't let it happen again. You're nothing to me.'

'That's fine,' said Alice, her chin dropping. 'I understand, but please let Lily go.' Alice took a step forward, but Anna backed away, teetering on the edge of the kerb where a river of rainwater ran down a gulley.

'Keep back, or so help me, I'll do it.' She waved the blade close to Lily's face, causing Alice to gasp, as if she'd not noticed the knife before. 'I almost feel sorry for you,' said Anna, turning on Jez. 'You'll wake up one day and find, like me, she's destroyed everything you ever dreamed of. And when that happens, I hope you'll think of me, and remember this day.'

'This isn't a game, Anna,' said Alice. 'You can't get away with this. And by the way, I'm not going to lie for you anymore. It's time to face up to the truth about what happened to Ellie.'

A flash of uncertainty flickered across Anna's face, picked out by the bright headlights of the police patrol car advancing on them at speed through the rain.

'I've taken the blame for Ellie's death for all these years, but no more,' said Alice.

'You killed my angel.'

'That's not what happened, and you know it.'

Jez snatched his hand back. 'What are you talking about?'

'I'm done living with the guilt,' said Alice. 'I wasn't even in the car when Ellie died. I took the blame because I felt responsible. But not anymore.'

'I don't understand. What are you saying?' said Jez.

'Anna found us in the workshop, and she ran out.

She made it to the car. I tried to stop her, but I couldn't. Ellie was playing on the drive, oblivious to everything.'

'Anna killed Ellie?' said Jez, re-imagining the awful scene that had played out, but now with Anna behind the wheel. 'And you took the blame?'

'I thought it was the right thing to do.'

'She's lying,' hissed Anna. 'She killed her, to spite me.'

'Enough!' said Alice, the force of her tone startling Jez.

'You confessed to the police because you felt guilty about your affair with Marcus?' Jez asked, incredulous.

'It wasn't an affair. It was one time, but yes,' said Alice, 'I assumed they'd charge me with something, and that would be my penance, a way of repairing the hurt I'd done to someone I cared about very much. Anna, you were the closest thing I had to a sister. I've looked up to you since we were children. You were clever, and bright, and full of ambition. You created your own business from nothing, married a man who cared for you more than you know, and gave birth to a beautiful daughter. How could you possibly think you were in my shadow? It was always me looking up to you.'

'It's not true,' said Anna, shaking her head, and her knees buckling. For a moment, Jez thought she was going to collapse, but she regained her strength, and stood tall. 'You wanted to destroy me.'

'I made one lousy mistake!'

'He promised never to see you again, but he went crawling back, after everything that had happened,' said Anna.

'I never wanted to see Marcus again, but he found the house, and broke in during the night. We were asleep, and he was drunk. Anna, you have to believe me. I never encouraged him.'

Anna glanced from Alice to Jez and back again, twitching like a cornered mouse. Then suddenly she dropped Lily, shoving her towards Alice. 'Have her then,' she howled. 'There's nothing left for me.'

'Give me the knife,' said Jez.

Anna shook her head, retreating into the middle of the road where a torrent of rainwater rushed over her bare feet. She gripped the knife tightly, fear and hopelessness written over her face. She looked like a little girl lost. She turned to face the car screaming down the street, its sirens blazing, and blue lights flaring. It wasn't going to stop in time. It was going too fast.

Anna lowered her arms to her sides, and the knife dropped from her hand. Her face softened, and she looked to the sky as if she was embracing her fate. She was right, she'd lost everything, and Jez realised now she was preparing to die.

He tried to scream her name, but it was lost in the sound of tyres squealing, and the roar of the siren. The car jerked to the right under heavy braking, but in the wet it hardly seemed to slow at all. It kept coming, skidding and sliding, heading straight for Anna. No way to avoid her. She closed her eyes, and threw back her head, waiting for the inevitable collision that never happened.

None of them expected the second car.

The red Volvo shot out of the drive, crashing through the gates, and glancing Jez's elbow with its engine screeching. It bounced into the road, landing heavily on its suspension, with Anna caught in its headlights.

In the last moment of her life, her head snapped sideways, eyes wide with surprise. She threw up her hands, as if somehow that would protect her from two tons of speeding metal.

The car struck her side on. She folded like a ragdoll. Her head hit the bonnet first, and her body was tossed into the air, turning head over heels, a fraction of a second before the police car rammed the Volvo with a terrifying wrench of metal and plastic that sounded like a bomb going off.

Anna's body landed in a heap of broken bones and sodden clothes on the far side of the road.

Jez stared numbly at the wreckage, watching steam rising from the front of the patrol car where it had stoved in the side of the Volvo. Its emergency lights still pulsed, washing the street in electric blue waves, but its siren slurred, and finally gave up all together. The Volvo had ended up a few metres down the street, straddling the central white line with its headlights picking out needles of rain.

At first, Jez detected no movement from either vehicle. The force of the impact had twisted metal, and mangled plastic. It seemed unlikely any of the occupants could have survived.

Then, the passenger door of the police car clicked open, and a hand appeared. An arm forcing the door out. Jez snapped into action, running to help a uniformed officer as he staggered free from the wreck.

His face was streaked with blood from a gash on his forehead, and he stood unsteadily. Jez guided him to the pavement, where Alice and Lily were standing, hand in hand, frozen in shock.

'Use my phone. Call an ambulance,' said Jez, shouting over the buzz that lingered in his ears. 'Tell them it's urgent.'

The driver of the police car remained pinned in his seat by the steering wheel, forced back against his chest by the impact. He grimaced in pain, but was at least conscious.

He screamed in agony as Jez peeled open the door, and leaned inside. 'Where are you hurt?' he asked.

'I can't feel my legs,' the officer wheezed.

His trousers were shredded and bloodied, messed up with what was left of the twisted and mangled dashboard.

'An ambulance is on its way. You're going to be fine.'

The officer snatched Jez's arm as he backed away. 'Tell them to hurry,' he said.

'They'll be here any minute,' said Jez, who gave him a tight-lipped smile as he prised open his fingers. 'I promise.'

Jez's feet crunched over broken glass as he approached the Volvo. Its engine was whining at a high pitch, as if it was stuck in neutral with the accelerator jammed on. He peered through what was left of the driver's side window. Marcus lay motionless, twisted at the waist with his lower half still on the driver's side, and his upper body sprawled across the passenger seat. His eyes were wide open, and staring vacantly into space.

Jez wrenched the twisted door open with brute force and determination. Overhead lights came on, illuminating the shred of deflated air bags, and the true horror of Marcus's injuries. His head and neck were bent unnaturally, and blood dribbled from his mouth. His foot was still pressed down fully on the accelerator.

If Jez had had any doubts about Marcus's intentions, and whether it had been an accident, they were wiped out in an instant. Marcus had deliberately driven at his wife with the clear aim of killing her.

'Is he badly hurt?' said Alice, startling Jez as she appeared over his shoulder.

He snatched the keys out of the ignition. The engine spluttered and died.

'Go inside and wait with Lily,' he said, guiding her away from the car. She was drenched, and as he put an arm around her shoulders, felt her shiver. 'Don't let her see any more.'

Alice nodded. 'I just want to know he's okay.'

Jez shook his head. 'No, Alice. Marcus is dead.'

57

Jez flinched as a nurse tied off the last stitch, and cut the thread.

'You were lucky,' she said, peeling off a pair of surgical gloves and dumping them in a cardboard tray. 'The knife missed all the main arteries.'

Jez inspected her handiwork, and lowered his arm into his lap. 'I never thought I'd be told I was lucky for getting knifed,' he said.

She smiled thinly. 'Try to stay out of trouble in future. You'll need to come back in a few weeks, but it should heal up nicely.' The nurse pulled back the curtains around the bed. 'You'll probably have a scar, but I think my sewing's pretty good.'

As she walked away, Alice breezed in with a coffee in a disposable cup. Her hair had been towelled dry, and she was wearing an unfamiliar pair of jeans and a chunky sweater.

She kissed Jez lightly on the lips. 'It's all they could

find to fit me,' she said, running a hand over her faded jeans.

'They suit you.'

She punched him playfully on the arm. The fact was, she looked pretty good in anything, even a pair of lost property jeans and sweater.

'Ow! Careful, they've just patched me up.'

'Sorry,' said Alice, examining Jez's arm. 'Neat job.'

'Are you okay?'

'Yeah. I think so.'

'Where's Lily?'

'Asleep upstairs. Someone's watching her.'

'Did you speak to the police yet?'

Alice shrugged, and took a sip of coffee. 'I told them everything,' she said.

'Everything?'

'Yes.'

'I wish you'd told me about Anna and Marcus before,' said Jez.

'How could I?'

'Didn't you trust me?'

'It's not that —'

'What then?'

Alice slumped on the bed. He shifted over to make room, waiting for her explanation. 'I didn't want you to judge. I needed a new start, and to put the past behind me.'

'You lied to me?'

'I never lied,' said Alice, hanging her head. 'I just didn't tell you the whole truth.'

'Isn't that the same thing?'

'I don't think so.'

'You never even told me Marcus was Lily's father.'

'What difference would it have made?'

'To me, a lot.'

'I couldn't,' said Alice. 'You know what I did. It was wrong. At the time I gave some serious thought to a termination, but I couldn't do it. And I'm glad now. Whatever I've done, it was never Lily's fault.'

'So, you started a new life?'

'I had to get away, and I vowed I'd never see Anna or Marcus again. The easiest thing was to deny what had happened, especially to myself.'

'And to me?' said Jez.

'It had to be that way.'

'Did Marcus know you were pregnant?'

'I never spoke to him again after … you know.'

'But he found you, Alice. He broke into the house, and he saw the photos of the three of us. He knew the moment he saw Lily that she was his. Don't you think he had a right to be told? He was Lily's father.'

'Maybe,' said Alice. 'But I made a decision, and I had to stick with it, for all of us.'

'It nearly got us killed.'

'I did what I thought was right. I couldn't have predicted that Marcus would find me again.'

Jez sighed, and folded his arms across his chest. 'I still don't understand why, after four years, he came looking for you.'

'I think he'd been looking for me for a long time. I'm convinced he thought there was more going on between us than there was.' Alice pulled her hair into a ponytail over her shoulder, smoothing it out with her hand. 'I'd seen the way he'd look at me, but he was my best friend's husband.'

'You still screwed him.'

Alice turned her head sharply. 'Only the once, and I never meant for it to happen. For Christ's sake, my mother had just died, and I went to the house to cry on Anna's shoulder. But she was out, and I found Marcus in the workshop. He was being so kind, and we opened a bottle of wine and ... I never wanted him. Not really. It should never have happened.'

'But it did,' said Jez. 'And Anna caught you.'

'And I've never been so ashamed. I tried to explain to her, but she was so angry.' Alice stared into her coffee, lost in her thoughts. 'I watched Ellie die in Anna's arms, and there was nothing I could do to stop it. It was all my fault. And so, when the police came, I told them I was driving. I thought it would take away some of the guilt.'

'Did it?' asked Jez.

'Not really, no. The police investigated, but said it was an accident. No one's fault. But that's not right. I was to blame.'

Jez ran a finger along the curve of Alice's jaw, her skin smooth and cold. 'You can't think like that.'

'If I'd not been so weak, Ellie, Anna, and Marcus would all still be alive.'

'Alice, don't.' Jez wrapped an arm around her shoulder, and tucked her head under his chin. 'You can't blame yourself. Anna and Marcus both bear a lot of responsibility.'

Alice said nothing. Hot tears streamed down her face.

'You should have told me when Lily went missing though,' said Jez. 'And you should have called the police.'

'I was scared, Jez. I couldn't bear the thought she'd hurt my little girl. I thought I could sort it out on my own.'

'Did you know it was Anna who wrecked Lily's nursery, and forced it to close?'

'What?'

'She knew her best opportunity to abduct Lily was while you were at work. But obviously, the nursery wouldn't let Anna take her without consent from us.'

'I had to leave Lily with one of the other mothers,' said Alice.

'Who was more easily persuaded that Anna was Lily's aunt come to collect her for you.'

'My God, I made it so easy for her. I'm so stupid.'

'You weren't to know what she was up to,' said Jez.

'But I fell for it.'

'I guess she took your phone?'

'Of course.'

'That's how she managed to find my number so quickly,' said Jez.

'She called you?'

Jez shifted uneasily on the bed. 'I found out about Anna through someone on Facebook, so I had a suspicion she was involved in your disappearance. I went to the house looking for you, but she threw me out. A few minutes later, she called my mobile. I had no idea how she found my number so quickly.'

'Why did she call? What did she want?'

Jez cleared his throat, and considered carefully how to answer. 'She invited me for dinner, and tried to seduce me,' he said, deciding that after everything, honesty was the best policy. No more secrets.

'She did what?' said Alice, jumping off the bed, her face reddening with fury.

'Look, there was nothing in it. We went for dinner, and she took me back to her hotel room.'

'Her hotel room?'

'Listen, Alice. Nothing happened. She tried it on, but I told her I wasn't interested.'

'Really?'

'Yes, really. She was playing games. You know what she was like. Don't let her get between us again. I don't know what was going on in that sick head of hers, but I didn't want any part of it.'

'You promise me you turned her down?'

'Yes. She tried to tell me you'd moved to Spain with Lily, and that I should forget about you both. I refused to believe it.'

'Which explains why she made me call you.'

Jez scratched his head, recalling the odd conversation on the beach after Anna had drugged him. 'You told me to move on with my life, to forget about you both.'

'Anna had Lily. I had no choice but to do what she told me.'

'You could have tried code,' said Jez.

'Code? Seriously? She had Lily. She could have done anything to her. I couldn't risk it.'

'I know.'

Alice finished her coffee, and dumped the empty cup in a bin.

'I'm sorry I didn't trust you,' said Jez.

'It doesn't matter.'

'It does. I jumped to the wrong conclusion about Marcus after he broke in.'

'I guess I should have been honest with you from the start,' Alice said, shoving her hands in her pockets.

'I was jealous, but only because I was so scared of losing you. You and Lily are the best things that have ever happened to me.'

'Do you still think so, even after everything that's happened?'

'Especially because of everything that's happened. I mean it,' said Jez. 'I couldn't bear the thought I'd lost you.'

'You didn't.'

'Thank God. But I'm never letting you out of my sight again.' Jez hopped off the bed, and wrapped an arm around Alice's waist. 'I mean it, Alice. I love you.'

She buried her head in his shoulder, and held him tight.

They stayed clutching each other until they were interrupted by a porter, who clattered past the bay with a noisy metal trolley.

'There's one thing I need to know though,' said Jez, pulling away.

'Go on.'

'Why didn't you just let me call the police after Marcus broke in? Everything would have turned out so differently if we'd just made the call.'

'And we'd be making weekly visits to see you behind bars, Jez. Are you crazy? It wasn't self-defence. You almost killed him.'

'I was trying to protect you.'

'No, you were trying to kill him. You over-reacted. But I wasn't going to let Marcus ruin everything a second time. I thought he was dead. No one knew he'd broken into our house, so I figured that if we dumped his body, no one would have been any the wiser.'

'But he wasn't dead. What we did was wrong.'

'I know. I seem to be making a habit of that. But it wouldn't have changed anything. Marcus would have ended up in hospital, just the same. Anna would have found out he'd tracked me down. Same outcome, Jez.'

'Even so, I feel bad. I don't even know how he found you.'

'I thought I'd covered my tracks, but maybe not so well. My guess is he found out where I worked. He knew what I did for a living. If he was determined enough, he could have worked through all the conveyancing firms in the county.'

'Do you think he did that?'

'Who knows. Maybe he followed me home. He might even have seen me with Lily, and put two and two together. Only Marcus knew for sure.'

'You said you'd told the police everything. Even what happened when he broke into the house?' asked Jez.

'Mr Hook?' Two uniformed police officers appeared from around a corner, and stood at the edge of the bay.

'Yes,' said Jez.

'If you're all finished here,' said the first officer, a young man with acne-pocked skin, 'we'd like a word about this evening's events.'

'Of course,' said Jez. 'I'll tell you everything I know.'

58

SIX MONTHS LATER

Lily poked the tip of her tongue between her teeth as she concentrated on fitting the key in the lock. Then, after a few frustrated moments struggling to turn it, the door fell open. She rushed inside with a whoop of delight.

'This is it, then,' said Jez. 'A new start.'

Alice squealed as he picked her up. 'What are you doing?'

'Carrying you over the threshold,' he said.

'You'll put your back out.'

'Shut up. It's romantic.' Jez staggered, with a mock grimace, towards the entrance of their new home.

'Hey, I'm not that heavy.'

He lowered her carefully onto her feet in the hall, where they stood taking in the enormity of the job they had ahead. Carpets needed replacing, woodwork painting, walls knocking down, and cupboards ripping out. Most of it cosmetic. A few months of hard work and a little cash would transform it into a home.

From above, Lily's heavy footsteps echoed through the empty house as she charged from room to room unable to contain her excitement. Alice meandered through to the kitchen, a 1970s monstrosity of Formica and mould-mottled tiles.

'Look, the previous owners left us a bottle of wine,' she said, picking up a dubious-looking bottle of white from the counter.

'That's sweet. They even left two glasses.'

'And a card,' said Alice, frowning at the envelope. 'Mr and Mrs Hook?'

'Only if you play your cards right,' said Jez, sidling up behind her and wrapping an arm around her stomach.

'Shall we open it now?'

Jez nuzzled his face into her neck. 'It's a bit early. Why don't we wait until Mum and Dad get here?'

'You're no fun.'

Lily crashed into the kitchen, skidding across the faded linoleum. 'Can I have the room with the big window? Please, Jez?'

'Of course you can, Lily-Bear.' Jez swept her off her feet and dangled her upside down, swinging her in circles until her face was red, and tears of laughter wet her cheeks. 'You can have whichever room you like.'

Lily squirmed free, and ran off again, disappearing up the rickety staircase.

'What is it?' said Jez, unable to read the funny look on Alice's face.

'Nothing.'

'I know it's a lot of work, but it'll be worth it. And it's so quiet here. The nearest neighbour's a mile away,' said Jez, looking to a window overlooking green fields as far as the tree-lined horizon.

'It's not that.'

'What then?'

'It's seeing you with Lily reminded me how lucky I am.'

'I'm the lucky one. And to think I nearly lost you. I'm never letting you out of my sight again,' said Jez, swamping her with kisses.

Alice batted him away, pulling away from his clutches. 'We're going to be okay here, aren't we?' she said, her face turning serious.

'Of course we are. It's a new start, for all of us.'

'I wish you hadn't had to sell your yacht. I know how much it meant to you.'

Jez shrugged. 'What was the point of having it if I couldn't sail it. The money's better off in the house. I'm sure Uncle Tony would have approved.'

'I'm sure he would.'

'Have you thought any more about the Broadstairs house?'

'Jez, don't.'

'Come on, Alice, we have to talk about this, for Lily's sake.'

'Just leave it, will you.' Alice stormed out of the room.

Jez caught up with her in the lounge, a spacious room with plenty of potential after they'd stripped the orange floral paper and replastered the walls. Alice was staring out of a window overlooking the overgrown garden out the back.

'Alice, this is Lily's future we're talking about.'

'We don't need anything from them. We're fine as we are,' said Alice.

'It's Lily's inheritance. Marcus was her father, and if we don't contest the will, all that money is going to charity. I've nothing against the lifeboat service, but think of the opportunities for Lily.'

'I said, we don't need their money.'

Jez sighed, and leaned against the jamb of the door with his hands in his pockets. 'The solicitors have put the house on the market for offers in excess of a million,' he said. 'Then there's Marcus's business, and their savings. It's a lot of cash.'

'No, Jez.'

He hung his head, defeated. 'She knows Marcus was her father, you know. One day she'll ask what happened to his money.'

'He's her biological father, that's all. As far as she's concerned, you're her dad,' said Alice. 'Marcus never had anything to do with her, and we don't need his money now.'

'This isn't about you. This is Lily's future. And anyway, you never gave him a chance to get involved. You never even told him about Lily,' said Jez.

'I've made my decision. You can talk about it all you

like, but I'm not changing my mind. Can we please just drop it now?'

'Fine,' said Jez. A sharp knock at the front door reverberated around the empty rooms. 'That'll be Mick. Let's talk about this later.'

'There's nothing to talk about.'

When Jez answered the door, a warm, spring breeze blew in, heavy with the scent of cherry blossom. Mick stood with his hands on his hips, baseball cap pulled down low on his head, and a cheesy grin on his face.

'Get the kettle on then,' he said. 'We're dying of thirst out here.'

'Just as soon as we unpack it,' said Jez.

Behind Mick, on the drive, three men in matching green overalls were busy around a box van. They lowered the tailgate, and with a well-practised drill, began unloading heavy cardboard boxes and pieces of furniture.

'Right, we'd better get a shift on then,' said Mick.

The whole operation to move their belongings into the new house took a little over three hours, with Alice orchestrating operations from the hall, identifying each box and directing it to the appropriate room. Most of their belongings were Alice's, from her previous life, before Jez. Their beds. The old oak dresser. Wardrobes and chests of drawers. Jez set up his TV in the corner of the lounge, opposite Alice's pair of matching sofas. But he consigned his Xbox to the loft. Wasting the day fighting imaginary aliens seemed so childish.

'Are you sure?' said Alice, with a crooked grin.

'Absolutely. Time for a new start, right?'

They rewarded Mick and his men with tea and a slice of Alice's fruit cake.

'Right, ready for the second load?' Mick asked, wiping his mouth with his sleeve.

He returned late afternoon, with the van fully loaded, followed by Jez's mother and father. Jez trotted out to meet them, leaning into his parents' car through the open window, and kissing his mother on the cheek.

'Welcome home, Mum,' he said.

Her smile was still lopsided, and her eyes portrayed little enthusiasm. She patted Jez's face. Her hand was cold and bony.

'Everything okay, Dad?' Jez asked, as his father hauled himself out of his old Rover, huffing and puffing with the effort.

'Your mother's a bit teary,' he mouthed.

It had been a huge wrench for them to sell their home with all its memories and associations, but it made sense that they move in, with his mother's ongoing care needs.

'It'll be strange for a few days, but ultimately you're both better off with us, where we can keep an eye on you,' said Jez.

He threw his arms around his father and pulled him into a hug. It seemed the right thing to do, and his father reciprocated, reluctantly, slapping him on the back.

Then Jez helped his mother out of the car and into a wheelchair they'd unfolded from the boot. 'Come on, Mum, let me show you around.'

He ignored the unimpressed look on her face as she regarded the weathered facade of the house.

'It's not much to look at now, but give it a few months and you won't recognise the place,' he said.

As they passed around the back of the removals van, Jez noticed it was packed full. His parents were supposed to have used the opportunity of moving to clear out some of their old junk. It would be a miracle if it all fitted into the tiny granny annexe on the side of the main house.

'You've got your own separate entrance,' said Jez. 'You can come and go as you please. There's also an entrance inside into our place, so you can pop in and see us whenever you like.'

Jez handed the key to his father, and bundled his mother's wheelchair over the doorstep, into a dusty open-plan living room.

'It's a long way from town,' his mother said, looking around the gloomy interior.

'But it's so peaceful out here, don't you think? And I know it doesn't look much at the moment, but once Alice and I have tidied it up, it'll be much better. I've brought some colour charts, so you can choose some paint.'

'Coming through,' said one of Mick's men, a tall, scrawny character with tattoos inked down both arms. He dumped a heavy box on the lounge floor.

'And once all your things are in, it'll feel much more like home.' Jez injected a note of optimism in his voice to counter his mother's sour expression.

Her recovery hadn't been as full as the doctors had first hoped, and his father was struggling on his own. He needed help with her care, and by moving them all in together, Jez could at least keep an eye on them both.

'Nanny! Grandad!' Lily tore into the apartment like a whirlwind, throwing herself at her grandfather, who snatched her up and tickled her until she was gasping for breath.

She pulled free, wiped her hair from her face with the back of her hand, and approached her grandmother with a grin. She took Lily's hand and held it to her cheek.

'Do you like our new house, Nanny?'

Jez held his breath.

'Of course I do, darling. It's perfect.'

'So do I,' said Lily. 'And we can all be together and see each other every day, can't we?'

'Yes,' said her grandmother, 'we can. We can see each other whenever we like.'

Jez slipped under the duvet and hunted out Alice's body for warmth.

'I'm exhausted,' she yawned.

'It's been a long day. No regrets?'

'No regrets.'

'You know we're going to make this work, don't you?'

'Of course,' said Alice, rolling over to face Jez.

He stroked a loose strand of hair away from her forehead. 'Are you quite sure about the will?'

'Jez —'

'It's the last time I'll bring it up, but you have to be one hundred per cent sure this is the right thing to do, for Lily, I mean.'

'I'm sure.'

'It's a lot of money. She could use it for a house when she's old enough, or to help her through university. She has a right to it.'

'No, Jez. That family has done enough damage to our lives. We're going to make a clean break. I'm not contesting the will.'

'Fine,' said Jez. 'You've made up your mind then.'

'One hundred per cent.'

'I won't mention it again.'

'Good.'

Jez chewed on his lip. Maybe Alice was right. They didn't need the Fensons' money. It would be a constant reminder of all the pain and hurt they'd been through. It was best to move on. They'd provide for Lily themselves, and make sure she never wanted for anything.

'Oh, I almost forgot,' said Alice, sitting up and reaching down by the side of the bed. 'I meant to give you this, but with all the excitement today it slipped my mind.'

She handed Jez a white envelope, printed with his name and their old address.

'What is it?'

'Open it,' said Alice. 'Your solicitor dropped it off first thing. I was keeping it as a surprise.'

Jez tore open the letter and yanked out a single sheet of A4 paper. He scanned the words, then re-read them three times until they finally sunk in.

'Good news?' said Alice, with a twinkle in her eye. She knew exactly what was in the letter.

'It's from the police,' said Jez. 'Confirmation that I'm no longer under investigation, for anything. No cases to answer, thank God.'

'I still can't believe they thought you'd killed me,' Alice giggled.

'It wasn't funny,' said Jez, pouting.

'I don't know. It's quite amusing,' said Alice, reaching for the lamp on the bedside table. 'Goodnight, Jez.'

As the room was plunged into darkness, Jez settled back on his pillow and stared at the ceiling waiting for his eyes to adjust. The silence was deafening. No traffic hum. No footsteps on the pavement outside. No chatter of late night drinkers making their way home. Even the dark out here seemed heavier. Thick and treacly, like molasses. It was going to take some getting used to.

The house popped and creaked, like it was settling in with its new inhabitants. Strange, unfamiliar sounds that came from above, below and all around.

Jez closed his eyes and let his body sink into the soft mattress, his muscles aching. For the first time in a long while, sleep came easily to him. His body relaxed and his breathing slowed.

INSPIRATION FOR BETWEEN THE LIES

The inspiration for Between the Lies came from an idea I had some time ago about a burglary going wrong. Like all the best ideas, it was a 'what if' moment.

What if a burglar was accidentally killed when they broke into a house late at night, and the death covered up?

After all, burglars don't leave details of where they're working that night, do they?

Next was planning a fiendish plot around that idea. I conjured up the characters of Jez and Alice, one of whom was hiding some kind of secret, although I had no idea what at first.

The characters of Marcus and Anna came later, as Alice's failed friendship and her misguided affair formed a backdrop to the novel. The rest came organically over time.

I'm not a quick writer, but Between the Lies proved to be one of the quickest first drafts I'd ever managed to complete.

The hard work came in addressing the many plot holes that became apparent when my Street Team of test readers first laid eyes on the manuscript.

It's since gone through several iterations, a full developmental edit, lots of drafts, a great deal of head scratching, and many late nights, honing the story and the words.

It took the best part of a year in the end, but I think it was well worth the effort. I hope you agree.

ALSO BY THE AUTHOR

Enjoyed Between the Lies?

His Wife's Sister

By A J Wills

He stole her childhood. Now she wants it back.

Mara Sitwell was only eleven when she went missing.

Nineteen years later, she's been found wandering through remote woodland, alone and confused.

She says she's been kept in an underground cell for all these years - but refuses to reveal anything about the man who snatched her.

What does she have to hide? And who's she protecting?

Her brother-in-law, Damian, certainly doubts she's telling the whole truth and fears she might even be a danger to his young children, especially when his wife insists on moving Mara into their home.

To save his family, Damian will have to prove what really happened to Mara all those years ago.

But the truth is never easy to uncover when it's been buried so deep. . .

AVAILABLE FROM AMAZON

A HUMBLE PLEA

Honestly, you can't go to a restaurant or even service your car these days without someone asking you to leave a review. And don't get me started on those customer satisfaction surveys.

But actually, book reviews are really important. Your reviews and ratings tell me – and others - you enjoy my stories.

Knowing my stories provide some escapism keeps me going when I'm slugging away late into the night, hammering on the keyboard, looking for inspiration.

I don't have the backing of a big publisher with a gazillion bucks to throw at promotion.

It's just me.

But I have you. And readers trust other readers.

So, if you do have a moment to spare before you dive back into the Amazon store, please leave a rating and review.

It needn't be long or fancy. Just a few words to tell

others what to expect - just don't spoil it for others by giving away the twist!

And if you're a social media user, please let your followers know you enjoyed it.

I'd be most grateful and you'll have the satisfaction of knowing you're sustaining this humble self-published author to write more.

Thank you and happy reading.

Adrian

Printed in Great Britain
by Amazon